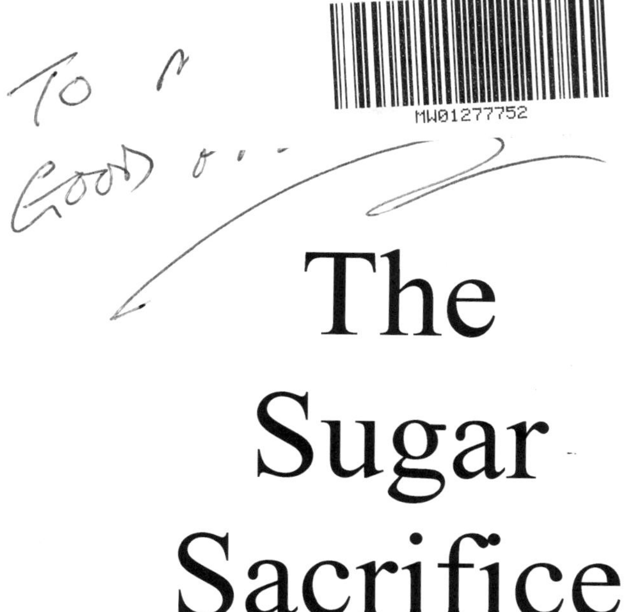

The Sugar Sacrifice

Lyle Garford

Except where actual historical events and characters are being described for the storyline of this novel, all situations in this publication are fictitious and any resemblance to living persons is purely coincidental.

Published by:
Lyle Garford
Vancouver, Canada
Contact: lyle@lylegarford.com

ISBN 978-0-9952078-2-0

Cover by designspectacle.ca

Book Design by Lyle Garford
lyle@lylegarford.com
www.lylegarford.com

First Edition 2017
Printed by Createspace, an Amazon.com Company.
Available on Kindle and other devices.

Dedication

This one is for my racquetball and squash friends.

Prologue
June 1792
St. Lucia

The Captain made his way to the end of the dock as dusk brought growing shadows to the harbour. He was scanning all directions for signs of trouble with each step while the man waiting for him with a travel valise in hand nervously did the same. The Captain felt tired and drained of energy to a depth he had not experienced before as he reached out to shake the man's hand. He studied the man's features, seeing fatigue and tension etched on his companion's face. The Captain knew it was mirrored on his own.

"Are you certain of your course of action, Captain Deschamps? I still think they will come after you, just as I am sure they are even now looking for me," said Colonel Jean Joseph de Gimat, Governour of the French island of St. Lucia in the Caribbean. "And what of your men? Are you still confident of them?"

Marcel Deschamps, the greying, but dapper and fit Captain of the French Navy frigate *Marie-Anne,* now into his early fifties in age, gave a weary shrug in response. "To be honest, I am not certain of anything. A year ago I wouldn't have thought what is happening now possible, but obviously I was wrong. It's no matter, though, as I am willing to take the risk. I don't think these bastards Montdenoix and Linger even know who I really am, at least not yet. They may have succeeded in stirring the colony up, but they aren't as smart as they think they are."

"Captain, we *both* thought they were

buffoons, but somehow they managed to convince the garrison of the fort on Morne Fortune to change sides and fly the tricolour flag of the Revolution. Sooner or later they will turn their attention to you. You command the most powerful warship in St. Lucia and I don't think even your devious skills will keep you safe. And if they find out what we have done they will stop at nothing. We both know they will be looking for it probably sooner than later."

The Captain nodded. "I am not afraid, Governour. We have talked of this before. The fact remains I am best positioned to get it safely away and nothing has changed to warrant a different approach. Besides, if things worsen as we suspect then someone has to step into the breach to help the remaining loyalists here and deal with it all. As I said, I remain prepared to take this risk."

The Governour studied the Captain's face for a long moment before reaching out to place a hand on the Captain's shoulder. "You are a brave man, Marcel. Well, the ship is waiting for me and I must flee. If they catch me lingering here I'll be hung on the spot."

Turning, the Governour stalked up the gangplank and signaled to the clearly impatient Captain of the small mail packet ship he could finally depart. Captain Deschamps was left standing by himself and feeling alone as he watched the ship leave the harbour of Castries, the capital of St. Lucia. The packet ship Captain was fortunate enough of a breeze was present, despite the stifling heat of a summer evening, to enable a relatively swift departure.

Having found ways to remain assigned to St.

Lucia for many years, the island had long since become Captain Deschamps home. But the sudden departure of the Governour brought an unsettling feeling his island home was now a strange and foreign place. When he was certain the ship was well away he gave a deep sigh, struggling to master his unspoken desire to simply flee too. But he knew this was impossible, so he turned to make his way back to his ship. As he retraced his steps he began scanning all directions for trouble once again.

Chapter One
December 1792
St. Lucia

The sound of the sudden, grating fall of the gleaming blade as it dropped down its guide was replaced by a harsh and resounding thud as it struck the base of the framework holding it all in place, jarring the senses of everyone nearby. One of the workers installing and testing the apparatus in the public square stepped forward, beginning yet another detailed examination of the various pieces holding it together. Calling two other workers over to him, he pointed at a spot he seemed dissatisfied with. After a quick, muttered conversation they all nodded agreement and he reached for a hammer, pounding at a supporting cross beam which appeared a little out of place while the other two watched him. After finishing the small adjustment, they hoisted the blade and let it fall three more times before finally looking more content with their work.

The three men all stiffened as they turned to face the officer that had been watching them when he moved to join their group. They had reason to be on their guard, as this man's hard, thin-lipped countenance matched his behaviour. Still physically strong despite being over forty in age and taller than all three of the workers, the officer was well known for using his overbearing physical presence to dominate everyone.

"Are you finally done?"

"For now, yes, Captain La Chance," said the worker with the hammer. "There is one other final piece I want to adjust, but I need a different tool from the ship, so we will return later. This may seem like a straightforward device, but it must be properly set up if you want the blade to do its job without problems or delay. I have learned much over the last several months while working with these new devices and the most important lesson was to take my time and do it properly from the start."

"Fine, fine. And the blade is sharp?"

"But of course. We worked it over yet again last night. You do know it will require some periodic maintenance depending on how much it is used?"

The officer gave them a cold smile. "Oh, I fully expect it will get some use and you will need to maintain it. How much remains to be seen. You may all return to the ship, but have your work completed today."

As the three men gathered their tools and left Baron Jean Baptiste Raimond La Chance, newly appointed Captain of the French Navy frigate *La Felicite*, smiled once again and examined the device before him with a professional eye. Machines designed to separate a man's head from his body were in use in different forms and various countries for centuries. Captain La Chance felt proud it fell to the enlightenment of the French people and their Revolution to refine the design to its current form.

In most parts of the world little concern was focused on whether or not an offender suffered or felt pain when being executed. With this new device, called a guillotine, deliberate care was being taken to ensure a swift end to an offender while inflicting as little pain as possible. Unlike earlier versions relying on axe heads and blunt force to do the job, the relatively thin, sharp, and angled blade together with its sheer weight falling from a great height ensured no need to let the blade fall a second time to finish the job, if it was properly maintained.

Satisfied, Captain La Chance turned away from the guillotine brought with him on the long journey from Brest in France to St. Lucia and found the watching crowd packed into the square was growing even bigger. The soldiers holding the crowd back were showing obvious anxiety about its size and weren't hesitating to use the butts of their weapons to club the more boisterous members of the crowd back when they got too close. The square was right beside the jail just off Peynier Street in Castries and was left empty for the specific purpose of public executions. Most of the previous executions in St. Lucia were accomplished by hanging the offender. A gibbet used until now sat dismantled off in a corner of the square.

The novelty of this new device clearly piqued the interest of the crowd, which was filled with an almost equal mix of both white and black faces. What was interesting for Captain La Chance was the mixture of reactions on those faces, ranging from outright horror at what they were seeing to absolute glee over the potential entertainment to come. The remainder in between those extremes seemed to wear equal mixes of outright fear, dismay, and fascination with what they were seeing.

A warm gust of wind blew through the square, making the new tricolour flag hanging from the flagpole beside the guillotine flap with the breeze. As Captain La Chance stared up at it he felt another surge of pride to know the new Minister of the Navy for the Republic, Gaspard Monge, chose him specifically for this mission. As he gazed upwards he saw in the periphery of his vision two other men were walking over to stop at his side and he turned his attention to them.

"Well, gentlemen, what do you think?" said the Captain.

"It has certainly caught everyone's attention, Captain. Perhaps for good reason," said Emile Martin with a smirk, one of the two civilian members of the tribunal Captain La Chance headed.

"We are ready to begin our work, Captain. What do you see are the next steps?" said Jeremy Bernard, the third member of the tribunal.

The Captain shrugged as he gave the two men a cold smile. Both still looked and behaved like the weak, petty clerks they were before the Revolution and he knew they needed his leadership.

"We must establish ourselves in the administrative headquarters. I think from my brief glimpse of the outside of the Governour's quarters it will suit our purposes. Since this island no longer has a Governour we may as well move in. It was important to set up the guillotine before all else to send a message to the reluctant ones about who is now in charge here."

Emile Martin waved a hand toward the device beside him. "Do you think we will actually need to use this much here, Captain? I thought the National Convention conferred the title of "The Faithful" on this island. They wouldn't have done this without reason, I should think."

"You are correct, sir. We received ongoing support for our cause from this colony, even back in the early days of the Revolution, unlike Martinique and Guadeloupe and the others. Why, many of the slaves on this island simply walked away from their masters as far back as 1790."

"Well, at least we are welcome here if nowhere else, Captain."

All three men knew well how true this was. Prior to arriving in St. Lucia Captain La Chance stopped first in Dominica, another nearby Caribbean island. The Captain bore a commission to take charge of St. Lucia until a new permanent Governour could be appointed and sent out, but part of his instructions were to stop on at least one British held island to introduce himself. The government was anxious for a report on what kind of reception he got to give them intelligence on how receptive other world powers in the area were to the change in administration. La Chance scowled at the memory before relenting as he saw how taken aback the two men were by the look on his face.

"Sorry, gentlemen, I am not displeased with you. It was the memory of how I was treated by Sir John Orde on Dominica. I know, I haven't told you much of the encounter. I was too angry, to be honest."

"Yes, we could see that," confessed Jeremy Bernard.

The memory still rankled. The Governour met him in Fort Young, the strong, dominating fortifications overlooking the capital Roseau and its deep-water harbour. The Fort was in an excellent strategic location, but the Captain found little time to admire it as he was soon marching back down the hill to his ship, clenching his fists in anger. He shook his head in reminiscence.

"The man has a reputation as a seasoned British diplomat, but there wasn't any diplomacy involved in his dealings with me. I couldn't believe how rude he was. He practically threw me out of his office."

"You'd think they would at least have the presence of mind to see which way the wind has blown and do what they must to build a relationship with us. We represent the new power in France, after all."

"Well, I confess I was a little disturbed at just how many ships flying the Bourbon flag were in Fort Royal harbour on Martinique when we stopped there too. I am thinking Sir John was aware of this and it may be the British still have a lingering fantasy the royalists there will find a way to turn back the clock here in the Caribbean."

"So what is your plan to deal with them, Captain?"

La Chance smiled. "The power of ideas will be their downfall. I could not hope to defeat them with the forces at my disposal, but cannon balls are not the only weapons we can wield. Montdenoix and Linger assured me our pamphlets are already enjoying a positive reception here on St. Lucia even though we have only just released them. Once we are certain of the reaction and can be assured of success here, we will find ways to deliver more to Guadeloupe and Martinique."

The Captain could see the two men were

doing their best to maintain bland looks, but having spent weeks sailing out from France with them he knew when they were being skeptical. He also knew why they felt this way.

The flurry of pamphlets and proclamations he quickly issued on arrival in St. Lucia walked a fine diplomatic line when it came to the sensitive issue of slavery. Over time the mulattoes, slaves with one white and one black parent, had come to form a significant group within the overall population. Because they carried at least some white blood in their veins, white slave owners believed the mulattoes would have higher intelligence and ability to learn. As a result, many held varied degrees of education and training in a wide range of skills. A smaller group within this population had actually been freed by their owners for various reasons and now even owned their own slaves.

The Captain's pamphlets assured this group the new French republic would respect their right to the freedoms of citizenship. The problem was the pamphlets also reassured the plantation owners their right to keep slaves, including mulattoes, would be respected. How this seeming contradiction would be reconciled was left unclear. Captain La Chance knew the possibility existed he could be challenged on the point, as the links between republican thinking and the abolitionist movement were clear. The Society of the Friends of the Blacks was a force in republican circles, having advocated abolition for several years. Captain La Chance remained unconcerned, knowing he could simply brush it all off as something for the National Convention to sort out.

The other reason for their skepticism was his characterization of the September 1792 Battle of Valmy as the turning point which would ensure the survival of the republic. While true the success of the republic over the vaunted Prussian army made many skeptics sit up and take notice, there were already warning signs more battles were on the horizon. The biggest reason for their doubt, however, was his announcement of the imminent arrival of a powerful expeditionary force to support his efforts. All three men knew no such force existed.

But as a true believer in the Revolution, Captain La Chance didn't care about their skepticism. His supreme confidence the power of ideas would win the day gave him strength. Beset by enemies on all sides, the new Republic was left with little choice but to rely on them to deal with problems outside the borders of France itself. General Rochambeau himself devised the strategy Captain La Chance was employing in order to buy time. The Captain believed the strategy, coupled with a big dose of fear of the guillotine beside him, was going to serve him well.

"Come, gentlemen, its time we talked with our agents Hubert Montdenoix and Fleming Linger. They have promised me a full progress report and details on the other matter they were tasked with accomplishing."

The guards roughly shoved aside the waiting crowd to make a path for the three men to walk to the nearby Governour's office on the far side of the public square. The expectant faces were silent as they passed, but an excited buzz of conversation grew seconds after they went by.

Their eyes needed a few moments to adjust from the bright sunshine of the day to the cool, dark interior of the entrance to the Governour's offices as the soldier standing guard outside let them in. Captain La Chance knew the sturdy stone building also held the main jail for the town. An officer and an officious looking clerk were waiting inside and both stiffened when the men introduced themselves. The clerk's demeanour became deferential in an instant.

"Gentlemen, they are expecting you. This way, please," said the clerk, leading them to a large meeting room in the rear of the building on the second floor. Across the hallway was an open door into another equally large room, occupied by a desk that dominated what was obviously the Governour's office.

The two men sitting in the meeting room stood the moment the newcomers were ushered in. Although the heat of December in St. Lucia was bearable, unlike the summer months, the room seemed stuffy even with shutters in the rear wall open to collect the breeze. The first thing Captain La Chance noticed were the piles of paperwork stacked on the table in front of the men. After introductions were made they all sat at the table.

"Gentlemen, I am curious," said Captain La Chance. "Why are you not using the office with the desk for your work?"

The one identified as Montdenoix offered a cryptic smile in return. "Captain, we prefer to maintain as low a profile as possible. In our line of work it always pays to keep it this way."

"Line of work?" said Emile Bernard.

The Captain coughed and turned to his colleague. "The fewer details you have about these fellows, the better, sir. Let us just say these men are *agents* of our masters and leave it at that, please. And bear in mind everything you hear in this room is to be kept in strict confidence."

As the man nodded in understanding the Captain turned back to the two agents. "So, gentlemen, you know I actually am in the same line of work as you and I do understand. Come, where do matters stand? I know you gave me a quick summary, but now that we have more time I'd like a full report. My colleagues need to hear this too."

The one called Montdenoix responded without even looking at his colleague, leaving no doubt as to who was the senior of the two agents. Stocky and muscular, Montdenoix had a military bearing and the Captain immediately sensed it was earned.

"Sirs, we are glad to see you. As you know, we have been successful in our efforts to grow republican sentiments on this island. By and large the population is quite supportive. Having said this, we are finding the situation has become rather fluid here. In a way, we have been too successful."

"Really? What does that mean?" said La Chance.

"Ever since our success back in June gaining the army's support and forcing the departure of the former Governour, there is very little productive work being accomplished on this island. Many slaves are no longer working for their masters, having taken our rhetoric about the rights of man seriously."

Captain La Chance raised an eyebrow in question. "So? What is the specific concern?"

"Well, food production is not at the levels it once was. Some of the slaves have little plots of land they till and there is fish to be caught in the ocean, so dire starvation is not imminent. But there are many hungry faces to be seen everywhere, as there is not enough to go around. Where food before was just ridiculously expensive, it is now beyond outrageous in cost. The salt fish the owners use to supplement the food of the slaves is very costly because it comes from the American traders. Some of the slaves have actually gone back to their masters to ensure they continue to be fed. On the other extreme, some of the slaves have taken to bearing arms wherever they go. They claim it is to protect themselves and what little property they have."

The Captain frowned. "So what have you done about all of this?"

Montdenoix shrugged. "We are walking a fine line, Captain. We can hardly compel the slaves to go back to actually serving as slaves again, now can we? At least, we can't do that and remain true to the principles of the Revolution. We have tried to encourage the plantation owners to find ways to lure them back, but most are resisting the notion. They claim they will make no profits if they start paying the slaves even token amounts. With sugar prices as they are, they may well be right. But if you can believe their audacity, some of them are even seeking compensation for the loss of their slaves."

Captain La Chance shrugged. "This is of no consequence. Slaves are just slaves and that hasn't changed. The real problem here is with the royalist plantation owners and not with the slaves. The slaves are merely doing what any of us would do in their position. So, you have records for me, I assume?"

"But of course, Captain. We have done as we were ordered. My colleague Fleming here has compiled a complete list of all plantation owners and their locations for you. I am pleased to report at least half of them profess support for our cause."

"So they say. Well, their actions will speak much louder for them soon enough. Your lists identify which ones are the problems, I assume?"

"They do, sir. You should know we also have a separate list of the plantations where the owners have already taken flight. Unfortunately, many were able to flee with their resources. We believe many left for Martinique and Guadeloupe, as a number of them have properties there too."

Captain La Chance frowned as he sat in thought for a moment. "You weren't able to forestall this from happening?"

Montdenoix shrugged. "Captain, we could not be everywhere at once. Besides, our brief was to find a way to turn the tide in favour of the Revolution here once and for all, and we have succeeded in this. By the time the army commanders sorted out who could be relied upon and took steps to stem the flow it was far too late. We have a list for you of the officers you can count on for support."

"And what of your other tasks?"

"Sir, we have successfully managed the colony as ordered ever since the Governour fled, although I confess dealing with all these bureaucratic details and this mountain of paperwork is far less to my liking than our regular duties. As I said, we are very glad you are here to assume command. I gather you know the orders you brought with you direct us to return to France for some new tasks?"

"Yes, I am aware of your orders. I share your distaste for dealing with paperwork, so I too am glad my commission to take charge here is only temporary. I have been led to believe my replacement will be here in February next year. These gentlemen here with me have the job of taking on the day-to-day administration of St. Lucia and to sit in tribunal to deal with some of our more reluctant citizens. I am actually tasked with consolidating what you have achieved here and more importantly, carrying the struggle to other islands."

"Well, we wish you gentlemen success. We will work with your colleagues to ensure a smooth transition and be on our way home soon."

Captain La Chance leaned forward, an intent look on his face. "There is one other matter to discuss, of course. How have you fared with him since your last correspondence?"

The man's eyes narrowed in response. "Captain Deschamps continues to prove obstinate, I am afraid. He remains in jail along with a number of other particularly vocal owners we were left with no choice but to incarcerate, given the probability they would cause us grief."

"Your last report to the Minister was a little vague on the specifics of your approach regarding the Captain?"

"Yes, well, one doesn't want to detail some

of the less savory aspects of an interrogation in case it falls into the wrong hands. I— Captain La Chance, are we authorized to speak of this in front of your colleagues?"

"Yes, yes, they know. Please continue."

Montdenoix nodded. "I assure you the question of what he did with it was put to the Captain most strenuously, on several occasions over a period of weeks, after his crew mutinied and turned him over to us."

La Chance smiled. "Mutiny is a harsh word to a navy officer. I would prefer something like *joined our cause*."

The rest of the men dutifully chuckled as Montdenoix held both palms out and offered a rueful look in return. "Indeed. In any case, he has proved quite resilient. As ordered, we ceased active interrogation of him in September to await your arrival. He has been rotting in jail ever since."

Captain La Chance sat forward once again, looking thoughtful. "No change of heart, then? Hmm. Look, are you certain he was placed in charge of it?"

"Captain, we are. We know the Governour didn't take it with him as we have questioned the Captain of the packet ship he took flight on. We have reliable witnesses backing up what this man told us. We also have reliable witnesses from the crew of the *Marie-Anne* who have confirmed their former Captain was definitely up to *something* around the time the Governour fled. So, yes, Captain, we have no doubt this man knows what we want. It just remains to get the information out of him."

"Indeed. I am surprised he has held out this

long. Well, we will just have to renew our efforts."

Montdenoix looked troubled. "I am sorry we have failed in this one aspect, Captain La Chance. The truth is the need to succeed is critical. You recall I mentioned earlier the economy here is struggling badly? This is all having a bad impact on our revenues, sir. Revenue from tolls and duties are down significantly. Either people simply don't have the money to pay or they are getting even better at avoiding them, or maybe even both. Sir, we have managed to pay the army *some* of what they are owed by appropriating what we could from the recalcitrant owners we locked up, but we are rapidly running out of options. In truth we have faced difficulty from day one given we started off with virtually nothing."

Captain La Chance frowned as he sat back, deep in thought for a few moments. "Yes, you are right. It is critical we succeed on this. One way or another the plantation owners will be made to fill in the gaps, but this may take time."

After pausing to think again for one final moment La Chance shrugged to let his indifference show. "Yes, well, our friend Citizen Robespierre stated it best last year in the Constituent Assembly, as I recall. *Perish the colonies, but not the principle* I believe he said, or something like that. If he is not concerned with the changes we have wrought from introducing the rights of man to the slaves then I won't be either, and if we must sacrifice the sugar and the wealth it brings for a time until we find a better way to manage this, then so be it. We must sacrifice *whatever* is necessary to achieve our goals."

Sitting forward once again he changed the

topic. "But what of this possibility Deschamps is a spy for the British? I know you were pushing him on this point, but has he confessed to this? Does he know about the letter?"

"No on both counts, Captain. We decided to save the fact we have the letter as a card for you to play. But we do agree with Paris the man has to be a spy. We know the intercepted letter you brought came from this island and it obviously contains a message in cipher. The fact it was on its way to Barbados is telling. I showed it to the new Captain of the *Marie-Anne* and his people yesterday, and they swear it is the handwriting of Captain Deschamps, despite efforts to disguise it."

"Well, then," said Captain La Chance as a smile returned to his face. "Perhaps we should point this out to our British spy. I suggest my colleagues remain here with your man Linger to get on with the details of the handover to us. This will leave you and I free to take the letter and have a friendly conversation with Captain Deschamps."

***

Captain Marcel Deschamps lay on the bunk in his cell in a dazed stupor, willing himself to find refuge in the oblivion of sleep despite it being filled with disturbing dreams. Having already consumed the one meal he was given for the day little else was available to do, although calling the disgusting slop he was consistently fed a meal was questionable. His iron discipline was still intact enough he already finished forcing himself to do his daily exercise routine once again. He thought about engaging in yet another conversation with the inmates sharing his cell or those in the other cells, but no topic he could think of not already debated to death came to mind. The dreary sameness of their days with no end in sight to their imprisonment was unhinging many in the jail.

A few of the inmates were actual petty criminals, but most were leading royalist supporters on St. Lucia. Their crime was to be in the minority and too vocal about what they saw as problems with the changes being forced on them. For this, most were incarcerated along with their entire family. Several of the women were taking it hard, suffering in particular from the utter lack of privacy.

Captain Deschamps had long since lost exact track of the days since his incarceration in late June. Being beaten senseless at random times introduced uncertainty, despite his best efforts to keep track. The others in the jail had not been abused to the same extent, but they too had lost precise count of the days and weeks.

He did know they were now in the winter months on St. Lucia, perhaps December or January. The stifling heat and still air in the jail in June was so bad when he first arrived the simple act of breathing was a struggle. But the temperature at present was almost bearable, if nothing else was. The stench of human excrement radiated from the pail in the corner of the cell. This was emptied only once every day, if the guards remembered. The reek of unwashed bodies permeated everything else. Insects were everywhere. As the Captain flicked a big, crawling bug off his arm he realized he couldn't remember the last time he actually felt clean. How he survived cuts received in the beatings they forced him to endure while not suffering infections was a mystery.

The distant sound of the only exit door from the cells enclosure being opened caught everyone's attention, putting all of the inmates on edge. Most of the time a door opening wouldn't be cause for excitement. After the random beatings endured by Captain Deschamps stopped several months prior for unknown reasons, visits to the cells by their captors soon resolved into only utterly boring, predictable, and undeviating daily routine to feed them and remove the waste buckets. The only real exception was always when a new group of inmates were brought in to the already crowded prison cells. But a deviation from the established routine could mean anything and without fail it stretched the nerves of the inmates taut every time.

Captain Deschamps remained where he was, eyes closed. Part of him dreaded the possibility they were coming for him, while unbidden the thought it would be good if they were indeed after him flitted across his mind. As he willed the thought away he knew it wasn't the first time he actually hoped they were coming to put an end to his miserable existence.

He could hear two sets of footsteps coming down the stairs and ever closer, finally stopping outside his cell. He sighed as the harsh metallic grate of the key turning in the lock and the rusty creak of the cell door sounded.

"Deschamps. Let's go," said one of the jailers.

His heart sank at the words, but he knew the people counting on him to be strong included his own loved ones. Bracing himself mentally, the Captain sat up with deliberate care and swung his legs off the bunk to the floor. Two pairs of rough hands seized his arms and jerked him to his feet. As the two burly soldiers serving as guards dragged him roughly out of the cell enclosure a few of the remaining inhabitants called out words of encouragement.

"Be strong, Marcel! Don't let these bastards intimidate you!"

He soon found himself in the all too familiar interrogation room on the second floor of the jail, used with him so many times before. The two soldiers slammed him into the same wooden chair as previously and one tied him to it with his arms behind his back while the other held him in place. Satisfied, one of the soldiers left the room while the other went to a door on the other side of the room. After knocking on it the soldier stepped to the side and stood impassively watching his prisoner.

As Deschamps waited he looked around and squinted in pain, noticing a difference this time as the shutters on the only window to the outside world were partly open, letting in a bright stream of sunlight. Although he couldn't see out the window because of where he was sitting, it wouldn't have mattered as his eyes were burning from the bright light.

He was still trying to accustom his eyes to it when the door to the room opened and two men came in. As they came into view he struggled to focus and realized the first man was, as expected, the bastard named Montdenoix who interrogated him before. As he shifted his gaze and saw the other man he couldn't help sucking in his breath in audible dismay.

Captain La Chance came over to stand before him, smiling as he folded his arms. A look of obvious, cruel pleasure was on his face. "Marcel, it has been too long. I am pleased to see you again, especially given the circumstances."

"La Chance, you pig," said Captain Deschamps as he glared back, struggling to master his emotions as he did. With deliberate effort he stretched as far forward as his bonds would let him and spat on the boots of the man before him.

"Marcel, is that any way to greet an old friend?" said La Chance, staring down at the spittle briefly before unleashing a devastating punch to the exposed midsection of his prisoner.

The pain exploded in his body as he gasped in agony, almost blacking out and slumping against his restraints. Before the pain even began subsiding Deschamps felt La Chance grab a handful of his prison shirt and use it to wipe the spittle off his boot while his two captors began talking with each other.

"Captain La Chance?" said Montdenoix. "I didn't know you and Captain Deschamps were acquainted."

"Yes, indeed, we go back a long ways. Don't we, Marcel? You bastard, I've been looking forward to this for weeks."

With no response from the prisoner La Chance looked back at Montdenoix with a cold smile. "His family and mine have been *acquainted*, as you say, for a long time. His father ruined my family, accusing my father of fraud and poisoning everyone against us. Our Captain Deschamps is from a family of high noble lineage, higher than my family, and they used this to their advantage. Life became a struggle as a result. Marcel and I knew each other when we were growing up, and let's just say this bastard continued the family tradition of persecution."

"I see," said Montdenoix, eyeing Captain La Chance with concern obvious on his face. "Well, it would seem our prisoner is paying attention to us again, so let us get on with this, shall we? If I may, we cannot let personal concerns get in the way of doing our duty."

La Chance gave Montdenoix a stiff look. "You have no need to teach me my duty, sir. I am just enjoying the fact this duty is enabling me to do things I've wanted to do for a very long time."

Deschamps gave a start as a rough hand grabbed his chin and pulled his face up, forcing him to look at the two men.

"Still conscious, are you?" said La Chance, as he let his grip on the prisoner drop once he was certain Deschamps would remain looking at him. "Good. Well, we need to have a little talk, Marcel. Actually, you are the one to do the talking here, as I'm sure you know. I'm also certain you know what we want, so why don't you just tell us and save yourself?"

Deschamps remained silent for a moment before sighing. Drawing on his reserves of strength he sat straighter as he finally responded. "I have no idea what you are talking about. I don't even know why I'm here or what right you have to imprison me."

The two men both laughed, although the laughter held no warmth. La Chance shook his head, still chuckling as he pulled some letters from his jacket pocket.

"So this is how you want it, eh? Fine by me. Look, this first letter I have here is all the authority I need to deal with the likes of you. This confirms the action taken by my colleague Hubert Montdenoix here. You were found to be supporting royalist agitators actively trying to subvert the legitimate government of France and its colony St. Lucia, hence your denunciation and incarceration. Our masters have considered the facts and delegated deciding your punishment to me. But that's not all! We have even better things to discuss with you."

As La Chance put a knowing smirk on his face and put the first letter back in his pocket, Captain Deschamps couldn't stop himself from snorting in disgust. "You bastards call yourselves *legitimate*? You are traitors."

The hard slap to his face rocked his head back and he groaned from the shock of it. Montdenoix gave him no time to recover as he grabbed a fistful of his hair and slapped him hard a second time, bringing stars to his vision.

Montdenoix leaned close to his face. "Listen, you idiot. Watch your tongue or face the consequences."

The mirth in La Chance's voice was obvious as he leaned forward close to Deschamps's face to continue. "So as I was saying, you have other things to talk to us about. Far worse things, actually. Being just a royalist supporter is bad enough, but being a spy takes you to a whole new level."

Deschamps couldn't help himself from stiffening a little as his captor spoke, and La Chance saw it.

"Oh, you know what is next, don't you? Yes, I can see it in your eyes. We have you, Marcel. Our friends were in the office of the former Minister for the Navy, you see. We didn't know who his minion out here was for certain, but we knew there was one. Lots of signs pointed to you and the evidence was overwhelming. And then, there was this!"

As La Chance held the envelope up for him to see, Deschamps felt his heart sink. He could see the address was to a nondescript trading house in Barbados and Deschamps knew the envelope all too well, since he was the one who addressed and sent it. But he composed himself and looked back at his accuser with as bland a face as possible.

"I'm supposed to recognize this, am I?"

"Ah, but you do, don't you, Marcel? Yes, some other friends intercepted this for us and what did we find? What seems an innocent looking letter has a message in cipher written in secret ink between the lines. We know the origin of the letter was this island and, what a surprise, when we showed this to your former first officer and your clerk they both swore this was your handwriting."

La Chance put the letter back in his pocket as he stepped back and spread his hands wide in mock dismay. "So you see, you have a real problem, Marcel. Merely supporting royalist agitators is one thing, but you are a spy. You are up to your neck in dung. But even now, you have opportunity to find our mercy. How, you want to know? It's very simple. Just tell us what we want to know, and we promise you will be shown more mercy than you deserve."

Deschamps stiffened and glared back at La Chance before responding. "I don't know what you are talking about."

"Captain," said Montdenoix. "Be reasonable. We know Governour de Gimat didn't take the money with him when he fled. We have questioned everyone involved. We also have the word of several witnesses you were up to something around the same time as he fled. Neither of us believes in coincidences, correct? So let's get down to business. I know my colleague here would likely prefer to let you rot the rest of your days in jail or even worse, but I can prevail upon him to, as he says, show mercy and set you free. You have my word on it. If, of course, you tell us where it is."

"If either of you think I would be prepared to accept your word for anything, you are both even more delusional than I know you already are. I don't know what you are talking about."

"Well, there you have it, Captain La Chance. As I said, he is an obstinate fellow, even now."

"If this is the way he wants it," said La Chance, with a shrug. Turning he walked over to where the soldier still stood awaiting orders. Deschamps couldn't hear the brief conversation, but he knew what was coming.

Pulling out a short, two foot long club from where it hung at his belt the soldier strode over to Deschamps and walked around him a couple of times, as if deciding where to start.

The first blow hammered unexpectedly on the front of his right leg on the shin, where minimal padding between his skin and the bone of his leg gave no cushion for the strike. Deschamps couldn't stop his inarticulate scream of pain in response. The scream was renewed as the next blow landed in the same area on his opposite leg. The blows continued to rain down indiscriminately all over his body for another minute before mercifully the beating finally ceased.

Barely conscious, his body a mass of bruises and indescribable pain, Deschamps was aware his captors were once again talking to him, but the words weren't registering in his brain. He felt his head jerked up by the hair to face them as a bowl of water was dashed into his face. As he focused on what they were saying he realized the bonds tying him to the chair were being undone.

"Well, Marcel, I do hope you enjoyed that as much as I did. Actually, I'm rather hoping you'll continue to be obstinate, so we can keep doing this. And I assure you, now I'm in charge here, we certainly will."

The agent Montdenoix coughed into his hand to gain attention. "Captain Deschamps, I do hope you understand that despite whatever history there obviously is between you gentlemen, our purpose here is to just have you tell us what we want to know. This is our job. And we will be merciful if he does, *won't we*, Captain La Chance?"

Deschamps watched as La Chance turned to Montdenoix, obviously trying to keep a scowl off his face before finally responding.

"Yes, yes, of course, Hubert. But I think Captain Deschamps needs to fully understand what his fate will be if he continues to show us a lack of cooperation."

Signaling to Montdenoix, the two men

finished untying him from the chair and after seizing him under the arms they lifted him up. Weakened and unable to resist, Deschamps winced and groaned in pain at the sudden movement. The two men dragged him over to the window, arriving in time to hear the distant, harsh thud of something hitting a piece of wood hard. La Chance threw the shutters open wide and Deschamps winced once again as the full sun of a bright day temporarily blinded him.

As Deschamps's eyes grew accustomed to the light he saw La Chance's face creased with naked malice as he moved to within inches of his own. "So, Marcel, look what I brought with me from home. I'll bet you've never seen one of these before, but you know what it is."

Deschamps went cold when he focused on the guillotine on the other side of the square, as he did indeed know what he was seeing. The workers were back testing the device and already raising the blade for another trial.

"So, yes, you need to cooperate and tell us what we want. Despite what my colleague here says I am now in charge here. Sooner or later I will lose patience with your lack of cooperation and when I do, this will be your fate. It will be too merciful and quick a death for my liking, but there is one possibility I enjoy the thought of. I'm told there is always a bare few seconds, perhaps two or three at most, when the head still appears conscious after the blade does its job. I plan to be there so the last thing you see will be *me* as I grab your severed head and spit in your face."

"*Yesss*, well, I think our prisoner gets the

point, Captain La Chance," said Montdenoix, unable to keep a hint of annoyance from his voice. "Perhaps we should let him return to his cell to consider his options, eh?"

La Chance took a moment to master himself, the naked hatred on his face slow to disappear.

"Yes, yes. I agree. Besides, he stinks and I've smelled enough of him for today. And there *is* always tomorrow. Let's go get a drink."

As they signaled the soldier to come over and take Deschamps back to the cells below, the rasping, metallic sound of the blade falling followed by the jarring thud of its impact came from across the square once again.

Chapter Two
December 1792
Antigua

The two men were both sweating profusely. They circled each other with wary focus as the sun glinted on the knives each man held in their right hands. Evan knew his opponent was struggling from thirst and beginning to tire fast, the same as he was. Both men were looking for an opening to attack, but the problem was neither was giving opportunity to do so. Despite having only one arm, Evan adapted long ago and was accustomed to maintaining his balance despite the loss. He wasn't outmatched in the fight because his opponent was using only one arm too.

Evan's opponent, a tall, dark haired and lanky black man, grunted and did a sudden feint to his right a bare second before kicking a cloud of loose dirt at Evan and ducking low. A strike with blinding speed under Evan's guard to his exposed lower right body was the real attempt.

Evan saw the move and knew it to be a feint, though. Dancing backward he spun in a quick circle to bring his right hand with the knife to bear in his own lightning fast counterstrike to the back of his off balance opponent. To Evan's frustration his slash met only thin air, as his foe recovered enough to pull away and begin the dance once again.

The struggle continued without letup in a whirlwind of sudden feints and countermoves for what seemed an eternity. The end, when it came, wasn't what the two men expected.

Launching a furious attack, Evan pushed his

opponent back with a series of quick thrusts only to have them barely miss each time. His opponent shifted unexpectedly, pushing hard to move forward with his own counterstrike right at the same time as Evan tried to shift his own attack. The unstoppable momentum of the two men brought their bodies crashing together in a bone rattling collision and their heads smashed into each other at the same time with an audible cracking sound. Both men crumpled to the ground, holding their heads and groaning. After a long minute Evan finally spoke.

"Christ, that's going to be painful for the next week at least. I think I may end up with a lump on my forehead."

"Too late for me, Evan. Damn me, it feels like I've already got one coming up."

The two men looked at each other as one and burst out laughing as they sat holding their heads. When the laughter finally subsided Evan groaned again and got to his feet. Trying in vain to brush the dust off his clothes he gave up and instead tried grooming his light, sandy brown hair with his hand to stop the sweat from falling down his face. His opponent did the same and the two men walked over to the edge of the clearing they were in where a small table and two chairs sat in the shade of a large tree with brilliant red flowers. Two mugs filled with water from a jug sitting on the table awaited them. After downing a mug each Evan turned to his opponent.

"Here, James, let me help free your arm. It'll be easier if I do it."

James grunted in agreement as he poured himself another mug and turned so Evan could get at the knots binding the black man's left arm to his side to untie it. Changing his mind, Evan decided to simply take the wooden safety sheath and the heavy padding added to the end of the knife off one of the practice blades they were using to simply cut the ropes. Once removed the two men began stripping off the improvised padded shirts used to keep them from injury. The shirts were completely soaked and slick with sweat.

"Well, despite the outcome, I'm glad we started doing these one arm practices, Evan. As dangerous as they are, it makes me just that much more capable to deal with whatever some bastard tries on me."

Evan Ross smiled in agreement as he finally got free of the constraints of the heavy padded shirt. Evan lost his left arm after being shot by a British Navy deserter over eight years ago. A Lieutenant in the British Royal Navy at the time, he was abandoned in the hospital attached to the Royal Navy base at English Harbour on the Caribbean island of Antigua by a Captain who didn't want him.

He needed a long time after his injury to grow truly accustomed to having a missing limb. Phantom pain bothered him for a time, but the nightmares and unexplained anger he sometimes endured took much longer to subside. He did his best to master it all, though. Eight years later he was so fully adapted to his loss and having only one arm he scarcely thought about it.

The black man with him, James Wilton, had been a Master's Mate on the same warship as Evan eight years before and was injured in the same fight.

The son of a Royal Navy officer and a black slave woman his father had freed and married, he chose to follow in his father's path in life. Shot in the thigh, James joined Evan in the hospital. The two men grew to be firm friends, unusual as this was and despite their disparate backgrounds. The trauma and recovery from their shared experiences proved an unshakable bond. When in public the two men referred to each other formally as Commander and Lieutenant, but in private they maintained no such distinction and they were simply Evan and James. The two friends were in despair for their futures until Captain Horatio Nelson entered their lives.

Nelson was tasked with assuming command of the Northern Leeward Islands squadron of the Royal Navy, based in English Harbour, and of the extensive dockyard repair facilities it housed. One of his primary tasks was to stamp out rampant American smuggling of trade goods in order to evade the King's taxes. Local plantation owners were all too willing to be the buyers.

With no spot available for them to serve on warships under his command, Nelson used Evan and James as spies to gain the information needed to stop the smuggling. In the process, the two men uncovered a combined American and French plot to destabilize the British islands in the area by arming runaway slaves, with the goal of profiting from the ensuing mayhem. With their success putting a stop to both, Evan and James were awarded promotions. Evan had served as Commander of the Navy Dockyard ever since, with James promoted to Lieutenant and serving as his First Officer.

The two men, both thirty-one years old, were still serving in their respective roles and this was unusual. In normal circumstances British warship Captains effectively wore two hats, one as Captain of their ship and the other as an intelligence officer. The Admiralty, however, saw value in the unique approach taken by Nelson and, having no other opportunities to hand for the two men given the nation was at peace, their assignment as intelligence officers kept being extended.

The cover story was Evan held responsibility to manage the Dockyard, with the help of James. In reality, over time a growing variety of covert tasks were sent their way to perform. They were constantly seeking information from anywhere they could get it, standing on guard against anything with potential to affect British interests in the Caribbean. While nominally they reported to the senior warship Captain on station in Antigua, in reality they took direction from their spymaster Sir James Standish, based in Barbados. Senior British diplomats around the Caribbean knew who they and their master in Barbados were, constantly seeking their advice while bringing information about developments in their respective domains to the intelligence officers attention. This meant dealing with a never-ending, virtual torrent of correspondence, which was the lifeblood of their work. Information was gold. Lately, the torrential flow was growing at an exponential pace.

But their job wasn't all about dealing with paperwork and this was why the two men were exercising their skills with knives. Over the years the two men found themselves in more fights, mostly in taverns, than either could remember. Trying to get information from people who sometimes didn't want to supply it could be a dangerous business.

Evan and James decided early on they were both going to make the best of their assignment as spies. The two men soon realized they could be involved in unconventional fights on an ongoing basis and this, combined with the need to remain fit, meant development of an exercise routine and weapons practice appropriate for their work was needed.

"Yes, you know I appreciate these one armed fights with me, James, even if we do end up with some bruises," said Evan. "Everyone else has an advantage over me, so I've got to be ready for anything. But you really think this helps you too?"

"Sure. If I've learned anything its that I have to be ready for anything, including the possibility one arm could be injured and I may have to fight with just the other. I like everything we've been doing, even if people don't understand why we are doing it. Moving these sessions to our back yard away from all the prying or curious eyes was a good idea."

"I agree. And keeping at this has certainly kept us both fit," replied Evan, looking at their surroundings before taking another long drink of water. Evan meant it, too. The daily exercise brought both men to a peak of fitness surpassing virtually everyone around them and the reality was they were fitter now than either man was ten years before. Both Evan and James actually looked forward to the strenuous routines and were unhappy if they missed even a few. The two men originally began practicing within the confines of the Dockyard itself, but they soon realized this location wasn't going to work. The problem was the unconventional nature of what they were doing.

Traditional Royal Navy combat training always included the use of weapons in hand-to-hand situations as part of the regular routine for sailors and officers alike. The standard cutlass drill along with use of pikes, sea pistols, cudgels of various lengths, and boarding axes were all common fare. Even boxing was included for fitness. But the two men's routine included regular practice with all of this and more.

Hand-to-hand combat with knives was definitely not part of the standard routine. Neither was practice with actually throwing knives at an opponent or the unconventional bare hands fight routines they began experimenting with. Their deviation from standard boxing moves to include strikes to opponents using their feet and practicing punches involving use of the base of the palm of their hands and not a fist drew attention. Some of the Navy officers passing through the Dockyard and seeing them at practice were particularly disdainful.

After the third pointed comment directed their way about ungentlemanly conduct Evan knew they needed to find a better spot, because the kind of fights they were usually in demanded anything *but* gentlemanly conduct. The backyard of the home the two men shared, half way between the Dockyard and the small village of Falmouth Harbour, was the perfect solution. The clearing in the rear was hidden from the road travellers used by several large trees and small brush, but was big enough to accommodate all of their needs. A pair of large timbers with their base sunk deep into the ground served as targets for multiple purposes. They began slowly expanding their repertoire of unusual tactics as they settled in. James even became proficient with the use of a crude home made garrote, a thin but strong piece of rope connecting wooden handles on either end.

"Well, I think two hours of this is enough for me today, James. You want to wash up first?"

James slipped his shirt over his head as he replied. "Nope, the wash tub is all yours. Manon is working at the Inn today so I'll just go use one of their tubs to clean myself up. They've got some music happening tonight so we thought we'd stay for dinner and enjoy it. Are you two coming?"

Evan smiled in contemplation of the idea. The thought of a pleasant evening at The Dockyard Dog Inn, the best such establishment in Falmouth Harbour, was appealing. After a moment to think he shook his head, though. "We'll see. I've got a meeting in St. Johns early tomorrow so probably not."

James raised an eyebrow at this. "Another job for us?"

"Maybe. The Governour's note didn't give details, just the request to be there. Well, have a good time."

"Oh, so it's really not just an excuse for you and Alice to have the place all to yourselves," said James, a teasing grin creasing his face.

Evan laughed.

***

A half hour later Evan finished heating water to pour into the wide, large barrel custom made for bathing. While many still believed bathing was something to be done once per year at most, attitudes toward cleanliness were changing. Life in the tropics meant sweating was inevitable and after years spent among unwashed bodies confined in close quarters on warships, Evan had developed a preference for cleanliness and opportunities to sponge his body clean were welcome.

As he was about to step into the steaming water with a piece of precious soap imported from home he heard the door to the room open. Turning, he saw Alice standing in the doorway, wearing a big smile on her face.

"*Ohh*, a naked man," she said, closing the door and walking over to where stood. "Even better, a *handsome* naked man."

Evan gave her a rueful smile and a kiss as she reached up and ran one hand across the hard muscles of his chest and shoulder, clearly enjoying what she was doing. Evan was two inches shorter than his friend James, but he was still above average in height and it meant Alice brushed against him as she stood almost on tiptoes to kiss him. Evan enjoyed her touch and he dropped the soap in the water, reaching out to cup her face in his hand to give her another kiss.

"My God, you are still as beautiful as the day I first saw you."

Alice and Evan were lovers and had lived together ever since she helped him make covert connections with slaves around the island, gathering the information Nelson needed to put a stop to American smuggling in 1785. Alice was uniquely placed to do so as when they first met she was a slave prostitute at a tavern in St. John's, the capital of Antigua. As the unacknowledged black daughter of a slave woman and John Roberts, the largest white plantation owner on the island of Antigua, she was given a hard choice. Her father also owned the tavern and her options were either servitude in the fields at the mercy of his overseers or life as a prostitute in his tavern. As reward for her help Evan used gold captured from French and American agents trying to destabilize Antigua to buy her freedom. Much of the gold also went to setting her up as part owner of The Dockyard Dog Inn in Falmouth Harbour. As a free woman she could have done anything, but she chose to stay with him. The truth was they fell in love with each other.

Evan had needed to think about the relationship. While her skin colour was irrelevant to him, many in society would consider such a union unthinkable. When it came to sailors, though, the Royal Navy overall was egalitarian. While the vast majority of men in the Navy were white and English, men of all colours and from all over the world populated British warships. Some officers were exceptions, but to most the only thing of consequence was whether a sailor was doing his job. Evan was well aware of the depth of prejudice toward non-whites of any sort permeating society, especially in the Caribbean. But as someone schooled in the ways of the Navy from a young age, Evan decided early in his career to pay no attention to the colour of anyone's skin for any reason, seeing little purpose in doing so.

Evan's biggest decision was whether to make the relationship permanent, because they both wanted it to be this way. The question to consider was whether there would be an impact to his career, which also made him to think long and hard about how important his career actually was. Taking a black woman's hand in marriage was unusual, but he needed look no further than his friend James to know he was not setting a precedent. In the end Evan decided Alice must come first and one day he proposed to her. To his surprise she turned him down, while making it clear the love she felt for him was unchanged. Her reasons reflected the hard, pragmatic outlook on life forced on her by her father.

Evan was aware Alice knew he wanted a ship, and in truth, this was more than simple desire. Both Evan and James, sailors to the core, were still lusting for a ship even after several years of their shore assignment. But with the country at peace, opportunities were few. Evan and James also became victims of their own success, as the Admiralty wasn't about to break up a good team of spies producing results without reason. Alice told him her fear was sooner or later he would indeed get a ship, and be given orders to sail away from her. She didn't want him forced into making a hard choice, despite assurances his mind was set firm. They were fortunate to be together for many years as it was, but the world was changing and with possible war on the horizon he knew she was right to fear it happening. In the end they simply continued living in the moment, hoping some day a resolution would be found.

Evan smiled and shook his head to clear away the memories, bringing himself back to the present. "Well, my love, since you are here you can help scrub my back. James and I had a long practice session today and I need a bath."

"What a good idea," she said, as she gave him the wide smile he so loved to see on her face. "In fact, I have an even better one. But first, I don't think I really need this dress for the job of making you presentable."

As she pulled it off, leaving her completely naked, Evan grinned and pulled her close, enjoying the feel of her lithe body and full breasts. He ran his hand behind her up to the cascade of black, gently curling hair falling down her back and pulled her head close for a much longer kiss.

When she finally pulled away she looked at him in mock exasperation. "Well, now look what you've done. I'm all hot and sweaty too. Say, do you think there could be room for both of us in this tub?"

Evan grinned and laughed.

***

The Governour's meeting room in his main offices in St. John's, the capital of Antigua, was reasonably pleasant to sit in for a change. Open shutters lining the far wall of the room on the second floor of the stone building meant a pleasant, but gentle breeze could drift in. The stone walls ensured the room was cool enough and pitchers of water to drink helped Evan to manage the heat of an unseasonably warm day for December, even though he long since abandoned any thought of wearing his

Navy uniform to such meetings and no one expected it of him anyway given his role.

What made a real difference this day was the limited numbers of people in attendance. Meetings the Governour held almost always included a host of various military personnel along with any number of influential plantation owners always wanting a say in anything with the potential to affect them. In a room packed with men sweating in their uniforms or suit coats, even a strong breeze stood no chance of offering relief. But as Evan took his place he noticed right away no one appeared to be enjoying the pleasant December day. Grim and worried looks were clear on the features of the men at the table.

The new Governour of Antigua, William Woodley, was chairing the meeting, and the dark look on his plump face was setting the tone for everyone else. In fact, however, he was far from new, having already served once before as Governour of Antigua from 1768 to 1771. Only three other people sat at the table along with Evan and all of them were military personnel.

The only other Navy officer present was Evan's immediate superior for matters related to the Dockyard. Sixty three year old Baronet Captain Sir John Laforey was taller than average with a lean faced countenance to match his usually aggressive demeanour. He proved a welcome replacement to his predecessor Captain George Rand. Where Captain Rand took an active dislike to Evan, Sir John was happy to support anyone capable of furthering his personal goals. In Sir John's case, this meant making him money.

Sir John was well known throughout the Navy, with a career starting during the Seven Years War and continued throughout the American Revolutionary War. Internal Navy politics and numerous disputes over prize money kept him sidelined for several years until the disputes were finally settled and he was sent to Antigua as senior Captain for the Northern Leeward Islands Squadron. The rumour was he wouldn't be a Captain for much longer, given his seniority. Unlike his predecessor, Sir John understood the value of intelligence and its role in helping to line his pockets. Evan was given free rein to do his job without interference as a result.

The other two men were full Colonels in the army, one commanding the large fortifications on Rat Island protecting the harbour entrance to the capital St. John's. The other was in charge of the remaining smaller fortifications around the island and the small garrison at Shirley Heights, overlooking English Harbour and the Dockyard.

"Gentlemen, thank you for coming," said Governour Woodley. "I wanted to get together with all of you to discuss the situation. In fact, I think we should do more frequent meetings given what is going on in the world."

"Governour, has there been a specific development to cause concern for the meeting today?" said one of the Army officers.

"Well, I met with the plantation owners council earlier today and have the usual justifiable concerns from them about the ongoing situation in St. Domingue, for which we need to discuss our preparations, and one development there in particular.

Hmm, that's not quite true, there is one other thing which could be of interest to you specifically," replied the Governour, turning to give Evan a direct look.

"Sir?" said Evan, sitting forward and raising an eyebrow to indicate his interest.

"You all know how worried the owners are about what is going on in St. Domingue and their fear of contagion, of course. One of them mentioned to me earlier today he has possible word of the first such sign."

This time Sir John Laforey raised an eyebrow and Evan could see from the look on his face he was trying to convey his disbelief. "Governour, we've discussed that with them before. We are over twice the distance from St. Domingue to Jamaica. If some fool were trying to export this bloody revolution of theirs to our domain, Jamaica would be a far more logical place to start. Have we received word from them on this?"

"No, but this doesn't mean it isn't happening. Since we are on this topic, I may as well finish dealing with this point. Commander Ross, the word is there was open talk recently in some tavern, by a couple of black men no one seemed to know, about The Rights of Man and how slavery should be abolished everywhere."

"A tavern? Where, sir?"

"Some place in Jolly Harbour, south of St. John's. Do you know it?"

"Sir, we know it well. A place where it's best to be prepared for anything if one really must enter it. We will get right on this and if there is something afoot we will deal with it."

"Governour," said one of the Army Colonels. "I have to agree with Sir John. It makes no sense for abolitionist agitators to deliberately target us. The French have far greater issues on their plate than trying to make our lives miserable here on Antigua. I don't know how they would get here even if they were trying it."

"I do, sir," said Evan, as they all turned to him in surprise. "Sir John and our squadron are doing a fine job of patrolling our waters to keep us safe, but there is a deserted beach for every day of the year on this island and there are a finite number of warships to do the job. There are many ways for someone determined enough to reach our shores to actually get here. The most likely would be fishing boats."

"Fishing boats?" said the Governour.

"Certainly. Every island has a host of small vessels and they often range far and wide to make their catch. They have to go where the fish are, you see. They encounter fishermen from other islands on a regular basis. Information is always exchanged about what is happening elsewhere. In truth, it's a rudimentary communication network, for use by anyone who needs to communicate with someone elsewhere without a lot of notice being taken. I confess I've used their services on more than one occasion. But sometimes, *people* are exchanged too. These are people who for whatever reason can't stay where they are and most often are runaways. If they can make it to another island where no one knows them and they aren't being hunted, they can try to blend in and gradually begin a new life. And to answer the question I'm sure you are thinking, this isn't just speculation on my part. My colleagues and I know of a few such examples here on this island. We watch them and as long as they haven't committed a major crime they should pay for, and aren't committing any crimes here, we have left them be."

The Governour frowned. "Are you sure this is wise, Commander?"

Evan kept a bland look on his face as he responded. "These people have established ties with local people we use as our sources to keep our finger on the pulse of what is happening on Antigua. We believe the information we get from our networks, which keeps us from being murdered in our beds in some unexpected slave uprising, is more valuable than a few escaped slaves from other islands."

The Governour paused to consider this before offering a sheepish smile. "Good point, Commander. Well, please do look into this and let us know if we have a problem."

The Governour sat back and looked at the men around the table. "So, gentlemen, as I said the real reason for this meeting is to discuss the situation, which appears to be worsening. You recall we've been hoping for better news from St. Domingue given the French sent another seven thousand troops to the island to help deal with the situation. Well, it hasn't helped. I've received a confirmed report the rebels have not been checked and, in fact, now have firm control of over about one third of St. Domingue. Apparently some buffoon named Leger Sonthonax has taken over as Commissioner and, instead of attacking the bloody rebel slaves as he should, he is harassing the plantation owners because he thinks they are all either Royalist sympathizers or they are secretly supporting a Spanish takeover."

Almost as one the men around the table sucked in their breath in collective dismay. One of the Army Colonels groaned. "Good Christ, what a mess. God only knows how this is going to end. I wonder if we're going to have to go in there eventually and sort it all out?"

In private, Evan was wondering exactly this, too. The effects of the French Revolution, with its publication of The Declaration of the Rights of Man and the ongoing turmoil wrought by the July 13, 1789 storming of the Bastille, rippled far and wide from the shores of France. In the Caribbean, the impact was like a major earthquake on St. Domingue, the valuable French western half of the island of Hispaniola shared with the Spanish colony of Santo Domingo in the east. The reason St. Domingue was so important was the scale of the sugar operations on the island, as they produced by far the most sugar of any island in the Caribbean.

"The depth of French stupidity on this matter knows no bounds," said the Governour. "You'd think that with over a half million slaves in St. Domingue, and apparently some forty thousand of them now in open armed rebellion, this idiot would see the problem. My understanding is there are only perhaps thirty five thousand white owners and overseers in total in St. Domingue to manage the entire lot! But I gather this fellow is another one of these bloody abolitionists and he somehow thinks it will all be just fine. So the fool divides his resources and has more of them trying to keep the royalists in line than he does bringing the escaped slaves back under control. Perhaps if he finds himself being murdered in his bed, as Commander Ross says, he might change his thinking."

"At least *we* are still holding the line on that nonsense," said one of the Army officers, allowing the heat of his feeling to show in the tone of his voice. "Thank God the House of Lords put a hold on the stupid resolution to support abolition approved by those idiots in our own House of Commons earlier this year."

The men around the table nodded, but Evan was lost in thought. He knew the situation in St. Domingue wasn't as simple as the Governour was portraying it. One of his primary tasks as an intelligence officer was to stay in contact with British diplomats in the Leeward Islands and sometimes beyond. The constant stream of correspondence with them together with several visits over the years to connect with them in person gave Evan an excellent understanding of the situation. And on St. Domingue, this was complicated beyond belief.

When the 1789 Revolution happened the wealthy white owners were overjoyed, as they saw opportunity to gain independence and loosen the shackles imposed by Paris. In short order they took over the local National Assembly, freeing it of nominees owing allegiance to Paris, and began making rules to suit their needs. The unique element at play was the fact not all of the plantation owners were white. Over time former black slaves, freed by their owners for a variety of reasons and free mulattos, offspring of a black and a white parent, came to own businesses and plantations of their own. What seemed so strange to Evan was these former slaves and people with parents who were still slaves now owned slaves themselves, and could be as harsh as any white plantation owner. Evan's jaw dropped when first told this group of roughly thirty thousand people were at a point where they owned one third of the land and one quarter of the slaves on St. Domingue.

Evan was also unsurprised to learn nothing was going smoothly in the local Assembly, as the white owners held no interest whatsoever in looking out for anyone's interests but their own. The men of colour, as the blacks and mulattos were known, were given opportunity to participate, but proved unwilling to cooperate unless their interests were met too.

By 1790 the slaves had realized their situation was getting worse, not better, as the local owners were running their operations with even harsher treatment than before, being freed of even the minimal accountability to France necessary in past. The men of colour were also frustrated they weren't being given the recognition or respect they expected and felt was deserved.

In August of 1791 it boiled over in a widespread uprising. Almost two thousand whites were massacred, while over two hundred large sugar plantations and several hundred smaller coffee plantations were destroyed. Over fifteen thousand slaves went missing. The violence continued, as no one was willing to compromise. Evan was dismayed to learn the number of slaves deserting to join the rebels was now so large, knowing it to be a bad sign.

With every reason to bring the wayward colony back under its control, Paris authorized deployment of the seven thousand troops to the island. But on a wider scale, there were rumours the Spanish on the other side of Hispaniola were indeed eyeing the French colony with the idea of finding a way to join them together under their control. To Evan's mind this gave the French Governour Sonthonax reason to be concerned and wary about the situation he was in. With the prospects for even more conflict on the horizon, Evan knew several plantation owners on St. Domingue were fleeing with their slaves to America.

As for the British, Evan saw nothing to indicate a direct interest in elbowing their way into St. Domingue, but he was suspicious. The island was productive in the extreme, and the wealth to be gained by controlling it could be enormous. Evan knew from experience naked greed was a powerful motivator. But as the Governour pulled out a letter and held it up for all to see Evan brought his attention back to the discussion.

"I should also mention, gentlemen, the insanity within France itself is apparently continuing apace," said the Governour. "I just received word from Sir John Orde in Dominica that some arrogant clown named La Chance showed up claiming to be the first of a wave of representatives from the new French administration, come to take over the various French possessions here. He told Sir John it was in our interests to build a relationship with the new masters in France and made a bunch of vague threats about what would happen if we didn't. Sir John threw him out without ado, of course."

The Governour laughed as he spoke. "I know Sir John well. I rather think the New Years Day Rebellion he faced back in 1791 on Dominica has not faded from his memory. He still thinks the French were somehow behind it all."

The men around the table smiled dutifully as the Governour continued. "Anyway, the point is that as near as I can tell the situation in France itself continues to go downhill fast. As for St. Domingue, well, need I say more? So the real purpose of this meeting is just to make you aware and to suggest the time has come for us to make these meetings much more regular. I trust you have your respective forces as prepared as possible?"

"Governour," said Sir John Laforey. "Please rest assured the Royal Navy stands ready to defend us against whatever madness comes our way. In light of what is going on we have been drilling our men more frequently than normal. We are not at war with the French yet, but we are ready for it."

The two Army Colonels both nodded and in turn assured the Governour they were doing the same with their men.

"Patrols here on the island, gentlemen. Do they need to be increased?"

The two officers looked at each other and, as one, turned to Evan. The officer in charge of the Rat Island Garrison finally spoke, a thoughtful look on his face. "Right now, I suggest no, as to this point we have had no more than the usual drunken fights from sailors or soldiers to contend with. However, we may have to change our thinking depending on what Commander Ross finds when he investigates what is going on in Jolly Harbour."

"Gentlemen, I will report as soon as I am able," said Evan.

"Very well," said the Governour. "I suggest from here on we do a meeting once every two weeks, same day and time here. I realize this may seem a bit much, but if we have problems coming our way I'd rather be on top of it immediately. Any concerns?"

The men around the table shook their heads and Evan rose with the rest of them as one to leave.

***

Within minutes of arriving in his office in the Dockyard Evan found James standing in his doorway wanting to talk to him.

"Evan, I have a report of something I think we need to check out. I got word from one of the barmen at that shack passing for a bar in Jolly Harbour of a couple of questionable black patrons talking about revolution, among other things."

Evan agreed, after filling James in on the meeting with the Governour. "Yes, let's pay it a visit this evening. We'd better be ready for anything."

After debating what being ready meant, they settled on bringing cudgels as their primary weapon. Essentially a thick, three-foot long stick, Evan and James deliberately cut theirs shorter by six inches to accommodate close quarter action of the exact sort they feared they might encounter. Both had thick leather straps threaded and tied off through holes in the handle. The cudgels were carried in a loose sheath behind their left shoulders, held in place by cunningly designed straps running from their neck to under their right arms and around their lower torsos. They also both carried their favourite seven-inch blade knives, easy to reach as they were strapped to their legs in homemade sheaths and concealed inside their boots. Neither wore their uniforms.

Leaving their horses tied to nearby trees the two officers walked to the ramshackle tavern they could see perched on a small rise overlooking the curve of Jolly Harbour beach. The building was in bad need of paint and repair. But it obviously remained serviceable, as a number of patrons could be seen in the light of lanterns through the open shutters sitting at the tables inside. A buzz of conversation and occasional laughter grew louder as the two men got closer to the door. James forestalled Evan from opening the door.

"Let me go in first, Evan. The barman doesn't know you well, but I know him. He'll point us in the right direction when I walk in."

Evan nodded, but followed James close behind into the bar. Within seconds the raucous noise of the crowd faded away to a dead silence. Evan knew where the bar was and watched the barman move surreptitiously into an area where the lantern over the bar threw less light. With an almost imperceptible jerk of his head, the man did exactly as James predicted.

As one the two officers turned to look in the direction he indicated, focusing instantly on two men sitting at a table by themselves in a far corner of the room. Both men held mugs of ale in their hands and were turned to look at the newcomers along with everyone else. Evan walked over to their table, with James close behind, appraising the two men as they went.

Evan knew these were the men they sought. As they made their way over the rest of the patrons in the bar quietly threw coins on the tables and left, leaving their still full mugs where they were. Even without this sign these two men obviously stood out, as both bore the dark, coal black features of slaves straight from Africa. They were both big and heavily muscled from work in the fields.

Evan decided on a direct approach. "Gentlemen, I think you may be the newcomers we heard about. We thought we'd come and have a talk with you. Can we buy you a drink?"

The two black men both wore unreadable looks on their faces as they looked at each other before turning back to Evan. The one closest to him finally spoke in halting English, with a thick, strange accent making it difficult to understand him.

"Why you want talk us?"

Evan shrugged. "We like to get to know new people on the island. In particular, we want to know whether or not someone is going to be a problem. So can we buy you a drink and talk about it?"

"Yes," said the man as he turned and nodded imperceptibly to the man across the table from him. As he did, without turning to look, he threw his mug hard into Evan's face.

As Evan recoiled and tried to recover himself, he was given no time to do so. His foe boiled out of the chair to shove Evan hard on his chest. From the corner of his eye Evan registered that James was already engaged with his own opponent. Evan fell backwards out of control, smashing into another bar table and rolling off of it. This saved him, as by this time the slave produced a long, wicked looking knife from somewhere. His attempted slash barely missed disemboweling Evan.

Evan used the momentum of his roll to get to his feet and as he did, he pulled his cudgel out in time to parry yet another hard slash of the knife already coming at him. The slave pressed him back with a series of vicious slashes, trying to keep the advantage, but all the while Evan was assessing his opponent and he soon realized the man was without any combat training whatsoever.

After parrying several even wilder slashes Evan decided he knew enough of his opponent to change strategy. With a subtle shift to the side after one such effort, Evan didn't step backwards as his opponent expected. This left the slave off balance and exposed in an over extended position. Evan brought the end of the cudgel down hard on the back of the hand holding the knife, hearing the audible snap of the bones in the man's hand as he struck. The knife clattered to the floor and fell out of reach.

"Ahhh—" screamed the slave, but to Evan's shock he recovered himself fast and delivered a devastating punch to Evan's stomach with his undamaged other hand.

Evan fell back and hit the wall, in excruciating pain and wheezing for air. The slave paused for a bare second to assess his shattered hand. Reaching out before Evan could react he grabbed the cudgel, ripping it from Evan's hand. With all the force he could muster the slave raised the cudgel, intending to crush Evan's skull with it.

In desperation Evan tried one of the new tactics he and James recently brought into their routine. With his hand and fingers stiffened as hard as he could make them he darted under the man's guard and stabbed his arm straight ahead, striking the slave hard in his exposed throat. The man choked inarticulately, clutching at his throat. The strike was enough to deflect the aim of the blow from the cudgel, which slipped from his foe's hand, but it still glanced hard off Evan's left shoulder where his arm had been severed.

"Christ!" shouted Evan. Pain exploded in his shoulder, as the amputation area was sensitive, even several years after the injury. But he focused again and reached down to his boot, pulling the concealed knife from its sheath as the slave choked and gasped for air.

As Evan straightened up the slave recovered enough to reach out with his remaining good hand, grabbing Evan by the throat. Evan couldn't believe the strength of the man's grip and he knew if he let him continue he was in danger of being choked to death. With no choice, Evan plunged the knife deep into the slave's heart.

The man stiffened and for a long moment his grip wouldn't loosen. As the slave finally dropped to the floor like a stone Evan struggled to regain his breath, still holding the knife dripping with the man's blood. As he recovered, Evan became aware the fight on the other side of the room wasn't over yet and he turned to help James, knowing to be ready for anything.

Evan saw in an instant James hadn't been able to pull out his weapons as the two men were engaged in a brutal, hand-to-hand fight. The two men traded a series of punishing strikes to each other's bodies. James appeared to be inflicting more damage than the slave, but every punch James got in return was heavy. As Evan moved to join the fray James employed a practiced tactic, turning slightly and hammering his booted foot with devastating force on top of the other man's unprotected foot, scraping hard down the man's shin as he struck.

The slave howled in pain, but as he dropped he tried punching James in the groin. James grunted sharply in pain too, appearing to suffer a glancing blow. Clearly angered, he reached back and grabbed his cudgel even as the slave moved to punch James again. With his left hand James grabbed the back of the slave's head, pulling the man hard towards him. As he did, he struck with the cudgel using all the force he could muster. With an audible crack, the slave's head went completely limp and James flung him hard to the floor.

"Bastard!" shouted James, dropping the cudgel and massaging his groin in pain.

Rubbing his sore shoulder Evan came over and stood beside James, who was still doubled over trying to regain his breath. Reaching down Evan felt for a pulse in the slave lying on the floor, but he already knew what he would find from the odd angle the man's head lay at. Blood was oozing from where the blow crushed his skull.

"Well, you did for this one, James. Mine is

rotting somewhere in hell, too. Damn it, I wanted at least one of these bastards as a prisoner to do some talking."

James finally responded slowly as he straightened up, still wincing in pain and rubbing his groin area. "Christ, I don't think I'll be making Manon happy tonight. That was just a glancing shot, too."

Evan couldn't help laughing and James gave him a rueful grin as he continued. "Don't think either of them were going to cooperate even if we could have got them under control, anyway. Goddamn, good thing we've been practicing, Evan. These two were both big, nasty brutes. Strong as hell."

Both men turned as the barman, walking over to stand behind them, spoke up. "Well, I have to say, this was the most entertainment we've enjoyed around this place in weeks. Got to admit, you two are a pair of mean and tough bastards, aren't you? I was putting my money on these two finishing you off."

Evan and James both laughed as they nursed their bruises.

***

After making arrangements for the watch to come and haul the bodies away, Evan and James made their way home, wincing from their injuries as they went. Both men desperately wanted nothing more than a hot bath to ease their pains and to fall into bed.

"So what are you going to tell the Governour, Evan?" said James.

Evan shrugged. "There isn't much to tell, except that everyone's fears may be justified. Personally, I agree with Captain Laforey it is highly unlikely these two would have been specifically sent to create havoc around here. They are more likely to be rogue runaways escaping the madness of St. Domingue who also happen to be sympathetic to the revolutionary nonsense out there."

"But we can't discount the possibility someone with an agenda sent them out, can we?"

"No, we can't. It may be there is someone with a brain behind this. Maybe there are similar runaways appearing on other islands. I will be recommending the Governour send word out and that everyone maintain watch for more. Those two weren't ordinary runaways and yes, I do think something could be going on out there."

"Symptoms of a larger problem with what is going on in France, Evan."

"Yes. I don't think you and I are going to lack for things to do for a long time."

As they rode up and gave their horses to the boy they paid to care for the small stable they maintained, they found Alice waiting at the doorstep for them and talking to a Marine from one of the ships in the Dockyard.

Behind her Manon Shannon appeared in the doorway, having heard the two men arrive. She was the other resident of their home, sharing her bed with James. They met several years before when Evan and James were on St. Lucia trying to stop a family of French nobles providing arms to runaway slaves throughout the islands. The daughter of a retired Navy purser and a slave woman freed by her father, she followed James and her heart to Antigua from St. Lucia.

The Marine held a sealed letter in his hands and he presented it to Evan as the two officers walked up. "Commander Ross, this came in for you on a mail packet ship from Barbados. The Captain advised your orders are to open this immediately."

Evan's face was grim as he tore the envelope addressed to him open. It contained a single sheet and it took little time to read the single paragraph it contained. As he finished he looked up at the Marine and nodded.

"Thank you. You may return to the Dockyard and advise the Captain we will be on board within four hours. I need some time to get cleaned up and to write a report before we go."

"Sir, departing so soon won't be possible. The Captain said a yard was badly damaged in a squall on the way here. The Dockyard is working on the problem as a priority. The Captain expects it may be two days or more before he is ready for sea," said the Marine.

Evan sucked in his breath in frustration. "Well, we'll see about that in the morning. Hopefully we can speed things up. You are dismissed."

"I notice you said *we* would be going, Evan?" said James, as the Marine saluted and left.

"Barbados, just the two of us. Sorry, ladies, not a trip for you this time. Something's up."

Evan held the letter out for James to look at as he continued. "No details here, but Sir James has advised there is a problem with *Marston* and he needs our help. Fast."

The two women looked puzzled at the reference, but James stiffened in response. *Marston* was the code name used for their informant on St. Lucia, Captain Marcel Deschamps.

Evan reached up to gently caress Alice's cheek, as he could see the look of worry on her face. "I'm sorry, my love. I don't know how long we will be gone. Duty is calling."

Chapter Three
January 1793
Barbados

Evan and James were both on deck as dawn broke and the packet ship lookout hailed sight of the island of Barbados in the distance. Evan knew they would be in port before midday and for Evan, it couldn't come soon enough. The repairs to the packet ship took far longer than anticipated, but there were no other vessels available to ferry them to Barbados sooner. Evan knew Sir James would understand the reasons for a mid January arrival, but the frustration at the delay was still with him.

"So where are we staying, Evan?" said James, giving voice to the exact question Evan was mulling over.

"Good question. This packet ship doesn't have much to offer and I doubt he will be in port long anyway. I think we'd better just find accommodations at an Inn and be done with it. We don't know how long we are going to be here anyway."

They were still in the same spot on deck later when the Captain finally found an open patch of space to nestle into, not far from two big frigates and an even larger but old two-decker warship dominating the broad expanse of Carlisle Bay. Numerous much smaller warships and merchant vessels dotted the bay. Others could be seen tied up on the docks lining the river shore feeding into the bay while a few lay on the shore itself as testament to its service as a careenage.

The packet ship Captain was apologetic.

"Sorry to anchor so far out, gentlemen. I know it's a long row to shore, but we will get you there shortly. The Admiral on station comes first, and he won't be happy with me if I keep him waiting for his correspondence."

Evan smiled and assured the man he understood. But the Captain was true to his word and an hour later they found themselves dropped with their kit bags on the dock beside Wharf Road in Bridgetown, the capital of Barbados. Much like St. John's in Antigua, the town was a bustling hub of commerce and people, with the only difference being Bridgetown was considerably larger and more spread out.

"You know of any Inns around here, James? Every time I've been here I stayed on ship."

James smiled as he pointed toward a side street and they began walking. "Why, yes, there's one not far away I can personally recommend. It's called The Fouled Anchor."

Evan turned to look at James, raising an eyebrow as he did. "Is it suitable for our purposes? We don't advertise the fact we're officers much, but there may be people who would recognize us and wonder why we would be staying in some disreputable establishment frequented by sailors."

"That won't be a problem, since this place actually *is* quite reputable. It's mostly patronized by officers looking for more comfortable accommodations that what the ships offer."

Evan kept the skeptical look on his face, but let the hint of a smile show. "And how exactly is it you are familiar with this place?"

James grinned. "I was a Master's Mate before I met you, remember? The other warrant officers and I ended up there on shore liberty once. Better quality women frequenting this place, you see."

Evan laughed. Within minutes they were across the threshold of the Inn. The building was large, but nondescript looking from the outside. The tavern's separate entrance was a short distance down the street. Inside they were given a clean and pleasant room to share, with a shuttered window and a view down the street of Carlisle Bay in the distance. After storing their kit and washing up, they made their way to the street. The Inn was not far from their destination, an unremarkable but for its size two-story stone building a few blocks away on Broad Street. Evan walked right by it before he realized this was where they wanted to go.

"Have you not been here before, Evan?"

"No," he replied, as they mounted the stairs to the second floor. "The Captain has only just moved in here recently."

Sandwiched between a host of law and notary offices was an entrance door with a sign indicating this was the home of SJS Consulting. Walking in, they found a small room with a desk crammed into a corner off to the side, along with a few chairs for visitors to sit in. On the far side of the room was another closed door. One wall of the room was lined with books while file folders stuffed with papers covered most of another wall. The desk itself was covered with stacks of paperwork and behind the desk sat a thin, middle-aged clerk in a suit. As he turned away from the paperwork he was reading, he stared at them over the glasses sitting on the end of his long nose. He looked them up and down hard and, obviously not recognizing them, a small frown appeared on his face.

"Gentlemen? Can I help you?"

"Yes, please. We are here to see Sir James. I am Commander Evan Ross and this is Lieutenant James Wilton. We are expected."

The man's face brightened right away. "Oh, Sir James has indeed been hoping for your arrival soon. I'm sorry if I seemed suspicious, you aren't in uniform and of course we have not met before. I am his confidential clerk, Harrison Black."

"A pleasure to meet you, sir. Is Sir James in?"

"Unfortunately, no. There is a scheduled meeting every week of all Captains on station he is attending at the moment. Given his role, he is required to provide an update for the Captains at each meeting."

"I see. When do you expect him back? Can we arrange to meet him?"

"Sir, I expect him back soon, but I cannot commit to a specific time. These meetings can be either brief or almost endless, depending on what is going on at any given time. I think it would be best if I give him your contact information and let him find you when he is available."

After giving the man details of where they were quartered, they promised to stay there awaiting the arrival of Sir James. Realizing they were both hungry, they went straight to the tavern at The Fouled

Anchor Inn.

The inside proved a welcome relief from the glare of the midday sun. Despite it being January, Evan knew Barbados was closer to the equator and even the few hundred nautical miles of distance made a difference. Both men ordered food and glasses of rum mixed with water to diminish the impact of the heady, but smooth Barbados rum.

They managed to find a table near one of the windows with the shutters open to let in the breeze. Fortunately, the table was also in a corner, meaning the wall was to their backs and they could see everyone else. As the bar wasn't full and no one was nearby they could hold their conversation unhindered by concerns anyone would overhear them. None of the patrons, most of whom were Navy or Army officers, bore any sustained interest in the two men wearing nondescript clothing anyway. James attracted a little interest as the only black patron, but the few who did look over were soon back talking animatedly to their companions. The crowd wasn't limited to military personnel, as a few groups of businessmen were sprinkled in.

Both men ordered the same food, consisting of a large bowl of fish chowder to accompany their main dish of flying fish fillets and bread. Evan and James were starving by the time their food arrived and they fell to with gusto. The chowder was delicious, with big chunks of fish and rich tasting lobster mixed in with a few vegetables and potatoes. A yellow pepper sauce the server provided on the side proved an excellent complement to the fish and bread. Evan smiled when the sauce arrived. After taking a sniff of it he grinned even wider.

"Excellent, this is what I was hoping they would have. I enjoyed some of this the last time I was here. I can *smell* how spicy these peppers are. I suggest start with small doses, James. This is stronger than what we get on Antigua."

James laughed as he spooned a generous dollop onto his meal. "I can take it."

As they were finishing Harrison Black walked into the tavern and looked around. They all saw each other at the same time, and Evan and James rose to greet him as the clerk strode over and shook their hands.

"Gentlemen, I'm glad to find you," he said, glancing quickly around to check if anyone was listening. "Sir James has returned and offers his apologies he did not come to greet you here. He feels it would be better were you to return to the office where you can talk without the fear of eavesdropping."

The two officers paid their bill and followed the man out. Back at the office, the clerk knocked on the closed door to the inner office and hearing an answering hail, he stepped in to announce the two men. After a moment of muffled conversation he left, leaving Evan and James to enter. Once in the room they found a greying, but still fit and distinguished older man in his early sixties rising to greet them.

Evan and James first met Captain Sir James Standish several years before. Captain Horatio Nelson introduced them in 1785, the year Evan and James helped Nelson to bring American smuggling under control and put a stop to a French and

American plot to destabilize the British sugar islands. Sir James, a British spymaster already well established on Barbados, was in need of help as his territory was far too much for him to cover alone. Evan and James were recruited to continue serving in an intelligence role, reporting to Sir James. They assumed the task of monitoring intelligence matters and offering advice to diplomats in the northern Caribbean, while Sir James continued to deal with intelligence for Jamaica and the southern Caribbean. The only exception to the arrangement was when a direct, active presence was required to address a situation. As a retired naval Captain, Sir James no longer held a desire for more active service.

"Commander Ross, Lieutenant Wilton, thank you for coming to Barbados. And I'm sorry I apparently interrupted your meal."

"Sir James, we came as soon as we could. Our packet ship needed repairs and they took far longer than we wanted," said Evan.

Sir James waved a hand to dispel Evan's concern. "Gentlemen, I am in need of your help. I could have put all this in a letter, but we have much to talk about and given what is going on in the world I felt it necessary to make time to discuss this face to face with you both. And, as you know, we have a problem with *Marston* to address."

He paused a moment to sit forward, a bleak look on his face. "I think it is not a question of *if* we will be at war soon, it is *when*. Our masters in London are growing ever more concerned about the direction the new French administration is taking, and we are not alone. It would seem a pack of extremist lunatics is winning the day in France over any semblance of moderation. In particular, there are fears the French attitude toward monarchies will inspire similar lunatics in other countries. This means we must be ready for war when it comes."

The two officers looked at each other as one, before Evan turned back to Sir James. "Sir. Command us, we will do our duty."

"I know. Your networks on Antigua and the other islands in the area will serve us well if it comes to war. I will be providing a fresh supply of gold before you leave to keep your networks happy. Among other things, we absolutely must keep a weather eye on what is happening on St. Domingue in future. I fear this island is going to be a major problem. I know you get regular reports from trading ships sailing in and out of there, but in hindsight I should have asked you to try and establish more direct contacts on the island itself. I'm afraid if we do end up at war with the French the insanity happening on this island is going to draw us into the fray whether we want to or not."

As he paused once again he put a hand to his forehead in sudden remembrance. "God, where are my manners? It's a little early, but would you like a glass of something, gentlemen? I could certainly use a drink."

Both officers agreed and Evan spoke up as Sir James poured them a glass of wine each. "Sir James? Your note mentioned a problem with Captain Deschamps? Is this something we can help with?"

"Yes, indeed. Well, the need to get together and talk about being prepared for the future was enough on its own to warrant asking you to come to Barbados, but the situation with the good Captain alone also served as reason to bring you here."

As Sir James paused to sip his drink Evan thought back to his various contacts with the French spy. The first time Evan interacted with him was almost his last, as the Captain deemed Evan a hindrance to his plans and tried to have him murdered. The second time found the two men unexpectedly working together to put a stop to a plot to sow revolution throughout the Caribbean. Having succeeded, the two men parted on a much more cordial basis.

The last contact from Captain Deschamps, though, was the most unexpected of all. Evan received a mysterious invitation to visit the Captain in St. Lucia almost two years ago. No reason was given as to why he wanted to see him, but the Captain suggested Evan should dream up some excuse to visit the local British Consul in Castries. Upon arrival the Captain used all of his devious skills to ensure no one saw them meet. Evan was flabbergasted when the French spy offered to be an intelligence source for the British.

The man's desire made sense, though. Evan knew he was a staunch royalist, loathing the radicals implacably gaining control of his homeland. When Evan asked him why he still served, the Captain told him the concern was what would happen to other royalists like himself in the Caribbean. With his experience the Captain knew he could look after himself, but his sense of duty wouldn't let him leave behind others in the royalist cause less capable.

The offer was warily accepted and Sir James decided to take the lead on maintaining communication with Captain Deschamps, given how valuable the information coming from him was. The decision was made easy because of the much faster communication possible due to St. Lucia being far closer to Barbados. As the most experienced intelligence officer Sir James was also most qualified to gauge whether Captain Deschamps was telling the truth and not playing some devious game.

"So, yes, gentlemen, we have a problem. The last correspondence I received from Captain Deschamps was dated several months ago, back in late June. And, I only received one letter."

Sir James paused a moment, obviously wanting to let the significance of this sink in. Both Evan and James stiffened in response as they turned to look at each other once again.

"Yes, gentlemen, I see you recall the arrangement we set up. Captain Deschamps was very diligent about sending both an original and a copy of every message over the last two years, with each being sent via different routes to ensure at least one got through. So at first I wasn't *too* concerned, although this was the first time this happened. But then I got confirmation the royalist French Governour of St. Lucia fled to the Spaniards in Cuba in fear of his life. The reason was the garrison somehow was convinced to switch to the revolutionary cause. Because of hurricane season it was mid October by the time I got wind of this, so I immediately sent a query to the Captain. I got no response. I didn't want to risk sending any more correspondence, because if he was under surveillance they might be looking for suspicious letters as evidence. I asked an American merchant Captain I've used in the past to discreetly look into what was going on and he only just came back to Barbados recently. There does seem to be a new Captain serving on the *Marie-Anne* frigate. There is also a rumour Captain Deschamps is in prison, but he can't confirm this. And finally, we have a report from Sir John Orde in Dominica that there is a new French administrator with radical leanings on the scene in St. Lucia."

"Yes, Sir James, we heard about this new administrator," said Evan. "Sir, this is very bad news regarding Captain Deschamps."

"Indeed. But there is more you need to know. His last correspondence with me openly expressed concern about what was happening on St. Lucia. Both he and the Governour were aware of revolutionary agitators active on the island and they were taking steps to keep them in check, but he confessed the situation was fluid. He also stated they were taking precautions in the event matters did not go well. What he specifically wanted from me was some help to evacuate the remaining royalist supporters if the need arose. He also stated we would find it very rewarding to do so. And, yes, those are the exact words he used and what they mean I don't know."

Evan frowned. "Sir, I know the Captain has a degree of personal wealth, but I can't believe he would be talking about using his own money. Is he perhaps talking about some major information we don't have, but could find useful?"

Sir James shrugged. "The Captain is well aware money is a great motivator, but who knows? You may be right, it could well be he learned something we might desperately want to know. Either way, we cannot simply ignore what has happened and by now I'm certain you've both figured out what your task is. I need you gentlemen to go to St. Lucia and sort this out."

"Do you have any specific orders, sir?"

Sir James paused and held his hands wide, palm open. "There are too many possible scenarios which could be in play to give you anything more than general direction. We will have to find some way to get you to St. Lucia and back. Find the Captain, find out what is going on, and do it fast. This has already gone on too long. Figure out what he was talking about in his letter. If he is indeed in prison or in need of our help, then help him. The man has been a valuable asset to us for over two years now and I will not see him abandoned at the first sign of trouble. This may mean you two are sailing into dangerous waters here, but this is what you signed up for. You will simply have to deal with whatever situation you find as you see fit."

Sir James leaned back in his chair, pausing a moment as a thoughtful look stole over on his face. "Hmm, you will need some sort of cover story. I will leave this to you. I know you have both been to St. Lucia before, and you in particular, Commander Ross, have been there in an official capacity. But this was some time back and I don't think most of the people you dealt with at the time are there any longer, so you likely have little fear of being recognized.

Regardless, you speak French and this will serve you well."

"Actually, Sir James, I've been taking lessons and I'm pretty good with the language now, too," said James.

"His woman speaks French quite well," said Evan with a smile.

"Sounds like the best way to learn it to me," said Sir James, with a small grin of his own.

"Sir James, we understand. If you have nothing further for us we will make arrangements to return to Antigua and be about it immediately."

"I know time is of the essence, but I have been working on something which may help and if I succeed it will, I think, make waiting just a bit longer worth while. I don't want to say anything more for the moment, so please just remain in Barbados while I sort this out. I will send word to your lodging when I'm ready."

"Sir," said Evan in acknowledgment, seeing Sir James appeared to have nothing further to say. The two men rose from their seats and saluted as they left.

***

They spent the next day, with little else to do, watching the sailors and shore personnel loading ships with supplies or doing small repairs. Both agreed it seemed clear everyone was moving with more purpose than would be normal. Few people were smiling and everyone seemed gripped by some invisible tension in the air. They found the same in town. Small groups of soldiers were everywhere, moving about the town with resolute looks on their faces.

Evan and James used the time to discuss how they would have to approach going to St. Lucia as they walked about. While they were not at war, Evan knew any Englishman appearing would be unlikely to receive a friendly welcome on the island. The two men agreed the only way to make it work was to try and sign on with an American or Dutch merchant ship willing to take a couple of passengers without questions being asked.

The advantage both men knew they had was Paddy Shannon. The former Royal Navy purser settled on St. Lucia years before after losing a leg during the American Revolutionary War and was father to James's girlfriend Manon. Paddy still served as an occasional conduit of information for Evan and James, although the grim realization his last contact with them was several weeks prior crossed his mind. Evan knew he didn't need to speak of his concern, as James without doubt was thinking the same thought already. James acknowledged with a grunt his agreement Paddy would be their starting point to find out what was going on when Evan mentioned it.

The next day the two men were finishing breakfast and sipping the remnants of their tea when Harrison Black appeared once again in the doorway to the tavern, announcing the Captain was ready to see them.

"Well, thank God he hasn't kept us dangling long," said James, as the two officers followed the clerk back to the office. Sir James was finishing brewing some tea and the three men took the time to fill their mugs before settling in.

Sir James wore a huge grin as the two men sat down. "Gentlemen, I'm pleased to advise I have met with success. But I guess I should check with you one last time, in case you've changed your minds. Can I assume you gentlemen would still like a *ship* to call your own?"

As the spymaster roared with laughter, looking from one man to the other, Evan knew the incredulous look he was wearing on his face was mirrored on the face of James. Sir James held up a hand to forestall them from responding.

"Gentlemen, I'm sorry, I couldn't resist a little fun at your expense. I *know* the answer, of course. This reward for your efforts is far too long in coming. You know we've discussed the problem of your ability to go where you are needed without having to wait on someone else's schedule or needs in past. Well, the Admiralty has finally seen fit to agree. I guess a looming war is a great motivator. But after approving the idea the First Lord left the details to the Admiral and I. It took some convincing, and the knowledge he has more warships coming his way to command, to free up the vessel I kept in mind for you. It's one I know you are both familiar with. I hope the *HMS Alice* will meet your needs?"

Evan couldn't stop his jaw falling open and he turned to find the same disbelieving look on James's face as Sir James chuckled once again. The two men were well aware of *HMS Alice* and her capabilities. They had used this ship as passengers and seen action on her before off the coast of St. Lucia while working with Captain Deschamps years before. That it bore the same name as Evan's lover was pure coincidence, but Alice herself had graced the ship with her presence and approval as they sailed to St. Lucia on their mission. Evan had been in actual command of *HMS Alice* for a few brief days, after stepping into the shoes of the commanding officer when he fell in battle against an American spy smuggling arms to St. Lucia. The command was short lived as a favourite of the squadron commanding officer was placed in charge on return to Antigua.

Evan finally found his voice. "Sir James, I think it safe to say you have managed to give us the best news the two of us have heard in a very long time."

"Well, enough having fun at your expense. Unfortunately, she needs repairs. What you need to know is the *Alice* conveniently was in an accident recently. She ran aground rather badly on a reef off St. Kitts. The former commander and the sailing master should have been paying attention to it, for they knew it was there. Note I said *former*, as the Admiral was not happy. The Commander was at the end of his normal tenure anyway so he received orders to return to England to a desk job. The same applies to the sailing master, but that's not all. There were ongoing reports of there being a lot of disputes among the officers and warrants for some time now. The Admiral got fed up and decided to disperse the lot of them, which I know is unusual for warrant officers in particular, but then who is going to argue with an Admiral?"

The spymaster laughed at his own joke before continuing. "So the *Alice* is on her way to Antigua for repairs in the Dockyard even as we speak. They stopped for a while in Basseterre to apply a temporary patch over the damaged area. It seems the damage is worse than perhaps thought, which forced the Commander to confess and thus gave the Admiral reason to act. She is also due to have her bottom cleaned, all of which will take time. The story we will put about is she sustained far worse damage than she actually did, which may not be far from the truth. A public decision will be taken to remove her from active service because of that and sell her. You, using the cover of a private trading company Mr. Black is going to set up for you, will purchase it and allegedly convert it to a trading vessel. In reality, she will continue to remain a commissioned warship in His Majesty's service. We can't have her armed to the teeth as she currently is, but you will retain some of your armament in secret. The purpose is to get to and from where you need to be in a ship that can fit in with your potential cover story as fast as possible. Is this making sense? Speak up if you have questions."

"Sir, it is," said Evan. "The only thing bothering me at the moment is people. From what you are saying it sounds like we will be running with a far smaller complement than would be normal? Do you foresee us using Navy personnel?"

"Good questions. Yes, the Admiral and I discussed this. You will have to make do with a much smaller complement. The idea is to have enough men to sail the ship, not necessarily fight with it too. You need to look like a penny-pinching merchant, right? So I think no more than twenty-five or maybe thirty or so men in total, officers and warrants included, will be necessary. And yes, we think these men need to be Navy. They will have to be sworn to secrecy, and I think the way to do this while ensuring they comply is to bribe them. In other words, we offer them merchant ship rates of pay. If they want to keep the extra money coming in, they keep their mouth shut. The budget to maintain the *Alice* will be managed from my office, of course."

"Sir," said James. "This will certainly help. What about prize money? I know we aren't meant to be a fighting ship, but who knows what the future holds?"

Sir James nodded. "Yes, indeed, I raised the point with both the First Lord and the Admiral here. Everyone is in agreement normal rules of the Navy should apply if indeed we find ourselves at war and you somehow end up bringing in a prize ship. I think we all agree everyone needs a little motivation."

Evan was still processing the thought he was soon to be in command of his own warship when a large question mark appeared in his head. "Sir? I already have my First Officer sitting here beside me and I assume new warrants will be found and assigned to the ship. What about the existing crew, though? Will any be retained for our use?"

"Ah, you've come to the point of contention I discussed with our Admiral here. He found it useful a ready number of prime hands were available to be reassigned to fill gaps in other warships. I protested and said you needed people who knew the difference between a topsail and a foresail. The thing was he maintained there were concerns about some of the members of the crew, too. Well, he's the Admiral so he got his way. However, I believe you have a good relationship with Captain Laforey in Antigua?"

"Sir, we do."

"Excellent. Well, the Captain will be receiving orders from the Admiral to assist you. You will have to fend for yourself with the man. If you can find some way to make it worth his while I'm sure he will be appreciative. However, there is one other thing I'd like to suggest to you as it applies to your crew."

"Sir?"

"I think it may be important you consider what skills your crew has to offer. Oh, I'm not talking about ship handling or skill with naval weapons. I'm thinking more along the lines of the kind of skills a gentleman wouldn't consider having. After all, the business we are in isn't exactly gentlemanly, now is it? To be clear, I am thinking about what you might need in St. Lucia when you get there. For example, if Captain Deschamps is indeed in prison, you might find it useful to have someone at hand who can unlock his cell door, you follow?"

"I do indeed, sir, and I agree. A skilled lock picker or two could prove useful. Perhaps someone with skills in silent entry to a building would help too."

"How about a forger, sir?" said James, rubbing his chin in thought. "The world runs on paperwork."

Sir James laughed. "It does indeed, and I see you both agree."

"Where are we going to find such people, sir?" said Evan, before putting his hand to his forehead. "But of course, you've already thought of this, haven't you?"

"Well, there are likely more than a few to be found on the various warships in harbour, but as I said the Admiral isn't keen to lose any people just now, even ordinary seamen. Fortunately, I have other friends here on this island and trying to pry men away from the Admiral isn't our only option."

The spymaster smiled.

***

The next day Evan and James presented themselves to the sergeant in charge of the guard at the entrance to Barbados Garrison, the extensive main Army complex a short distance south of Bridgetown. The man scrutinized their letter of introduction to the senior Colonel in charge of the Garrison and looked them both up and down, staring with dubious concern at their lack of uniforms, before shrugging and telling them to wait. He disappeared inside, finally reappearing after fifteen minutes. The skeptical look on his face remained, but he signaled them to follow him into the complex.

Once inside St. Ann Fort and the main Garrison building they were led to a bare room with nothing other than a large table and a half dozen chairs sprinkled around it. Telling them to wait once again, the sergeant disappeared. A short time later the door opened and a tall, mustachioed officer appeared with a soldier following close behind. He sat down and stared at Evan and James for a moment, his face frozen, before finally speaking.

"Right. My name is Lieutenant Ford. Which one of you is Commander Ross?"

After Evan identified himself and introduced James, the Lieutenant continued. "Our Colonel has asked me to see to your needs. He tells me apparently you two are Royal Navy and your commanding officer has requested we see if we can supply you with some people."

The Lieutenant leaned back in his chair, his face hardened as he assessed Evan and James once again. "The strange part is the Colonel tells me I am to find what you want wherever I can, which includes seeing if some of the scum too stupid to follow orders and paying for it by rotting in the Garrison jail cells might fit the bill. I can't imagine why you would want any of those fools, but my job is to follow orders and, unlike them, I will do so. So, what exactly are you looking for?"

Evan leaned forward to respond. "Men with lock picking skills in their past. Burglars. Pickpockets. Forgers. If you could provide three or four men with these skills we would be most grateful. It would be even better if you can find some with more than one such skill."

Evan offered a smile as he continued, while the Lieutenant's eyes bulged wide. "You should assure them we are not judges, and have no interest in whatever incidents they may have been involved in prior to now. We are strictly looking for their expertise. If they meet our needs, we are prepared to offer them an opportunity to join the Navy. I know this may not necessarily sound appealing, but the pay will be better than ordinary seaman's pay and, if I understand army pay scales correctly, it will also be better than what they are getting now. They will also have opportunity to be doing less routine duty than now. *If* they meet our needs, of course."

After a few moments digesting it all, the Lieutenant shook his head as if to clear cobwebs from his mind. He pulled at his long moustache for a few moments longer, obviously in thought, before slowly turning in his seat to look at the soldier standing behind him. The man was standing guard by the door, stiff at attention, and staring straight ahead.

"Well, Smith? You heard them. I brought you with me in case I needed help with identifying people they might want. Anyone come to mind?"

The soldier remained staring straight ahead a few moments, his mouth working as if he wanted to speak, but something kept him holding his tongue. He finally stiffened and stood even straighter as he spoke.

"Sir. Yes, sir."

"Well?" said the Lieutenant, with obvious impatience as he scowled at him. "Get on with it. Who do you have in mind?"

The soldier paused for another brief moment before reaching his decision and turning to look straight at the Lieutenant. He blurted out his response in a rush. "Sir, *I* have— some of the background these gentlemen are looking for. And I know others, too."

"*You?* Huh," said the Lieutenant, eyeing the man with a dubious look on his face. "I suppose that shouldn't surprise me. What others are you talking about? Give me names."

The soldier went back to staring straight ahead. "Sir, my mates Jack Hopkins and Tommy

Wishart. Between the three of us we have what they want."

"Good Christ, those two?" said the Lieutenant with an audible groan. "Right, go down to the lockup and bring them both here."

Shaking his head once again, he turned back to Evan and James. "I sure hope you two know what you're about. These three wouldn't be on my recommendation list for *anything*."

While they were waiting the Lieutenant left, only to return a few minutes later followed by another soldier bearing a tea tray with a pot and three cups. After the soldier left and as they were taking their first sips the door opened once again. This time two unshaven, rough looking soldiers came in followed by the guard Smith. As Evan scrutinized the three men he realized the two unwashed newcomers stank from being in the cells and not having bathed in some time. Unlike the shorter, but stocky guard these two men were taller and thinner. Smith looked to be a year or so older than the others. All three men were in their early twenties and they all presented the harsh demeanor of hungry wolves.

Evan asked the men to sit as the Lieutenant moved his chair to the side. After learning which man was which Evan began his pitch.

"Men, all you need to know at this point is I am a Commander in the Royal Navy and this gentleman is my First Officer. We have a proposal which may be of interest to all three of you, but first we need to satisfy ourselves you are what we want."

"Sir, if I may?" said Smith. "I told them what you said on the way here from the cells."

"Very good. So, I need to know what your skills are and what level of experience you have. A few details, please. One at a time."

At first the three men were hesitant, but the two newcomers took their cue from Smith. Evan soon realized the man seemed to be the unofficial, natural leader of the three. All three men gave similar stories, having been friends coming from poor families in a small town outside Sheffield in northern England. With few opportunities as they grew up, they turned to anything they could to keep themselves alive.

All three confessed to being thieves at one point in their lives and to having skill with silent entry of buildings, including the ability to pick locks when the right tools were available. Wishart and Hopkins both confessed to being pickpockets whenever the opportunity arose, while Smith admitted to having worked as a certificate and document forger for a corrupt lawyer before the man was caught. After several minutes of probing questions by Evan he felt he knew enough. He turned to James and nodded his head toward the door. As they got up Evan looked at Lieutenant Ford.

"Sir, I need to speak to my colleague in confidence for a moment outside. We will be back shortly."

With the door closed behind them and far enough away Evan was certain they wouldn't be overheard, Evan looked at James.

"Well, what do you think?"

James shrugged, but offered a small grin. "I'm quite sure this isn't the first or likely will be the last time any of those three have seen the inside of a jail cell. But that could be said of most sailors, of course. This fellow Smith looks like a crafty bastard to me. All three of them will bear watching, but I think they'll do."

"I agree. I think they are all telling the truth about their skills, too. I don't expect they know anything of sailing given they're from Sheffield, but we can deal with that. I guess the only thing that remains would be to figure out if we can motivate them to join us."

"Don't think that will be hard, Evan. From what I've heard life in the Army isn't any more pleasant than life in the Navy. I suspect these three will figure the Navy couldn't possibly be worse and just *might* be better. They'll sign on."

Evan laughed and they went back inside. After sitting down Evan sat forward to address the men, deciding to be frank. "Right, I expect none of you have any experience with ships other than as a passenger?"

"That's correct, sir," said Smith.

"No matter, you will learn. Look, here's the situation. I could simply tell this officer we want you three men and you would find yourselves as part of my crew. But I would much prefer you be willing volunteers. Obviously, we are looking for people with your kind of skills for good reason. It is likely we will find ourselves in difficult situations when using those skills because of the nature of our work and I need to know I can count on you. I can't give you any more details than this. You already know your pay will be better if you join willingly. You will have opportunity for prize money, but I wouldn't count on it happening.

But see here, you may be sitting there thinking life in the Navy could be some grand adventure as a result of what I'm saying, but don't count on this either. The possibility of action is as real as the possibility of routine boredom."

Evan paused a moment and turned to Lieutenant Ford. "Sir, if I may, why were these two men serving time in your jail?"

Lieutenant Ford grunted as he tried obviously restraining himself from laughing outright. "Drinking and fighting with other soldiers, of course. Why else?"

"No surprise," said Evan, as he turned back to them. "Right, all three of you do need to understand one last thing. My First Officer and I are not tyrants, but we expect obedience. Fail us and you won't find yourself rotting in jail. You *will* instead be strung up at the grating for a dozen or maybe more lashes with the cat. The Navy maintains discipline the same as the Army. The Lieutenant and I believe in being firm, but fair with the men in our command."

Evan sat back to gauge the three men's reaction as he finished his pitch. "Well, what's it to be?"

No one said anything until finally Smith looked over at the other two. "I'm for this. We should do it."

The one called Tom Wishart leaned forward to look at him in response. "Jack, how do we know we can trust these buggers? I—"

"*Wishart*, you goddamn donkey!" barked Lieutenant Ford. "You will show respect to these officers. Any more muck like that coming from you and *I* will be the one having you tied to the grating. And I guarantee you can expect it to be more than just a dozen stripes on your back."

"Sir, we are sorry," said Smith, in haste to smooth things over. "Tom is sorry, aren't you, Tom?"

"Sir, I apologize," mumbled Wishart, although he didn't look overly contrite.

"Look mates, we're in this together still, aren't we?" said Smith. "Let's do it. Hell, I'm doing it. Commander, you can count me in."

The other two soldiers turned to look at each other as one, before both turned back to Evan and acknowledged they would volunteer too. The one called Wishart was the last to agree and Evan wasn't sure the man was wholly happy with the decision.

Evan wondered for a brief moment at the dynamics of the relationship between the three soldiers, but dismissed the question forming in his mind, knowing he would find out soon enough.

"Welcome to the Royal Navy."

***

The next day Evan and James were once again seated in front of Sir James in his office on Broad Street.

"Gentlemen, I'm glad you met with success. Keeping a rein on those three you found may be easier said than done, but what can you do. Perhaps get them to train a few other members of your crew, once you get it all sorted out. Anyway, the message you sent indicated you have arranged passage for you and the men back to Antigua?"

"Sir, we are leaving as soon as we leave your presence. The Admiral conveniently has a ship on its way to Antigua and the Captain kindly agreed to let us take passage with him. Lieutenant Wilton and I want to be at our task as soon as possible, sir."

"Excellent," said Sir James, as a worried look stole over his face. "I think events are moving fast, maybe too fast, and Captain Deschamps is in need. Well, before you go I have a few things you will want."

Reaching into his desk drawer he pulled out two large, heavy looking bags clinking with the obvious sound of coins as he dropped them on the table in front of them. "Use this with care, gentlemen. The usual rules, of course. It should meet your needs for a while. Also, you will want these."

Pulling open another drawer on his desk he drew out two envelopes, giving both to Evan. Evan saw one was addressed to him and the other to Captain Laforey. Both envelopes bore the Admiral's seal.

"The one to Captain Laforey is making him aware of the situation regarding *HMS Alice* and has instructions for him to assist you as we discussed. The other envelope has your orders to assume command of *HMS Alice* when the time comes. You know what to do."

Evan looked down at the envelope in his hand as the weight of what the orders meant fell square on his shoulders. But he knew his years of hard work and training gave him the preparation he needed for the challenge of commanding a warship. *His* warship, with his responsibility alone for it and the lives of the men he would lead. Evan looked back up at Sir James.

"Sir, I do. We will not fail you."

Chapter Four
January 1793
Antigua

Captain Sir John Laforey pursed his lips as he sat in the aft cabin of his frigate in English Harbour and finished reading the orders from his Admiral in Barbados a second time. As he put them down in front of him on his desk, he looked up at the man sitting across from him.

"Well, congratulations appear to be in order, Commander Ross. It's a ship for you to command, albeit in unusual circumstances. If this isn't a sign things are getting worse I don't know what would be. And I see the Admiral desires me to help you."

"Sir."

Sir John pinched the bridge of his nose as he sat in obvious thought for a moment. "I find it interesting the Admiral has no men on his station in Barbados to spare, but can be generous with the men *I* command. Well, he's the Admiral and my job is to follow orders. This may take some time, though."

"Sir John, if I may?" said Evan, continuing only when he saw the Captain nod. "I was expecting this would be the case and will make do in the meantime. The *Alice* is not yet ready for sea anyway. Also, given the nature of the work we will be doing I think it important to take time and ensure I've got people with the right skills under my command. If we do find ourselves at war and I have the right people with me, there may be times when I am able to ascertain the whereabouts of enemy ships in the course of following my orders. Please be assured I will endeavour to get such information to you as fast as possible should it occur."

Sir John laughed and sat back in his chair. "You know, I confess I like you. You understand how things work. Yes, Commander Ross, I think we can work together on things like that if the time comes. If you can get us useful information I will do what I can to ensure you get a share of any prize money, even if you are not in sight when the action commences. I've fought many battles over prize money in my time and I don't think they want *me* arguing with them yet again over shares. So have a conversation with my First Officer about exactly the sort of men you want. He will be told to get them for you."

"Sir, I do have one specific request. You may recall there was a midshipman named Timothy Cooke working with Lieutenant Wilton and I for the last few years in the Dockyard?"

"Cooke? Yes, isn't he one of the young fellows my Captains and I just examined and passed for Lieutenant?"

"The same, sir. I would like to keep him with us if he is willing and this meets with your approval. I realize it's a bit unusual, but we have found it most helpful to have someone we can rely on to manage the Dockyard when Lieutenant Wilton and I are away. I've come to appreciate his qualities and I think he would be an asset doing the kind of work we do, too. In truth, we have used him to aid us directly on a few occasions, so I am certain he will meet our needs."

Sir John shrugged. "We have plenty of Lieutenants around and I don't have a spot for him just now anyway. What do you mean *if he is willing*, though? He's a Lieutenant and will do what he's told."

"Sir, given the unique nature of what we do I prefer to have the men under me volunteering and willingly doing the job."

Sir John stared at Evan for a moment before answering. "Well, you have a different way of doing things, but then *you* are different, aren't you? Suit yourself. If he agrees, let me know and I will have orders prepared for him to continue reporting to you."

Evan rose and saluted after expressing his thanks. Back in the Dockyard he strode past his office with purpose and a sense of foreboding toward the inner harbour. The list of tasks to perform and decisions to make since he returned seemed endless. A growing mountain of paperwork sitting on his desk was screaming for attention, but he also knew he wouldn't be able to focus properly until he learned the full situation with his ship.

At one of the docks he found James standing beside the Dockyard Shipwright. Both men were staring at *HMS Alice*, which was in the process of having everything not nailed down offloaded onto the dock by a small swarm of sailors and Dockyard workers. A huge, growing pile of crates, casks, and equipment was beside them. Evan groaned to himself when he saw it all, aware of what it meant.

The mournful look the head Shipwright gave him confirmed it. "I'm sorry, Commander Ross. Once I got a chance to look at the damage it was clear there was nothing for it. I don't know how the bumbling incompetents managed to sail it all the way here without the *Alice* sinking, for God's sake."

Evan took a deep breath to hide his disappointment before responding. "Not your fault. So obviously, as soon as you've offloaded her and got the masts out you're going to beach her and get down to business, right? Dare I ask, how long do you think before she's back afloat?"

The Shipwright, an grizzled older man with his hair tied back in a long sailor's queue, shrugged and took a moment to spit some phlegm off to the side, buying himself time to think before replying.

"Commander, I'm going to be honest with you. Normally this wouldn't be a problem, but with the possibility of war on the horizon suddenly everyone wants everything done yesterday. A lot of it is stuff they didn't get around to telling us about because they were all too busy chasing women or drinking, for God's sake. So I'm sorry, but my best estimate is maybe early April if you are lucky, even given the *Alice* is a brig-sloop and only has two masts instead of three. Unless, of course, you can get me dispensation from Sir John to move you to the front of the line."

Both Evan and James winced in unison, and they turned to look at each other.

"Damn, sir," said James. "What are we going to do?"

Evan looked at the Shipwright, the concern obvious on his face.

"Sorry, but I have to ask. You are taking into account we won't be putting all of the cannon back on the ship, are you?"

"I am."

Evan could only shake his head. "Damn.

Well, I don't know, but we'll have to figure something out. Sir John would have every Captain on station up in arms if he approved our needs over theirs, so getting a dispensation won't happen. Come on, Lieutenant, let's head back to the office."

Along the way they found the newly minted Lieutenant Cooke, still performing his duties in the Dockyard while awaiting an assignment. Evan ordered him to follow and the three men made their way to Evan's office.

Once they were settled in, Evan explained the full situation to the fair haired, handsome Lieutenant Cooke. In the four years since joining Evan as a midshipman, the once gangling teenager matured into a strong, lithe young man. Evan and James both soon learned he was steady and reliable as he cheerfully went about his duties. Even better, he was smart and he soon realized what Evan and James were really doing. He joined James on a few occasions trawling the taverns for information and did well with the guidance of James.

As with the day they first met, Evan once again made it clear the young man could have a choice. Evan was barely finished making his pitch when the new Lieutenant signaled his thoughts by grinning cheerfully.

"Sir? I accept. I've enjoyed my time here with you and Lieutenant Wilton and I've learned a lot. I'd love to stay with you."

"Excellent. You know, I haven't even told you the good news we are getting a ship yet."

The Lieutenant's eyes lit up. "A ship? Even better, sir."

"Yes, it's the *Alice*, but she won't be ready for service anytime soon. The problem is we have been given a mission to St. Lucia and we must leave as soon as possible. Right, I have a couple of jobs for you two. The first job is to find us a crew. Captain Laforey has agreed to help us, but we need to give them some idea of what we want in terms of people. You will need to work with his First Officer on this. You two know a lot of the sailors on the various ships on station. Put your heads together and give some names to the First Officer to consider. We need capable and experienced men, and by this I mean both as sailors and more. We need people who can handle themselves in a fight, and can also be relied upon to keep their mouths shut."

The two Lieutenants took a moment to ponder this. With a quick glance at Lieutenant Cooke, James turned back to Evan.

"Sir? I assume it's alright to tell them about the extra pay?"

"Hmm. Yes, if we must, but make it clear to them they are not to be telling the whole world. It would be preferable to ensure first they have some interest in a detached, small ship assignment. Make it clear this isn't expected to be the usual routine. If whoever you are talking to isn't enticed by this then perhaps don't bother talking to them about extra pay unless we really want them."

James nodded. "I like that, sir. What about the warrant officers?"

"Hmm," said Evan. "A gunner, a bosun, and God help us, a purser. If you can pry a carpenter out of them, or at least someone with skills in the area, please do. I suspect what will happen is they will end up giving us people who have been apprenticing in the roles."

"Sir?" said Lieutenant Cooke. "I take it we aren't going to have a Marine complement?"

"Correct. Oh, I almost forgot. See if you can find some Americans in their crews. A few of them would be useful."

Having Americans serving on Royal Navy warships wasn't as unusual as it might seem. Times were still hard in America and more than a few were willing to take the King's shilling to join the Royal Navy. Evan could see the two Lieutenants looked puzzled for a moment before understanding flashed on their faces almost as one.

"Yes, gentlemen, we may wish to pretend we are someone else on occasion. Having real American accents would help with the pretense."

"Sir? I'm confident we can get a good crew. You mentioned a second job?" said James.

"Yes, it's training. This will be ongoing, of course, but the immediate need is to work on those three men we brought back with us from Barbados. They need to be shown just how much they don't know about warships and about how to behave in particular. I suspect the first time I have to mete out punishment it will be to one of those three, but I would also like to be proved wrong. Lieutenant Cooke, you are perhaps best suited to this task so please get on them right away."

Evan turned to look directly at James. "As for you, I think you should take the lead on training Lieutenant Cooke and all of our new recruits in the new methods we have been working on. And yes, I mean *all* of them, including the less orthodox ones. I think it best everyone on the Alice be able to back everyone else up, so if I need some bloody Frog agent garroted with as little fuss as possible then I don't have to take time to think about who we've trained to do what."

"Makes sense, sir. Anything else we can help with?" said James.

"Not just now. While you two are dealing with all of that I'm going to beat this paperwork into submission. I'm also going to think about how the hell we're going to get ourselves to St. Lucia as soon as possible. We're going to have to buy our passage there on a merchant ship. The question is who will do it."

"Sir?" said James. "Don't know if you noticed, but the *Lady Croydon* just came into Falmouth Harbour last night. Not sure how long he plans to be here or where he might be headed."

Evan groaned. "No, I didn't notice. God, it would have to be that arsehole O'Brien, wouldn't it? Well, I suppose he will do, although he'll charge us a bloody fortune to do it. At least he'll get a lot less scrutiny than we would, because everyone knows him. I will track him down and talk to him."

"Sir?" said James. "There is one other thing we haven't talked about yet, but maybe we should. What about the women? They will want to come with us, especially Manon."

Evan winced. "I know. I've been trying not to think about it. You understand we can't be sure of their safety, especially given we don't know the situation there. Manon is going to tell us she is the best placed of all of us to get information, though, isn't she?"

"Yes. She will also want to see her father. We haven't heard from him in far too long. Sir, do you think we could just not tell the women where we are going?"

Evan sighed, sitting back in his chair and turning away to stare outside the window of his office in thought while absentmindedly tapping his fingers on the desk. Both Manon and Alice actively helped Evan and James in past with intelligence gathering on St. Lucia, and both enjoyed the taste of action and intrigue. Evan finally turned back to face James as he spoke.

"We could do that, but if Manon ever finds out she will probably murder you. And me. And you are right, there is the problem of her father."

James took a few seconds to rub his chin in thought, obviously struggling with the issue. Seeing the puzzled look on Lieutenant Cooke's face Evan turned to him.

"Lieutenant, you are wondering what we are talking about. His woman Manon, whom I believe you have met, is from St. Lucia. Her father is Paddy Shannon and he is still there. Both of them served as informants for us in past and Paddy still serves in that role today. As I told you earlier, we need to go to St. Lucia on what appears to be a rescue mission to save a key French informant. The question is whether we need to do the same for Paddy. We don't know the situation with him as we've received no correspondence from him for some time now and this is a concern. Both the French informant and Paddy may be in grave danger."

"Thank you, sir, you've made the situation much clearer. I can see it's a difficult issue. If it was my father in danger, I would be prepared to risk everything to help him too."

Evan and James looked at each other for a moment before nodding as one.

"He's right, sir," said James. "We tell her. I will take care of that tonight and I will ensure she understands the danger. But there is one other question, you know. What about Alice? She will want in on this too."

Evan sighed. "I know. God, leave her to me. I will talk to her."

***

After the two officers left Evan worked steadily for two hours on the accumulated paperwork. Bills for supplies, requests for work to be done on various warships, correspondence from the Admiralty Victualing Board, letters from diplomats around the Caribbean, and a host of other miscellaneous demands left him with tired eyes by the time the sun was beginning to go down. But after two hours of steady work the pile awaiting his attention was still over half the size from when he started. Evan thought about simply shoving it all away and going to see the Captain of the *Lady Croydon*, but he knew if the ship was recently arrived in port it wouldn't be going anywhere soon. He also knew exactly where to find Captain O'Brien later in the evening. With a sigh he resolved to keep at it for another hour.

As Evan finally locked his office for the day

and left the Dockyard he bypassed the path to the home he shared with James and their two women. Within minutes he was at the entrance to the Dockyard Dog Inn, a large and sturdy stone building in Falmouth Harbour commanding a sweeping view of the picturesque bay and the ships it contained. Evan studied the ships in the distance and smiled as he walked up, recognizing one of them as the *Lady Croydon* swinging at her anchor.

Stepping inside, the first person he encountered was Emma, one of the owners of the Inn. She and her husband Walton co-owned the Inn with Alice. All three were former slaves who had worked together at the Flying Fish Inn in St. John's. Along with Alice, Emma and Walton helped Evan put a stop to the French and American plot several years ago and in the process some of their enemy's gold made its way into their hands to buy their freedom. Enough was left over to partner with Alice to buy the old Falmouth Harbour Inn and rebuild it into the pleasant, well maintained Inn it currently was.

"Evan! We were wondering about you. James has been here since you got back from Barbados, but we haven't seen you. Is Alice joining you?"

Evan gave her a brief hug in response. "Sorry, Emma, I've been very busy and no, I'm here to see someone tonight. In fact, I see who I'm looking for right now. Please have someone bring me an ale and a refill for whatever Captain O'Brien is drinking."

"Right away," said Emma, as an understanding look stole over her face for a brief moment before she turned away.

Evan smiled to himself as he walked over to the Captain's table, well aware Emma knew better than to ask what was going on. The Captain stopped talking and appeared wary as Evan stopped beside him without sitting down. The two men with the Captain deliberately sat back in their chairs.

"Commander Ross, how good to see you," said the Captain, although the tone of his voice held no warmth.

"Seamus, welcome back to Antigua. It's been a while, hasn't it? If you can spare me a few minutes I'd appreciate it. I've got a refill on the way for you."

As he finished speaking a serving girl appeared at his side bearing a tray with the drinks, but Evan forestalled her from putting them down.

"Not here, please. Perhaps over there by the window where we can talk undisturbed."

The Captain, a wiry older man with a weathered face that spoke of years at sea, looked at the drink. "Appreciate, you say. Well, since you're buying, why not?"

After moving to the new table the two men looked at each other in silence as they waited for the girl to set the drinks down and leave. As she did Evan took one last look around to ensure they would be unheard. He was about to speak, but the Captain started the conversation.

"Just to be clear, Commander, if you're going to make my life miserable like the last time you saw me, you can keep your drink and I'll just go back to my shipmates for the rest of the evening. And for the record I really am here on legitimate business, so you are wasting your time sniffing around me."

"Seamus. The last time you were here you were merely doing your job, just as were we. The fact we caught you smuggling is your bad luck. Trying to argue the point in court was a waste of your employer's time and money, but this was your bad decision, not mine. Seamus, you may find this hard to believe, but I really am not interested in whether you are smuggling on this island at the moment. Seriously. So can I get on with what I need to talk to you about? Please?"

The Captain stared unspeaking at Evan for several seconds, a stiff expression on his face. Finally, he sighed and finished what was left of his old drink before pulling the fresh mug of ale closer. He held it up for a moment and nodded his head toward the mug before finally speaking.

"You're buying, I'm listening."

"Very good. By any chance are you planning a stop in St. Lucia on this trip?"

The Captain's eyes widened before he responded. "Maybe, but I was going to make other stops before I got there. Frankly, with the situation being what it is, I'm not entirely sure stopping on any of the French islands is a good idea, let alone St. Lucia. I'm taking a big risk as a British trader sailing into their waters and, given the premium they will charge me for any goods I might buy from them, it may be impossible to sell anything I acquire. With their economy a shambles it isn't clear to me enough people on their islands have the money to buy what I bring anyway."

"Despite the fact I agree with your analysis I

have a proposal for you to consider. If I could persuade you to make St. Lucia your very next stop, taking some passengers there and then back to here, would you be interested?"

"Passengers? Who, you and that black son of a bitch who works with you?"

"Yes, and I wouldn't recommend calling him that to his face. He might take exception, and I guarantee you would regret doing so. Anyway, there may be three to five others with me too. There may be a couple of women. Not sure yet."

"Huh," said the Captain, unable to hide that he was furiously thinking through the implications. "How long do we stay?"

Evan shrugged. "Two, maybe three days? I will have to assess the situation."

The Captain paused briefly to consider this before continuing. "Right, it would be useless to ask you what you want to do there, but I do need to know what the story is. How do I explain your presence? Are you all just more sailors on my crew? And what about the women?"

"All of the men except me are just more crew. I will be an English businessman, there to see if I can keep some deals I have made alive despite what is going on with the change in administration. The women will be servants."

The Captain grunted as he digested this while rubbing his chin in thought. After a few moments he asked one more question.

"When?"

"I'd like to be on our way in two days or less. Maximum three days."

The Captain sat back and, after obviously thinking hard for a few moments, he smiled. "This will cost you, you know. I have losses to recoup from the last time I was here. And we may be sailing into dangerous waters."

Evan couldn't help letting a wry smile cross his face before responding. "Talk to me."

***

The negotiation took a while, but in the end it wasn't as unpleasant as Evan feared it could have been. As expected, Captain O'Brien started by asking for an outrageous sum of gold. Evan chuckled and countered with a sum parsimonious enough to make the Captain groan. But the man stayed where he was and the back and forth continued.

Evan knew enough resources were in his possession to pay even the outrageous sum the Captain asked for, but he wasn't about to do it. Unforeseen future needs and the sobering thought of having to account for it all to Sir James in Barbados made him cautious, despite the funds being a secret allocation. At one point they reached what seemed an impasse until a novel idea occurred to Evan. He decided to float it to the Captain and was gratified to see it made him sit and think hard about it. After several more minutes of discussion they reached agreement.

Evan was aware he might be criticized, but the risk was acceptable. The Captain would ferry Evan and his men to St. Lucia and back in return for an up front, partial payment of a small amount of gold. Evan topped up the remaining payment of gold with an additional amount Evan would get back when the final element of the deal was fulfilled, which was the Captain would be allowed to smuggle a cargo of goods approved by Evan into Antigua unhindered, once and only once. For the Captain, the surety of Evan's extra gold to be deposited with a local lawyer proved sincerity. For Evan, he knew he would get his gold back because the Captain knew he could not escape the long reach of the Royal Navy if it came down to it.

On the surface the downside was the Crown was losing out on much needed taxes, but Evan knew one way or another the Captain would have to be paid. The gold he was paying was far less than what it would have been if the profits to be made from smuggling weren't a factor. The local plantation owners wouldn't complain at getting needed supplies at a much cheaper rate. Evan had spent enough time over the years dealing with Sir James in Barbados and Sir John Laforey to know neither would likely have a problem with it, given the resources all belonged to the Crown either way.

Evan was tired from his long day as the two men finally shook hands. He declined an offer from Emma to have the Inn's kitchen make him a meal, as he knew Alice would be waiting for him at home. But as he was standing to leave James and Manon walked in the entrance to the tavern.

As with every other time she walked into a room, none of the men in the tavern were able to stop themselves from turning to stare at the lithe young black woman. Even Evan admitted to himself she was a serious rival to Alice, but he knew where his heart lay. Not for the first time Evan wondered at how he and James deserved having the two most beautiful women on the island at their sides. As they came over the Captain and James stared hard at each other before the Captain left to return to his own table. Evan sat back down as James and Manon joined him. James confirmed Manon now knew the situation and, as expected, was enthusiastic in her desire to join them.

"Evan, I want to thank you for letting me come with you. I know we may be in danger, but my father may be too. I am worried for him."

"We know. You must not take chances when you are in St. Lucia. Well, we will have time to talk later about the mission. James, I have made arrangements with our friend, so it is settled. We leave in the next two or three days maximum."

James scowled in the direction of the departed Captain before responding. "The thieving bugger is without doubt overcharging us, but so be it."

"Yes, well, please do your best to refrain from throttling him before we finish this mission. Look, I'm tired, so I'm off home to see Alice and have dinner. You're eating here?"

"We are," said Manon, with a grin. "Enjoy your evening alone."

Evan laughed and pulled some coins out to pay his bill before leaving.

***

Evan was grateful Alice was ready with a pot of savory stew brimming with huge chunks of fresh grouper caught bare hours before simmering in anticipation of his arrival. He began trying to tell her of his day, but she forestalled him and pointed at his bowl.

"I know you are hungry. I was too and I've already eaten. Talk when you are done."

He reached out to stroke her arm briefly across the table before grabbing his spoon and digging into the perfectly spiced stew, complemented by slices of fresh bread she baked earlier in the day, which he slathered with butter. As he washed it all down with a mug of ale he sat back in tired satisfaction and began to relate how his day unfolded. While listening Alice cleared the table of dishes, before finally sitting down. As she did, Evan reached over to take her hand in his to tell her of the decision they would be taking Manon with them to St. Lucia.

"So I know what you may be thinking, my love. You will want to come too, and you aren't overly concerned about the danger, are you? I confess *I* am, though. The truth is the only reason we are taking Manon is because of the situation with her father. This, and the fact she is indeed well placed to get us information from her contacts there about what is going on, of course. But make no mistake, I think the situation there is volatile and we may be sailing into serious danger. I know you have helped too and have been through danger with us many times, but this may be different. So in truth, I am really hoping you are going to tell me you are willing to stay behind."

Alice squeezed Evan's hand and bit her lip before speaking. "I know, lover man. Yes, I was thinking I would like to come with you, but I understand and I don't want to add to your worries."

Evan smiled in relief. "Thank you, my love. This will make it easier. But there is one other thing I wanted to talk to you about. Alice, I will have a ship soon. Yes, there will probably be times I am away, but Antigua is my home base. I don't know how long this will last, but if there is a war coming I believe they will want me to continue doing what I am doing. This ship isn't being repaired to see service as a warship, it's being fit out to meet my needs as an intelligence officer. So I don't believe I am going to ever have to sail away and never come back to you. You know, maybe it's having a war on the horizon to help one finally see clearly what is important in life. So honestly, even if some day they do come to me and order me to sail away forever, I won't do it. I will resign my commission and leave the Navy. Look, you know what I am really talking about here. I asked you once to marry me and now I am asking again."

Evan could see Alice's eyes were brimming and she brushed away a tear she finally couldn't hold back before speaking. "God, I don't know what I did to deserve you. I— I don't know how to say this. You probably didn't notice I said I *was* thinking I wanted to join you going to St. Lucia, right? Yes, well, my thinking did change. You remember back in early December, the day you came home and we enjoyed a little fun in the washtub? You may also recall we didn't take our usual precautions. My time of the month was due a bit after that and it didn't come. I didn't think much of it, but its now just over a month later and it still hasn't come. Evan, I feel like I'm gaining weight around my midsection."

Evan was stunned by the implications of

what she was saying before he whooped for joy. Slipping from his chair to kneel on one knee before her while still grasping her hand, he smiled up at her and responded with his voice firm.

"Marry me, you wonderful woman. Marry me before I leave for St. Lucia."

"Yes!" said Alice, unable to keep the tears at bay any longer as Evan rose to his feet, pulling her from the chair, and embracing her in a crushing hug with his arm.

"I love you, Alice. You've made me the happiest man alive. My God, and I thought I was busy before this!"

They both laughed before he silenced her with the longest kiss of their lives.

***

The tiny church in Falmouth Harbour was less than a decade old. The funds to build it came from nearby plantation owners in the area, but they were slow to fund its construction because this particular church's primary purpose was to minister solely to the converted slaves in the area.

Evan was not a regular attendee at church and neither was Alice, although both held a firm belief in the existence of an all encompassing, universal spirit permeating the world and everyone in it. They both made their general belief clear to the young priest conducting services at the church, and although he did his best to remonstrate them for their lack of attendance, he seemed satisfied with their faith.

With this issue behind them the young man raised the delicate subject of their proposed union itself. Evan smiled to himself as he listened to him awkwardly trying to point out the societal pitfalls awaiting a naval officer marrying a woman of colour and at the first opportunity to speak he did so, assuring the young man of his resolve and his full awareness of the possible consequences.

Obviously relieved, the young priest agreed to conduct the service for them, but only after the publication of the banns. In the church this meant publishing notice three Sundays in a row to the parish of the proposed union, thus providing opportunity for anyone to challenge it. Alice was concerned, but Evan reassured her, knowing it would be unlikely a congregation full of slaves or former slaves would challenge one of their own marrying a naval officer of some stature.

Their friends were overjoyed at the news. Manon and Alice had become each other's best friends in the years since she moved to Antigua to be with James and burst with pleasure Alice asked her to be her bridesmaid. James reacted with pleasure at being asked to be the best man, but Evan could tell James struggled with mixed emotions over the idea of his friend getting married. Evan watched him studying how happy Alice and Manon were, and he wondered at how much he was putting his best friend on the spot. Evan knew he would sort it out, though. Their friends Emma and Walton were overjoyed too, and right away began making plans for an enormous wedding party at The Dockyard Dog.

Evan was vexed at having little he could do about the delay necessary due to the banns, knowing he would be sailing into possible danger soon. The first of the notices would be published the next day. But the frustration he felt was inconsequential compared to what he felt when he learned of a different delay.

The day before they were due to sail Captain O'Brien's crew discovered the integrity of one of his yards was deteriorated to a point it badly needed replacing. Without it, the ship's maneuverability and speed would be significantly hampered. Even with the surreptitious help from a couple of Dockyard workers Evan offered, it meant they would not be able to sail until almost the end of the first week of February at best. Evan and James furiously looked for a ship with the potential to take the place of *The Lady Croydon*, but nothing suitable was to be found on such short notice, even in St. John's. Evan was exasperated, but once again little could be done to change the situation.

Evan channeled his frustration into joining training sessions with James, who was already working with the three new hands they acquired from Barbados. At first tentative in handling the unfamiliar naval cutlasses which were standard weapons on any Royal Navy ship, the three men gradually became accustomed to them. With little else to do while they waited on the repairs, James made them practice the standard cutlass drill until their arms could barely lift the weapons.

With that organized Evan focused on training Lieutenant Cooke. Given the Lieutenant's long familiarity of naval cutlasses and other standard naval weapons no practice was needed with these, so Evan began teaching him some of the refinements in hand to hand fighting he and James developed. The young Lieutenant took to it fast, quickly seeing the rationale for devising creative new ways to deal with a foe.

With repairs almost complete a few days later, Evan knew the decision he was putting off would have to be taken soon. As he sat with James in the tavern at the Dockyard Dog he once again looked around to ensure they wouldn't be heard before speaking.

"James? What do you think of our three recruits from Barbados now you've spent some time with them? Can we trust them and are they ready? I'd like to bring them with us because I have no idea what awaits us, and we may need their skills."

James took a moment to sip his drink. "I think our initial impressions remain valid, Evan. The only one I'm not sure about is this bastard Wishart. He's got an attitude I don't like and he has to be prodded to do things way more than the other two. I know, I'm a First Officer and it's my job to make them do what we want. Liking me isn't part of what is required. But the other two have actually been quite taken with the training I've given them, enough I'd almost say they are at a point where they look forward to it. I think Wishart is just a lazy bastard at heart. But none of this means we can't trust them in the sense I think you are talking about. So yes, if you think we might need them then I see no harm bringing them along. Actually, I could use the time we are sailing to St. Lucia to give them more training in what it means to be a sailor."

"Very good, let's bring them. Lieutenant

Cooke stays here to run the Dockyard and begin training any sailors who come available. How are you doing with the recruiting, by the way?"

"Still waiting, Evan. We proposed a number of names and Captain Laforey's First Officer has proposed a few others. I've met with a bunch of them and so far I have no complaints. We have ten men for certain who have agreed to join us, but none of them know they will be getting paid better. Hopefully by the time we get back from St. Lucia we will have almost everyone identified and available to us."

"Excellent. Well, I got word today that Harrison Black has finally finished setting up our new company. I think for a name The Leeward Islands Trading Company has a nice ring to it, don't you?"

"Sure," said James with a grin.

"Good, because as co-owner with me the two of us are now in business. We have already acquired our first asset, the former *HMS Alice*. We have to slowly put the word out this is a private venture on our part and that henceforth its home will be Falmouth Harbour."

"No problem," said James, before staring over Evan's shoulder toward the entrance to the tavern. "Evan? Seamus just walked in and he's coming our way."

The Captain stopped beside the table, but made no move to sit down. "We sail an hour after dawn with the tide, unless you have some reason to delay."

"We'll be there," said Evan.

***

Alice was awake, despite the early hour and

the pitch dark of pre dawn, to help the three of them with their breakfast. All three were anxious to be away, having loaded their kit the night before in the buggy they would take to Falmouth Harbour and to the ship. Evan knew they were all on edge, not knowing what they would be sailing into, but grateful the seeming interminable wait was finally over and they could simply be about it. James and Manon went out to the buggy first in order to give Evan and Alice a private, last moment alone. Evan gave Alice a final kiss and held her close as hard as he could. Both were unwilling to let go.

As they finally broke apart Alice looked up at Evan, a tear threatening to fall from one of her eyes. "Come back to me, my love."

"I will. We have a wedding to attend."

Chapter Five
February 1793
St. Lucia

As they sailed slowly into Castries harbour in the bright morning sunshine of a mid February day the tension on board *The Lady Croydon* was a palpable, burning undercurrent. Despite it Evan saw several members of the crew that had not been to St. Lucia before were standing in open-mouthed awe at the scene, enjoying the stunning view as they sailed into the harbour's shelter. From the narrow entrance the harbour widened into a large bay. Gentle, rolling hills covered with lush tropical vegetation surrounded most of it, but in the distance the hills gave way to towering mountains also covered in green vegetation. The main docks of the port were to starboard and beyond this were the multi coloured buildings of Castries. Several homes painted with a riot of different colours dotted the hills on either side.

But most of Captain O'Brien's crew wore worried, tense looks, being aware a British flagged ship could find a cold reception. This alone was cause enough for worry, but their Captain told them nothing about the close-mouthed crowd of passengers they boarded in Antigua. Evan knew care was needed, as the crew would be all for running at the first sign of trouble. Evan couldn't blame them, either. The thought of rotting in a French prison cell for even an hour was not a pleasant one.

The last time Evan and James were in St. Lucia was for their clandestine meeting with Captain Deschamps over two years ago. On the surface little appeared to have changed, except two frigates and a smaller French warship were in the harbour along with the usual array of small civilian ships. The *Marie-Anne*, one of the frigates, was familiar to both men. On looking closer Evan saw the once trim, well-maintained ship was showing signs of age and neglect. While it still appeared serviceable and its forty guns made it a formidable foe, the change was impossible to miss. Paint was peeling on the sides of the ship and even from a distance Evan could see the deck held equipment stacked in unorganized, loose piles in places. Evan knew Marcel Deschamps was her Captain for many years past and would never have countenanced it looking as shabby as it now did. With dismay, Evan and James both realized as one the flag flying aloft was the revolutionary tricolour.

"Well, that's not good. But it's as we suspected," said Evan, as he turned to scrutinize the other two warships in harbour.

The other frigate was named *La Felcite* and appeared built to a slightly different plan, but was still almost the same size as the *Marie-Anne*. This meant she would likely carry a minimum of thirty-two guns and was thus able to deliver a heavy punch of her own. Although she appeared to be newer, oddly it too bore the same subtle signs of neglect. Like the *Marie-Anne* and the other smaller warship tied up at the dock, *La Felicite* flew the tricolour too.

The third warship was a corvette named *La Rose*. Evan paid particular interest to it as they came closer, realizing it looked roughly comparable in size to *HMS Alice*. This meant *La Rose* would bear a similar complement of weapons to what the *Alice* would normally carry and she would be a formidable foe in her own right.

As the two men continued studying the ships with interest Captain O'Brien sidled over to where they stood on the far side of his quarterdeck.

"Don't know if you two have seen them, but the welcoming committee has noticed us and is signaling we are to moor over there just beyond these warships. It looks like some of the usual Customs thieves are waiting for us. What I don't like is the number of soldiers waiting there with them."

"We're not a war with them yet, Seamus, and you are just a struggling businessman trying to make money, remember?" said Evan.

"Yes, I do remember. The problem is trying to make money and drinking my favourite ale are what usually get me in trouble."

Two French Customs officials boarded as soon as the crew finished securing the ship to its moorings, followed by four soldiers who stood sullenly looking about and eyeing everyone with suspicion. James left Evan's side and began busying himself as if he were a member of the crew before disappearing below. Evan tried to stand close enough he could listen to the Captain using his basic, but serviceable French to converse with them. After scrutinizing their papers in detail and a cursory look into the hold of the ship Evan assumed the Customs men were satisfied and would leave. The surprise came when they demanded the fee.

Captain O'Brien's jaw fell open and remained there for a long few seconds as he processed the exorbitant number given to him.

Recovering himself, he began arguing with the two Customs men. Listening surreptitiously, Evan was as surprised as the Captain, knowing the fee they wanted truly was ridiculous. The Captain finally threw up his hands and came over to where Evan stood.

"I'm sorry, I have to involve you in this. They want a ridiculous fee and there is no way I can afford to pay it. I complained I've never paid anything like this *ever* before, but they claim times have changed. They enjoyed telling me the fact we are British means we pay the highest possible fee, too. So either you pay it or I will be forced to turn around and leave."

"Don't worry, Captain. I won't enjoy paying it, but we must do it. I brought sufficient funds."

The two Customs officials eyed Evan with interest as the small, but heavy purse of coins he offered disappeared into their pockets. One demanded to know who he was, but they seemed to accept the Captain's explanation Evan was an English businessman here to see the local English consul about possible business opportunities in St. Lucia. The two men eyed Evan with puzzled curiosity as this was explained to them, but after shrugging almost as one they told the Captain they were free to go about their business and left with the still scowling soldiers in tow.

As he watched them leaving the ship Evan pulled Captain O'Brien to the side.

"Right. You know what to do?"

O'Brien scowled. "Of course. I go over to the *Marie-Anne* and I give some story about Deschamps being an old friend, and ask if he's on board. God knows why I agreed to this, but I'll do it. I'm going to supervise the men off loading some cargo for a bit and then I will go do what you want."

"I'm sure the extra gold I'm paying you has something to do with it," said Evan.

"You're staying on board for now?"

"We are. I want to watch and see who is watching us, if you follow. I'm going to be surprised if they *aren't* watching us. And I need to know what you find out."

As the Captain left the ship Evan made his way below deck to the small Captain's cabin where James and Manon were waiting. After briefing them he signaled for them to follow.

"Time to put the plan in motion. James, find Smith and have him meet us on deck. The other two stay here for now. Let's go."

***

The wait wasn't long. O'Brien supervised his men for fifteen minutes before casually wandering over to the *Marie-Anne* and engaging in a conversation with the French Marine posted on guard on the dock. Evan could see in the distance the Marine was doing minimal talking, before he finally turned and waved to someone on the ship. After a minute an officer made his way off the ship to the dock. The conversation with him was short and Evan could see the Captain holding up both hands palm outward as he backed away and left. As O'Brien got closer to *The Lady Croydon* and came on board Evan saw the conversation had left the man visibly upset with barely held in check anger. As he strode over to where Evan and James stood on the deck Evan could also see a small sheen of sweat glistening on the man's face. The Captain looked over his shoulder to see if anyone was watching them before he turned to the waiting officers.

"What a bunch of arrogant bastards," he said, the heat in his voice obvious. "That's the last time I do anything like this for you, goddamn it. The guard was suspicious the second I mentioned the name Deschamps and that's when he called the officer down. He accused me of trying to spy on them and it took some fast talk to calm him down. Then he told me to get lost or they'd throw me in jail."

"Did they say anything at all about Deschamps?"

"Well, I think I caught the guard by surprise at first because he reacted funny when I mentioned him. He said Deschamps was the Captain a long time ago and then he woke up and got suspicious. Then the officer got involved and that was it. This better be worth what you're paying me, because I'm not going back to talk to them again."

"All right, Captain, believe it or not I do appreciate you did this. Right, some of us are going to disembark and do some scouting around. Continue about your normal business. We all plan to be back on the ship before nightfall."

As the Captain nodded and went back to supervising the men on the dock, Evan turned to face James and Manon. He also caught the eye of Smith and waved him over too.

"What happened just now reinforces the need to be careful here. Smith, you are with me for today, but the others will stay on the ship. I might want them tomorrow, though. I haven't been able to pick out anyone watching us, but this doesn't mean they aren't there. We'll take a couple of sailors with us to the dock as we disembark in a crowd. Because I am reasonably well dressed in civilian clothes it's likely any watchers will focus on following me. I'll create a diversion to make sure I get attention while you slip away in the opposite direction. I'm going to just scout around town for today and see if I can get in to see this consul of ours. You two find Paddy and see what the situation is. James, if you deem it safe you can scout the bars and see what you come up with. Be back on board before nightfall. Questions?"

No one spoke, so they ordered two sailors to follow them and they all marched off the ship to the shore, joining the Captain and his men working on the dock. After stopping Evan folded his arms in an aggressive stance and plastered a scowl on his face as he stood in front of Captain O'Brien, who looked at him in surprise. Evan kept his voice barely loud enough to catch attention, but not enough for other people on the dock to hear what he was saying.

"Please, Captain, pretend to start an argument with me."

"Eh? What are you talking about?"

"I'm trying to create a diversion, damn it. Make it look like you're arguing with me. Wave your arms around and look angry. Just keep your voice low enough people can't hear you."

As understanding finally dawned the Captain struggled not to laugh before he began waving his arms in an appearance of frustration while talking with Evan.

"Well, this won't be hard, will it? I've got lots of practice having arguments with *you*. Anything else you need me to do? Go and fetch you some ale? Wipe your arse for you?"

"Most amusing, Captain. Just keep it up for a bit longer," said Evan, adding a big scowl to his face for the benefit of any audience.

After another minute Evan signaled enough and with Smith in tow he walked away. As he did Evan whispered to Smith to keep watch for followers.

Evan was soon struck by how subtly things were changed since his last visit to Castries, as they spent the next five minutes walking about before heading to the consul's office. The number of beggars in the streets was increased along with the roving bands of street urchins Evan knew would pick his pocket in an eye blink were he not wary. As he had noticed in previous visits few people were smiling, which seemed such a strange contrast given the tropical paradise they lived in. Evan felt a distinct undercurrent of tension emanating from people passing by.

Evan knew something else was different, but couldn't place it until with a start he realized the age of the people around him was vastly different from before. Numerous blacks of working age were walking about town, unusual for the time of day. Many were simply sitting watching the people going by. Several looked hungry and held out their hands in obvious hope he might give them a coin.

"Sir?" said Smith. "Scruffy looking bastard about fifty feet behind us. Dark hair, red shirt, hasn't shaved in a week."

Evan stopped unexpectedly to pretend to look at a fish stall while stealing a fast glance behind. The man Smith identified was too slow to react before Evan saw him, despite finding sudden interest of his own in a nearby stall too.

"Yes, I expected this would happen. Well done, Smith."

As they resumed walking both men sensed a sudden stirring in the people around them, as if a boulder was thrown into a pond and the ripples were making the people around them rise like a flock of startled birds. Puzzled, Evan was unable to determine the source. He looked at Smith, who appeared as surprised as Evan. They knew whatever was going on was nothing to do with them, as people were streaming past and disappearing around the corner of the street they were on. Evan shrugged and motioned for Smith to follow the crowd with him.

As the crowds grew Evan realized they were getting closer to the administrative heart of Castries, where the Governour's office, the main jail, the militia hall, and other government offices were located around a central square. The crowd was much thicker the closer they got. Evan began looking around for a vantage point where they could see what was going on, but all such choice spots appeared either taken or were rapidly disappearing.

"Sir?" said Smith, pointing toward a spot with promise and motioning Evan to follow him. Evan followed close as Smith used his elbows to brush people aside. A number of the blacks he shoved aside scowled at Smith, but appeared unwilling to challenge a big, white male who appeared more than capable of defending himself.

Evan's face froze as he came in sight of what attracted everyone. Seeing a real guillotine was a new experience for Evan, but drawings of it were in past editions of the newspapers and he knew what the device was instantly. The base of the device bore dark stains, which Evan surmised was blood from previous victims soaking deep enough into the wood it couldn't be removed. Files of soldiers held the crowd around the square back. The murmur of excited voices from the crowd grew louder, as a small cart pulled by a horse and buggy drew up near the device. Evan sucked in his breath as he saw the cart held three men and two women. One of the men was black while the rest were all white people.

All five of them were filthy and disheveled looking, with their hands tied behind their backs. The two women remained slumped to the floor of the cart while the men were dragged off. The hair of all five people was roughly shorn and cut short.

Once they were all off the cart a pompous looking French Army officer stepped forward and motioned to a soldier standing nearby. The man raised his musket and fired it in the air to silence the crowd. After a few moments the officer began reading a proclamation in a blaring voice. The four white people were all part of the same family and all were accused of sedition against the new regime. The revolutionary tribunal's finding of guilt and a conviction on this charge meant death, along with confiscation of their plantation and all of their assets.

The black man, however, faced a charge of spying. Who he was serving as an informant for wasn't mentioned, but the charge made clear the information was going to forces beyond the borders of St. Lucia working against the revolutionary regime. Either way, the penalty for him was also death.

Evan grew worried as he listened to the charge. He didn't recognize the prisoner, but this meant nothing. His primary sources of information were the informal networks of slaves and local people on all of the islands he was tasked with watching. The reality was the man could well be one of the informants providing him information in past. If so, and if the man had been tortured into revealing others in the network, people such as Manon's father Paddy were in dire danger.

Evan bit his lip in frustration, knowing it equally possible the man could have been working for someone else. The most likely possibility was the royalist refugees fleeing St. Lucia for other islands like Martinique. If they were plotting some kind of return in force to St. Lucia they would in particular need to know the military situation on the island. Another possibility was the Spanish, although Evan felt the chances of this were slim. The Spanish had no history with the island of St. Lucia and seemed occupied with simply maintaining their existing possessions in the Caribbean.

The inescapable conclusion was Paddy's life was at risk and, the sooner they got him out, the better. Even as the thought came to him Evan spied James looking at him from within the crowd on the other side of the square. Manon was beside him. Neither acknowledged each other, but Evan fervently hoped James was reaching the same conclusion and would persuade Paddy to pack up and leave with them immediately.

Evan turned back to the spectacle once again. Watching the executions held no interest for him, but the crowd was hemming them in on all sides and it would be a struggle to leave. While Evan was thinking about the ramifications of it all, the officer finished reading the charges and ordered the executions to proceed without delay.

Evan was familiar with the experience of public executions he had seen conducted before in Antigua. Watching the crowd he realized the people here were as varied in their reaction to what was happening as at home. The emotions on display ranged from outright horror to gleeful fascination on the other end of the scale. What did seem different was a subtle feeling the crowd was hungry for the spectacle, and was even welcoming what was to come. As the crowd grew more frenzied in anticipation he realized they were actually *lusting* to see it in action again.

The executions proceeded with efficient dispatch. As the blade dropped on the first victim the crowd let out a collective, inarticulate groan which could have been one of either pleasure or pain or even both. Evan shook his head in disgust as some in the crowd laughed throughout and made crude remarks about the spurts of blood jetting from the severed bodies. By the time the third prisoner was dispatched a small lake of blood began forming around the base of the guillotine. Despite being some distance across the square Evan could see a cloud of flies already swarming to take advantage of the congealing pool. He was disgusted with the scene and done watching before the blade fell on the last victim. Pulling at Smith's arm, he turned and forced a path through the bystanders.

The crowd thinned out the further they got away from the square. Despite his concern for Paddy, Evan knew sticking with the plan was necessary and he hoped James would do everything possible to protect Manon's father. Evan began mentally preparing himself for his meeting with the British consul, but Smith interrupted his thoughts.

"Sir? Our new friend is back following us again."

Evan kept walking without turning around as he made his decision.

"Hmm. I don't care if this man follows us to our next stop, but we will have to do something about him once we leave. We are going to see some people later who won't be happy if we lead a Frog spy to their doorstep."

"Would you like me to take care of him, sir?"

Evan gave Smith an appraising, sidelong glance as they continued walking and Smith gave him a bland look in return.

"We do need him to stop following us, but I would really prefer not to draw a lot of attention while we persuade him to stop," said Evan, as he stopped in front of the consul's office.

"This is my first destination. See here, it would also be quite preferable if he were unable to make a fuss about it later. Can you manage this without my help, Smith?"

"Sir. In the short time we've been under your command you and Lieutenant Wilton have proven to us you are men of your word. You really have been both firm and fair. I think you were consciously taking a chance on us and I would like opportunity to prove to you that your decision wasn't a mistake. So yes, I can deal with him."

The thoughtfulness of the sailor's response impressed Evan, sensing this man was unlike average sailors. But Evan also couldn't help a small smile as he raised an eyebrow in question.

"The Army was that bad, was it?"

"My God, sir. With all respect, you have *no* idea how bad."

"Sorry, Smith. It wasn't a fair question to ask, but we shall keep it to ourselves, eh? Right, I expect I'll be perhaps thirty minutes or an hour at most. I'll meet you back here on this spot then."

Evan watched Smith saunter away for a moment before entering the office in front of him. The man he was going to see was actually a French lawyer who, for a fee, agreed to serve as temporary British consul when the last British diplomat serving in the capacity was recalled. Despite their countries differences, diplomatic contact at official levels was always necessary.

After being kept waiting for almost thirty minutes Evan was finally ushered in to see the man. The lawyer greeted him with a wary, cold demeanour, but he saw how well dressed Evan was so he sat back and listened to Evan's cover story, saying nothing. The man began to thaw after Evan gave his false name and presented himself as a British businessman representing the Leeward Islands Trading Company, a firm more interested in making money while wanting nothing to do with politics. Making it clear he was simply adapting to which way the wind was blowing and wanting to deal with the new people in charge, Evan hinted his clients were wealthy owners and businessmen on other British islands. The suggestion profits could be found all around by arranging for a continuing flow of quality French products for the quiet consumption of his clients made the lawyer sit forward in his chair with interest. High quality French wines, cognacs, and cheeses topped the list Evan presented.

When Evan finished the lawyer sat back and smiled as he thought it through, obviously considering the potential to reap a tidy sum from his share of the proceeds. Rising from his chair he brought out a decanter from a nearby cabinet along with two cognac glasses. As he poured Evan a drink and resumed sitting he finally responded.

"Well, sir, I see possibility in what you suggest. I have to confess I feel a fool for not having thought of this myself. But the more I consider it I believe you are right. The current political troubles mean disruptions to supply, which in turn means opportunity for profit. So this will take time, but I am certain we can work something out to our mutual advantage."

"Excellent," said Evan, before plastering a concerned look on his face. "I confess, though, I am a bit troubled about our ability to really make this work. I hear so many wild stories about the politics here I'm not certain what to believe. And this morning when we came in we were charged the most ridiculous fees. I am hoping you could fill me in a little on what is going on here, and more importantly, you can assure me we can make this work without the nonsense of those fees. I would prefer not to have to engage in direct smuggling, to be blunt. Too many things could go wrong."

The real purpose of Evan's visit was to get an understanding of exactly what was happening on St. Lucia since the old Governour departed, and he sat listening as the man opened up and began giving him exactly what he wanted. The lawyer did his best to be circumspect, but couldn't hide his underlying contempt for the new regime as he quickly summarized what Montdenoix, Linger, and Captain La Chance had done. The two agents who set the stage for La Chance were already back in France, leaving the Captain in sole command. Evan mentally filed away the names of the two agents, in case one day he crossed their paths again.

"So what is this man La Chance like, sir? Is he someone we can do business with?"

The lawyer paused to consider his response. "Yesss, I believe so, but we must approach him carefully. He is perhaps more of a zealot than one could wish for. Best leave him to me. I will have to give thought to how we deal with the man. It may be better to seek assistance from some of his underlings or simply wait until someone more amenable comes along."

"I noticed the guillotine was in use today, sir. He is that much of a believer?"

"Oh, yes, the guillotine has been quite busy lately. The remaining royalist plantation owners who weren't smart enough to leave in time are awake at nights in fear they will be next."

"Indeed. And I see there seems to be military support for it all. I notice the warships in the harbour are all flying the tricolour. Actually, I've met the Captain of one of those frigates before, the *Marie-Anne* I believe it is. I guess he must have fled too, did he?"

The lawyer's eyes narrowed a little as he responded. "I usually don't pay much attention to their doings, sir. If you must know, I believe I heard a rumour there was a high-ranking former military person locked in the jail, but I have no idea if he is the man you are talking about. Were I you, sir, I wouldn't be asking too many questions about the military around here."

"Of course, sir," said Evan, offering an innocent smile to smooth it over and downing the remainder of his cognac. "Well, I have some other old friends to look up and the rest of my cargo to dispose of so I shall be off. I will await your correspondence once you have looked into things on your end. Once you have an idea of prices and availability we can work out details."

Smith was waiting in a patch of shade under a palm tree nearby as Evan stepped outside into the bright sunshine. As the man stepped forward Evan resisted the urge to look around.

"Well? How did you make out, Smith?"

"Mission accomplished, sir," replied the sailor, although on seeing Evan's look he knew more was expected. "I'm afraid it was necessary to do for him, sir. I'd hoped to give him a bad enough concussion he wouldn't remember anything about us, but he decided to struggle. He's hidden underneath a stinking pile of garbage in one of the back alleys. He'll be found eventually, but I'd say it's going to take time. I don't know why, but people don't seem to be very diligent about cleaning up around here. Maybe the slaves aren't being forced to do it anymore? In any case, I'm quite sure no one saw me."

Evan took a brief moment to give the man a nod of approval. "Well done, Smith. Right, let's go. Keep a weather eye out."

Evan's next stop wasn't one he wanted to make, as it wasn't part of his primary mission. But when Governour Woodley on Antigua learned Evan would be on his way to St. Lucia, the man implored Evan to see if he could find out what was happening to his half brother and his family who lived on the island. Evan warned the Governour he would not have time to ride out to the plantation the man owned, but the Governour extracted a promise Evan would at least stop at the house the family owned in Castries.

A fearful looking female slave answering Evan's knock at the nondescript, but well maintained house near the edge of town wanted nothing to do with him until Evan revealed they were Englishmen. With a nervous, quick look around she ushered the two men into the sitting room and left after telling them to wait. After several long minutes the door finally opened and a pretty, dark haired, but young white woman walked in. She was clearly nervous, but she gave both men a determined look. Seeing how well dressed Evan was she settled her gaze on him, but a slight frown appeared as she did.

"I understand you are English?" she said, her French accent heavy.

"Indeed," said Evan, rising to take her hand. "I'm sorry, but before I go further I must know who you are. I am looking for members of the Morel family. Are you one of them?"

"Sir, I am Marielle Morel. And you?"

"Then you and your family are who I am looking for. I am Commander Evan Ross, British Royal Navy. Governour Woodley on Antigua has asked me to— Good Lord!"

Evan was stunned as the woman crumpled and fell to her knees in front of him, clutching at his hand with both of hers. Tears were streaming down her cheeks as if a sudden storm burst on her face.

"My God, I can't believe this. Bless you for coming. Sir, I've been so afraid. Can you take me away from this godforsaken place?"

"I— please, sit here if you could," said Evan, as he and Smith pulled her to her feet and guided her to a chair. "What is happening? Where is the rest of the family? I was told to expect you and your parents."

"My parents are gone, sir" she replied, sobbing as she choked the words out while still clutching at Evan's hand, unwilling to let go. "Those maniacs took them away and then cut off their heads three days ago! I was at the plantation when they came for them, but my slave Martise and I hid. We were afraid they would come back so we made our way here. Martise saw my parents being murdered. I don't think they know we own this house in town, but sooner or later they will realize it and they will come for me too. Please, please save me. I don't want to have my head cut off."

Evan's concern melted at her pitiful state and knew he would have to find a way to smuggle her out. After reassuring her he would do so, her simple gratitude was heartbreaking to see.

"Bless you, sir. I will be forever in your debt. But my God, I know of others who need help. Can you do anything for them too?"

Evan shook his head, keeping a firm, but forlorn look on his face. "Not possible. I am here in secret and it is not my mission to rescue royalist supporters in need. You and your servant are the only two we can help. Marielle, if I may, you must not under any circumstances divulge who I am or what I am going to do for you."

The tears still streamed down her face, but she nodded her agreement. Evan thought hard for a few moments before he continued.

"See here, I am not certain exactly how long I will be here. I anticipated it would be no more than another two days, but I think it very possible we will have to depart tomorrow. If I bring you back to the ship now it may attract unwanted attention. You seem to have been safe here so I think you should stay one more night. Smith here will come to fetch you at some point tomorrow. You and your slave will not be able to take any of your belongings with you other than what you can carry in a small handbag. I suggest bring anything small and valuable to help you get by in Antigua. And for God's sake please do not wear your best dress to the ship. We don't want to attract attention, so you need to wear something nondescript. You understand?"

As the two men made to leave Evan paused at the door. "Marielle, one question for you. Have you ever heard of Captain Marcel Deschamps and if so, do you know what became of him?"

Recognition dawned on her face at the mention of the name. "Yes, Commander. I don't know him, but father spoke of this man. Once it became clear we should have left St. Lucia sooner father approached him for help. He was going to see what he could do, but then father told me the Captain was overcome by his own men and dragged away to prison. I haven't heard anything since."

Evan sighed. "Thank you, this is helpful to know. Watch for my man Smith and speak to no one else."

***

By the time the two men got back to the ship night was almost upon them. Evan fretted over the absence of James and Manon, but as he was about to leave in search of them James appeared and boarded the ship. Evan gave James a questioning look.

"Sir, I know you are wondering where Manon is. I left her with Paddy. He is being a stubborn old bastard, but I think we finally convinced him to come away with us after I told him what we saw today. He's still reluctant, but the spy they did for made both him and me nervous. Manon said she didn't recognize him, but he could have been someone new in the network since she left. And so you know, the reason we haven't heard from Paddy for a while is his usual sources are drying up. Ever since this guillotine appeared everyone has become real nervous about supplying information. Anyway, she wanted to stay with Paddy tonight to make sure he stays convinced to leave and to help him pack a few belongings. Given we don't want to attract too much attention to the ship until closer to when we are ready to leave, I agreed."

Evan grimaced in response, telling him of his day and of making a similar decision regarding the woman Marielle. "Right, I think it best we get out of here tomorrow. Did you catch anyone following you after my distraction here on the dock?"

"Not that I could see, but that means nothing."

"Well, I don't like what I'm finding on this island and I have a bad feeling about it all, but there is one other task I want to accomplish first thing in the morning before we leave. I need to scout the jail. It seems clear if the Captain is still alive then that is where he is. Looking at all the soldiers around here, though, I fear we are going to have to come back with more resources than we have now if we're going to free him. We shall see."

***

As soon as enough light was about the next day Evan, James, and the three sailors they brought with them stepped off *The Lady Croydon* onto the dock. As near as Evan could tell, no one appeared to be paying them any attention. With one final look around he turned to the four men.

"Right. James, you know what to do. Get

Paddy and Manon on this ship as soon as possible. He is not to take anything other than what he can carry. Smith, go and get those two women we spoke to yesterday and for God's sake don't be conspicuous about it. Just get them here fast. If we run into trouble we may not be able to wait for you, you understand?"

As Smith nodded impassively Evan turned to Wishart and Hopkins. "You two, you are with me. I need your expertise to do a fast reconnaissance of the local jail here. I believe a friend of ours is inside and we may need your help getting him out at some point. Let's go."

As Evan and the two men got closer to the jail Evan admonished them to be as nonchalant about what they were doing as possible.

"We've done this kind of thing before," said Wishart, a hint of annoyance in his voice coming through.

"Say *sir*, damn you," said Evan.

"Yes, sir."

The jail was a forbidding two story stone building with a large footprint, which shared a wall with the Governour's offices next door. The main entrance was on a side street away from the public square where the guillotine was located. Around the back a small courtyard was attached to the building with a small stable off to one side. A large entrance door with another two guards was set into the rear wall. A waist high stone fence surrounded the courtyard.

The two sailors with Evan muttered to each other as they sauntered past the main entrance. They stopped within a few feet of the door and the two guards standing on either side of it. Wishart distracted them by pretending to have something in his boot, while Hopkins got as close as he could to surreptitiously examine the entrance door lock. The two men used a similar ruse at the rear of the building to buy themselves enough time to do a thorough inspection of the area. After doing a full circuit of the building the two men motioned to Evan to step into the shade of a nearby tree. Looking around to ensure they were alone first, they made their report.

"Sir," said Hopkins. "This isn't going to be easy. Agreed, Tom?"

"I agree, *sir*," said Wishart, with enough of a hint of insolence in his tone to annoy Evan once again, although he decided to let it pass for now. "I'm pretty sure we can get both of those doors open even if they are locked. They look pretty simple, really. After all, who would want to break *into* a prison? The prisoners are always in cells and the guards are always there to stop them from getting out. We would need the right tools, though."

"Do you have them available to you?" said Evan.

"Well, I would probably want a specific tool I'm sure we can find or have made back in Antigua if we need to be quiet about it. If you don't mind the blunt and noisy approach we wouldn't need it. The real problem, sir, is the guards inside."

"Tell me more about what you think we will find inside, please."

Hopkins coughed in embarrassment. "Well, my mates and I *have* seen the inside of jails on more than one occasion, sir. One jail isn't really all that different from another, you see? The cells will be below ground level. I guarantee there will be at least two more men on the inside of the front door. Those would usually be the officers in charge. This rear entrance, hmm—probably another two men there as well, although they will be relief guards. They would take a break, spell off two of the guards out front and then those two would do the same with the others."

"What about the upper floor? Any guards up there, do you think?"

The two men looked at each other and shrugged. Evan grunted as he digested it all, realizing he should have been able to think of all this himself. He also knew he couldn't accomplish his mission without more help. After some thought, he gave the two men a speculative look.

"You two think you could give me a diagram of this place and what you think the interior might look like?"

The two men looked at each other one more time before turning as one back to Evan.

"Yes, sir. No problem," said Hopkins.

"Well done. Right, let's get out of here. It's time to leave this island."

***

Evan was back at the ship an hour after he left it, but the sailors reported no sign of either Smith and the two women or James and Manon. Evan felt a growing concern at their absence and he scanned the waterfront with care, but there seemed no sign of trouble. A Dutch flagged trading ship coming into harbour was in the final process of docking nearby. Captain O'Brien was pacing the dock and supervising as his men loaded the last of the goods acquired the day before, so Evan went to join him.

"Captain O'Brien, are you just about ready to depart?"

"The sooner we get out of here the happier I'll be. In other words, yes. I've been pushing the men hard to deal with the cargo and they are almost done."

Evan was about to respond when he saw James hurrying across the dock towards him. Even at a distance Evan could see from the frozen, desperate look on James's face something was wrong. James strode up and motioned to Evan to step to the side where they couldn't be overheard.

"Evan! Goddamn it, they're gone. I got to The Thirsty Sailor and found the place completely ransacked. Everything is destroyed and there is no sign of either Manon or Paddy. I asked a neighbour what happened and was told soldiers came in the early morning hours to take them away. Christ, what are we going to do?"

"Bastards!" said Evan. "God Almighty, I don't know. I need time—"

Before he could finish speaking a hand appeared on his shoulder. Evan turned to find Captain O'Brien trying to draw his attention. Standing beside him was an older man Evan did not recognize.

"Sir," said the Captain, the urgency in his voice quelling Evan's protest at being interrupted. "This man is the Captain of the Dutch ship that just came into harbour. *Listen* to him!"

"Sirs, I noticed your flag as soon as I came into harbour. You are in grave danger and must leave, *now*. Look, my wife is English and I tell you this because of her and the many friends I have on your island. I made a fast passage out from Amsterdam and obviously the news has not made it here yet. The French King Louis the Sixteenth went to the guillotine on January 21st. It was the final straw for your government. England and France declared war on each other on February 1st. I told my men to keep their mouths shut and stay on board when I saw you, but I can't guarantee it will stay this way long."

"Mr. Ross, I'm not risking my ship even a second longer," said O'Brien. "If it means our deal is off then so be it. The tide and the wind are with us. You two either get on board or you stay and rot in a French prison. Make a decision."

Evan was appalled, but knew the time to act was now. "Right, I agree, we get on board. Let's go."

James put out a hand to stop him. "Evan, I want to stay. I'll do what I can to find out where they are and if there is any possible way to free them I'll do it."

Evan's mind raced through the ramifications and he turned to James as he made his decision, reaching into his pocket to pull out a bag of coins.

"Stay safe, James. Use this as you see fit. I *will* be back in disguise with help soon, so watch for us. I guarantee you we will not stop until we find a way to free them."

Evan gripped James's forearm for a long moment before James turned and disappeared within moments into the town. Evan turned to the Dutchman and shook his hand.

"Sir, I don't know how to repay you for this. I will ensure our government knows of your kind act.

I would appreciate it if you would forget about everything you have just heard. Captain O'Brien, let's get the hell out of here."

As they were about to mount the gangplank to the ship Smith and the two women appeared, coming fast enough across the dock to turn a few heads at the sight.

"Thank God you are here, Smith. No time to explain, but we are leaving, *now*."

"Sorry to take so long sir," said Smith once they were all on deck and the gangplank was being hauled on board. "The ladies and I were just about to leave when there was a pounding at the front door I didn't like the sound of. We escaped out the back and it's a good thing we did, because it was a troop of soldiers. I heard them break in, but I don't think they realized we were there because no one covered the rear entrance and they didn't come in chase. Once we got out safely I checked around the front. They posted a guard at the entrance and I could hear them searching the place. I wasn't sure if they were going to raise an alarm so we took a roundabout route to get here and this is why it took so long."

"Commander?"

Evan turned to find Marielle standing beside him, tears once again in her eyes.

"I don't know how to thank you for saving us. You are my hero."

Reaching up, she kissed him on the cheek. Evan nodded, but turned back to watch for any trouble. The haste of everyone getting on board and the quick pace at which the crew cast off the lines mooring them to the dock and made sail was obvious.

Several people on shore and the surrounding ships turned their heads to watch, looking puzzled. Evan scanned the warships as they passed them by for any signs they were being readied for pursuit, but the faces onboard looked as puzzled as those on shore. As they left the harbour entrance and stood out to sea Evan breathed a sigh of relief they were free. But the knowledge his friends were in danger ate at him and he clenched his fist in frustration.

Someone, somewhere, was going to pay if they were hurt.

Chapter Six
February 1793
Antigua and St. Lucia

James did his best to keep a bland, noncommittal look on his face as he walked through the crowds in Castries, but beneath the surface he was seething. Frustration, fear for his old friend Paddy and his lover Manon, and, most of all, anger and the desire to lash out at whomever was responsible raged through him. James knew he needed to calm down and build some kind of plan. The thought of finding a tavern somewhere he could sit and think with a mug of ale in front of him appealed, but he knew a clear head was necessary.

The alternative was to keep busy while he thought his way through it by walking. After three hours of steady walking about he knew the layout of every street and alley in the town of Castries. The walk helped transmute the roiling stew of emotions engulfing him into a single, burning desire to save Paddy and Manon and a commitment to do whatever it would take to succeed. And with it came the basis of a plan.

James didn't have any friends on St. Lucia, having never spent much time on the island, but he knew this wasn't the case with Manon. She spoke of her friends often and, many times in particular, her best friend Janine. Knowing it would take Evan time to return in force, his obvious immediate problem was going be the need for food and shelter. James also wanted information, as to do anything to help Paddy and Manon he needed to know for certain where they were. He didn't know where to find Janine, but he did know where to start looking.

Fortune shone on him for the first time in the third tavern he stopped in. Presenting himself as a merchant sailor hoping for a ship while in conversation with the bartender he casually added he was hoping to find a woman he met the last time he was in town named Janine. The man's eyes lit on hearing the name, as it turned out she was a server in one of the nearby taverns James was yet to visit.

The Rusty Anchor tavern turned out to be an old, shabby sailor's haunt close to the waterfront and the main docks in an area dominated by buildings and sheds built to hold cargo transiting through the port. James found a corner table away from the few customers in the tavern at this time of day and eyed the pretty, black serving girl who eventually came to take his order. She was young and, as near as he could tell, close in age to Manon, so he asked for her name. She gave him a speculative, wary look, but told him her name was Janine and James smiled. Satisfied she was the woman he sought, he decided to risk revealing who he was.

Her face showed a mixture of surprise and wariness as he did. She gave a quick glance around to ensure they weren't being overheard before looking back at him. Her face softened and she bit her lip in thought a moment before giving him a tiny smile.

"My God, you are her man, aren't you? She told me of you. Look, you are in danger here. You know word has just come today that France and England are at war, don't you?"

"I do, but I am here with reason. I know you

are her good friend and helped Manon with information in past. I'm looking for your help once again, because I am certain they have taken her away. See here, is there somewhere we can talk without anyone knowing? Maybe later?"

Her eyes grew wide in shock at the news of Manon and she surreptitiously scanned the room one more time to ensure no one was paying them attention. "Yes. There is a shed behind this building containing stores and equipment. I will leave it unlocked. Come back tonight at dusk and I will meet you there."

"Very good. In the meantime, can I have some ale and food, please? I am a paying customer and I'm hungry."

She smiled for the first time since they met.

***

Despite being fairly sure she wouldn't betray him, James wasn't about to trap himself in a building with only one exit without being certain she was true to her word. He secreted himself in the thick of a nearby patch of brush to watch and wait. Insects soon realized where he was and did their best to torment him, but fortunately the wait wasn't long. As promised, she appeared carrying a small candle to light her way, but behind her was a dark male form. James was suspicious right away, but he could see the man was unarmed.

She opened the door of the shed and called out as she peered in. "James? I am here with my brother, so please don't be startled. James?"

James took a few seconds to gauge the situation. He wasn't concerned about dealing with the two people, as the knife he carried along with the smaller one strapped to his leg and secreted in his boot would more than serve if fighting his way out became necessary. The real issue was whether this was a trap and there were others in hiding, waiting for him to show himself. But he saw no indication of other people in the area and deciding to trust them, James came out of hiding.

Janine and her brother were appalled as James related the story of what he found at The Thirsty Sailor when he discovered Manon and her father were taken. Both were well aware of what their friend's fate was likely to be and they agreed to help in any way they could. The two of them were slaves, but they managed the tavern for an owner who rarely made an appearance in their lives as long as profits were realized. As they were the only two people ever entering the shed, it made an ideal location for James to use as a base to sleep and to see to his basic needs. At his request they agreed to use their contacts to try and find out what became of Paddy and Manon.

Before they left him for the night James made one specific request. Given the probability was strong Paddy and Manon were being held in the main jail, James knew a rescue attempt to free them from it might be necessary. Asking to speak to petty thieves incarcerated in the jail in past took Janine and her brother by surprise until he explained a map of the interior would be crucial to have. Once they understood, they agreed to help with this too.

James was tired as he finally lay down in the makeshift bed prepared for him in the shed. He smiled to himself, knowing a good start toward getting Paddy and Manon set free was underway. His worry over what was happening to them and how they were being treated couldn't be helped.

But someone was going to pay for this.

***

They sailed into English Harbour early in the morning and found a frantic, buzzing hive of activity. With news of the formal declaration of war having made its way to Antigua via a swift packet ship from England, the demands for repairs and requests for supplies to fill in gaps on the warships was at a feverous pitch. Lieutenant Cooke couldn't hide his relief at Evan's return.

"Thank *God* you are back, sir," he said, as the two men made their way to Evan's office for debriefing. "I have to say this has been a learning experience. You know, as a Lieutenant I do understand how this works. When a Captain isn't happy, I expect to be shat upon. I just wasn't expecting to be shat upon by *all of them* at the pretty much the same time."

"Welcome to the Navy, Lieutenant. But it's not going to get any easier and we are going back to St. Lucia soon. Very soon."

The Lieutenant's face grew grim as Evan relayed the news of his trip. The rest of the day became a blur of paperwork and meetings, with a host of difficult decisions taxing Evan to the limit. On his way back from St. Lucia he used his time to consider what his needs would be, so by the time he set foot on shore everyone around him was soon hard at work.

His major quandary was the need for a ship to meet his requirements, followed by the need for men. With the war on simply sailing into Castries harbour with an English warship was impossible. Captain Laforey's resources at his disposal were nowhere near sufficient to invade and hold St. Lucia while ensuring the defense of the islands in his own domain. Even were this possible, how to get his people out alive wasn't clear. But when Evan met with the Captain to report on the situation, the Captain provided a ready solution.

With increased patrols as a result of war being declared one of the squadron warships had captured an American merchant ship, chancing on them in the middle of trying to smuggle their wares onto a deserted beach on the north side of Antigua. The Captain smiled at Evan's request to temporarily borrow it.

"But of course, Commander. This is why I'm bringing it up. Just do me a favour and don't damage my capture. It'll fetch a tidy little bit in the prize court."

"Sir? What was his cargo, if I may ask?"

"Salt fish and wood, I think. Why? You want it, too?"

"Yes, please. I will need to look the part if I am going to sail in disguised as a trader."

"It's all yours, Commander. Do with it as you see fit, just bring me back the ship."

Having a known American merchant ship with authentic papers to return to St. Lucia was the perfect solution Evan was hoping for. Fortune smiled on Evan once again as the efforts to find men set in motion before his departure to St. Lucia were paying off. When Evan asked Lieutenant Cooke about it on returning to the Dockyard, he received a list of thirty men newly assigned to the *HMS Alice*.

"They provided everyone we wanted sir, although there were more than a few Captains tried to change their minds once the war was declared. Fortunately Captain Laforey was involved in the meeting I was at when the final decisions were made and he put a stop to that. You were right about the warrants, they are new to the jobs, but they are well-seasoned sailors and the rest of the crew is too. They're a bunch of tough bastards, if I may, but I know a good number of them and I believe they will serve us well. I think the possibility of doing something different intrigued them. And by the way, we were successful in keeping them all in the dark about the higher pay. None of them know."

Evan raised an eyebrow in surprise, but was pleased to hear it. "Excellent. What about the Americans? Did we have success finding any for our crew?"

"Yes, sir. Sorry, I forgot to mention this point. We have two of them. They are from up north, some small town just outside of New York. They naturally have the New York area accent, though, which is what you were looking for I believe."

"Very good," said Evan, as he sat and deep in thought for a moment longer. "At some point soon I am going to read myself in and take charge of them all. Let's make this sooner than later. I suggest assemble the men at eight bells of the afternoon watch in the Dockyard. Make it a place where other people can't overhear us please. But before you organize all of this, go and bring in those three sailors

Lieutenant Wilton and I brought back from Barbados. I have a job for them."

Within minutes Lieutenant Cooke announced his return. Evan asked him to stay as he explained what he wanted to the three men.

"Forged American birth certificates for such a large number of men, sir?" said Smith, his brow furrowed in thought. "I can use my friends here to help, but the delicate work will have to be done by me. This will take a bit of time."

"This is why you're going to start on it immediately. Please train your friends here in the finer points as you go. I will be providing you with some samples to work with in the very near future."

Smith's face brightened. "Samples would be helpful, sir, the more, the better."

"Also, you need to provide similar documents for Lieutenant Cooke, Lieutenant Wilton, and for me. We may not have the right accents to go along with the certificates, but if they help to fool our opponents even for a while it may make a difference. While you are at it, I need some false paperwork showing the *Alice* to be an American merchant vessel. I will have a sample of this for you too. You are dismissed for now. Lieutenant Cooke, one last request of you. Get someone to find the American merchant ship Captain whose vessel was seized by Captain Laforey and send him to me, as soon as possible. And have the ship's papers we seized given to Smith here."

Evan sighed and rubbed at the stubble on his face, but he knew he couldn't let up until what he needed done was set in motion. For the next two hours Evan busied himself writing reports and dealing with the massive volume of paperwork accumulated on his desk. The quick, verbal debriefing provided to Captain Laforey when he first came in on what occurred and details on the French warships in St. Lucia was sufficient in the short term, but the Governour, Sir James Standish, and Captain Laforey would all be expecting written reports as soon as possible.

Evan knew some of the details, at least, would be provided to the Governour before his report made it to his desk. One of his first tasks as he got off the ship was to make arrangements for Marielle Morel to be delivered into the care of her uncle, Governour Woodley. She stopped as soon as she realized they were about to be parted and she drew close as she turned to smile up at Evan.

"Commander, thank you for all you have done. Please, I would like to see you again."

Evan stopped and straightened himself, taking a moment to consider how to deal with her request, but he knew he needed to be open with her. "Madam, I appreciate your sentiment, but I must tell you I am spoken for."

He saw the disappointment flash in her eyes, but she bore it well. Before turning away she stepped even closer to give him a kiss once again. "I understand, Commander. But you are still my hero and I will tell my uncle this."

The reports were all beginning to blur before his eyes when he heard a knock on his door. A harried looking Lieutenant Cooke came in with a man Evan did not recognize when he told them to enter.

"Sir? This is Captain Wild. He is the Captain of *The Ocean Mist,* the capture Captain Laforey told you of. If I may, sir, I will leave you two and return to my duties."

Evan waved the Lieutenant away and motioned to the Captain to sit. The man looked at the chair for a moment before finally shrugging and sitting down, a look of dark insolence on his face. Evan decided to get straight to what he wanted.

"Captain Wild, bad luck on your part to be caught. You don't have to tell me you are angry with us, as I am already well aware. You are facing a serious loss. With both your cargo and your ship gone your life will be more difficult. However, I have a proposal for you to consider which could help you recoup at least some of what you have lost. Notice I said *some*. If you are interested then say so. If not, the door is over there. But before you respond, I need to know you are prepared to keep your mouth shut about what I am asking of you. I should warn you failing me on this point would be a very bad idea."

The man's face remained impassive for several seconds before he finally spat out a response. "God, you bastards make me sick. I'm just a small trader scratching out a living for my men and I. So first you ruin me and now you're going to take advantage of my need and screw me somehow."

"Make a decision, Captain," said Evan, his voice weary. "I've enjoyed a long bloody day too."

"Christ, what other decision is there to make? Of course I agree. I have no choice, you bastard."

"Wasn't my idea for you to try smuggling

goods to Antigua, now was it? Drink? I'm having rum and water," said Evan, as he got up and went to the cabinet he kept his liquor in.

The Captain rolled his eyes and sighed, but put out a hand for the glass. "All right, what do you want?"

"Sir, I need a ship to sail into St. Lucia and yours is conveniently available," said Evan, watching as the man's eyes registered surprise at the mention of the French island. "Yes, you heard me right. You don't need to know why I am going there. I have a crew and being the bright fellow I'm sure you are, you have realized I will be pretending to be an American merchant. We may be there a little while and this is why I am interested in you."

"To do what?"

"Why, to be yourself. Look, we can take a shot at pretending to be merchants, but I am concerned we may stumble over some simple thing only a merchant would know and reveal ourselves. So you come into the picture to deal with the Customs officers and the locals. Obviously, you'll have to concoct some story about why you came to St. Lucia unexpectedly. Maybe you can say you heard a rumour the island was in need of what you have to offer and with the war on you are hoping for good profits as a result. So you do your haggling with the local merchants and provide me with the cover I need. If you can sell your wares and actually collect your fees from them I'll even let you keep the money. So am I making sense so far?"

The man took a big sip at his rum before responding. "This will be dangerous. What happens if we are caught?"

"A bad situation for those of us who are British, I expect. You can justifiably claim innocence as a real American. Pretend I coerced you or something," said Evan, unable to keep a grin from his features.

The American Captain seemed equally incapable of keeping a scowl off his face, as he downed the rest of his drink and slammed the mug on the desk.

"So if I can't actually collect the fees before we get out of there I go home empty handed. More British bull!"

"No, no, no," said Evan. "You will be paid a separate fee regardless of that. Half now, half when we get back. If we do well, you end up with it all. It won't compensate for the loss of your ship, but it will be a start."

The Captain sat back in his chair, obviously thinking hard about what Evan said, before slumping forward and sighing. "How much is this separate fee?"

Evan smiled.

***

The negotiation with the Captain took a little longer than expected, as the man bargained hard, but in the end they reached a deal and even shook hands. Evan paid him a little extra to get more paperwork samples for Smith and his mates to use in making forgeries, but he knew it would be worth it. Evan wasn't sure how reliable the Captain would be, but Lieutenant Cooke was going to be watching the man for any sign of trouble when the time came.

Evan's next task, however, was the most important one to perform that day. Lieutenant Cooke gathered the men into one of the big, temporary carpentry sheds the Dockyard workers erected to help increase production when demands increased. With the Lieutenant standing guard at the entrance to ensure no one else could enter or listen in, Evan stepped forward to address the men.

Evan felt a moment of wonder as he stood before the crowd of men, *his men*, for the first time. He long hoped this day would come, but he would never in a thousand years have expected to be reading himself into command of a warship while standing in a temporary carpentry shed.

Reaching into his pocket he pulled out the orders Sir James Standish gave him from the Admiral in Barbados. Although he last used the stentorian quarterdeck voice every Royal Navy officer learned to develop of necessity a long time ago, the memory of how to use it was not lost. The men stood silent as he finished reading. Evan folded up his orders and put them back in his pocket while scanning the faces in the crowd.

Lieutenant Cooke was right as to a man they bore the look of seasoned sailors. Most appeared to be less than thirty years of age, but a few older hands were sprinkled in the crowd. Evan recognized a number of the faces, but couldn't recall having actually talked with any of them. The only exceptions were the three sailors Smith, Hopkins, and Wishart.

"Right. I have a few things I need you to know and understand. First, you were all told this posting with me would be different from the usual

Navy routine, but you weren't told much about why this was the case. You were also given opportunity to decline, which means at least so far you are all volunteers. The thing is, part of what *different* means is you will be expected to keep your bloody mouth shut at all times about what the *HMS Alice* and her crew are up to. My Lieutenants and I all believe in being firm, but fair with you. We do not like using the cat, but we will if we must. The thing is, you *must* understand about keeping your mouth shut, though. The safety of you and your mates depends on this. If you tell anyone anything about what we are doing, or have done, and you are found out, I guarantee you will be lashed to within an inch of your life. The fact your tongue may have been loosened by drinking enough rum to sink a rowboat will *not* save you."

Evan paused to let the point sink in. "So, before I go any further, and I know this will seem odd, but you now have one last chance to decline this opportunity. If you have a problem with what I have just said then leave, *now*. Give your name to Lieutenant Cooke at the door and go back to your ship. I will speak to your Captain and assure him you have done nothing wrong. Make your decision."

Several of the men stared at Evan in open curiosity, while many turned to look at others in the crowd. Evan could see all of them were thinking hard about what Evan was saying. But none of them stirred from where they stood.

"Very good. Welcome to the *Alice*, men. Notice I said *Alice*, and not the *HMS Alice*. We are going to be doing things requiring we not advertise whom we, or our ship, really are, despite the fact I assure you we are indeed a Royal Navy ship and a Royal Navy crew. So, I expect most of you know the *Alice* is still being repaired. We are going to sea very soon, however. We will be disguised as the crew of *The Ocean Mist*, an American merchant vessel we caught smuggling. We will be pretending to be merchants. The American Captain will be with us to help fool the French about this, which we will need to do because we are sailing into Castries on St. Lucia."

A number of the men gave a small start at this. "Yes, you heard me. Our mission is very straightforward. There are three people imprisoned on St. Lucia by the Frogs and we are going to free them. These people have helped us in past and now it is our turn to help them by getting them out. I believe many of you know Lieutenant James Wilton. He is already in Castries trying to get the information we need to free these people. I don't need to tell you this is going to be dangerous. We are not going in there to trade broadsides with anyone, but if the opportunity or the need to break some heads arises we will do so. We are going to do what it takes to get these people out and we aren't leaving there until we do."

Evan paused one last time, gratified to see several of the men were actually smiling because of the opportunity for action. "Look, there is one last thing I need to tell you. The *Alice* is not going to be armed like a normal warship. You will find we will still have some bite, but our main defence will be to run if need be. Once she is ready for service her home will become Falmouth Harbour, in keeping with the pretense she is as a merchant ship. Because of all this, it is not likely we will have prize money to share. If we are in sight when one is taken by another ship, though, we will get our share. To compensate you for the likelihood of slim opportunities for prize money, the good news is you are all going to be paid from this day on at merchant ship pay rates."

Several of the men stared in openmouthed awe at Evan as an immediate buzz of conversation filled the room. From the rear of the shed Lieutenant Cooke bellowed out his annoyance.

"Silence, damn you all! Commander Ross didn't give you leave to speak!"

Evan raised a hand to quell any further talk and waited a moment to get their attention back. "Just to finish on this topic, I will say if the opportunity to take a prize presents itself we will not hesitate. Right, this is all I have. Please do recall what I said about keeping your mouths shut. This includes telling anyone about your pay. You are dismissed."

By the time Evan left the Dockyard and made his way home to Alice his brain felt like mush. She could see how tired he was as he stumbled in the door. He knew she would be worried, but he could not hide the truth of the events on St. Lucia from her. As she put together a makeshift dinner for him he sat slumped at the table and told her the story.

He knew his returning to St. Lucia so soon worried her, in particular because this time he would be sailing into danger in a hostile port. But there was little he could do about it and as they fell into bed together the need to find solace in each other's arms overcame his weariness.

***

They sailed into Castries and docked in the

early afternoon on the last day of February. Evan made certain to make himself as scarce as possible when the Customs agents boarded *The Ocean Mist,* as he feared Captain O'Brien would be dealing with the same men as before when Evan was in Castries. Fortunately, these two were different and the soldiers accompanying them on board were as well, so he continued to busy himself with small tasks as he worked his way close enough to overhear what was happening.

Evan was pleased to see the American Captain was doing his job, as the Customs agents showed no suspicion on their faces and appeared to be seeing exactly what Evan wanted them to see. Even better, the agents seemed pleased at word of the Captain's cargo and assured him he would have no problem making a sale. The two American sailors from the New York area were given tasks to work on near the Customs men and were loudly talking to ensure their accents could be overheard.

Despite the war being on security didn't appear to be tightened as much as Evan feared, as the Customs men didn't bother even asking to see the paperwork of any of the common sailors. Even better, the inspection of the cargo in the hold was cursory, and it failed to find the casks of weapons secreted behind the real cargo. The odd fact of several more sailors being present on the ship, more than a merchant vessel normally would have, escaped their notice completely.

Despite a burning urge to get off the ship and find James, Evan knew patience was needed. The Captain spent the next two hours negotiating with some buyers and after offloading some of the cargo for their inspection, a deal was made. Evan busied himself on the dock, pretending to be a clerk assisting with the process while watching to see if they were being observed. By the time night was falling and they quit for the day Evan was certain the deception was a success. As they finished what they were doing James took advantage of the bustle to appear from the shadows and sidle over to Evan.

The two men sat in a dark corner of The Rusty Anchor to debrief each other, as far away from the other patrons as possible. Evan was elated as James slid a rough map of the prison across the table to him and explained its origins.

"This cost me a bit of what you gave me, especially to ensure no one would ask questions as to why I wanted it. I am really hoping we can trust the bastards giving us the information, but I can't guarantee this. The people helping me here at the Anchor *are* good friends of Manon, though, so I am optimistic."

"Excellent. Any word on the number of guards inside?"

"Yes. During the day there are more about, but at night they consistently reduce the numbers to one at either door outside, with only two guards inside. No officers at night. Apparently, these idiots think people like us wouldn't bother to break in when it's dark outside. Good news for us, bad news for them."

"Hmm. What about the second floor? Are there guards there too?"

"This would be a problem. The sources don't

think so, but they can't be sure. They know there is a big interrogation room on the second floor and they believe the rest of the rooms are offices. They can't be completely certain, though, since no prisoner spends any time up there other than to be questioned."

Evan rubbed his chin, the concern obvious on his face. "Huh. Well, we will have to detail some of the men to go up there and deal with whomever may be there. It just means we are going to have to be really quiet for as long as possible once we get inside. So, do we have any confirmation Paddy and Manon are actually in the jail?"

James looked worried. "Word seems to be they were brought there, but my friends here spoke to someone who *thought* they saw a woman being taken elsewhere. Don't know who it was or where they went. We are still trying to find out."

"Well, we're going to find out. I want to show this to Smith and his mates tonight so they can compare it with the one they made based on what they saw from the outside. Tomorrow we will do reconnaissance on the jail one more time. We're going to have to give the men opportunity to learn where they are going, too. Offloading the cargo is going to take more than one day anyway and we need to keep our cover intact, so I think we go in and do it two nights from now."

***

Smith and his mates stood looking at the jail from a discreet distance and conferred together one last time before they turned as one to Evan and James.

"Sir, the map is helpful and seeing it again is

good," said Smith. "We think the approach should be made from the front."

"The front? Why?"

"The officers who would normally be stationed inside the front entrance to greet any visitors won't be there when we go in at night. The guards that *are* inside will probably be lounging in the rear of the building, in this room the map indicates is likely for the guards to pass the time. It will give us that much more time to get enough people inside to deal with them. Also, there will be minimal moonlight tonight, so taking out the guard at the front door might not be as noticeable as it would when the moon is full."

Evan took a moment to consider that before he nodded agreement. The men were about to return to the ship when a flurry of activity erupted at the rear entrance of the jail. Several soldiers milled about, as a buggy with a cart to pull was made ready. Evan motioned to his men to remain and watch, as several other bystanders were doing. As he suspected, more prisoners were being brought out from the cells and, judging by the growing numbers of people streaming toward the main square, he knew yet more executions were going to happen. As he watched even more soldiers appeared from the militia headquarters nearby, marching towards the square to ensure order was kept.

Once again, there were five people going to their end. Soldiers dragged each of them out, one man on either side of each prisoner. With their hands tied behind their backs and blinking in the bright sunshine they weren't used to, the bedraggled prisoners appeared a pitiful lot as they were loaded into the cart. To his dismay Evan realized Marcel Deschamps was the last prisoner being dragged out the door and shoved into the cart. Evan cursed and looked at James standing beside him.

"Damn," said James, looking appalled. "What are we going to do?"

"Nothing," said Evan, clenching his fist in frustration. "Goddamn it, all we needed was a little more time. There isn't a bloody thing we can do. Come on, then. Let's get a spot in the crowd. We need to see this to the end."

As they stood and watched in silence the cart passed close by them on its way to the square. Evan was shocked at the change wrought upon the Captain. Evan's last memory was of a man healthy and strong in his appearance despite being several years older, but today he was a barren shell. Thin and unshaven, his was hair unkempt and roughly shorn short, like the other prisoners. Evan could see massive bruising on his face together with scars not present the last time they met.

Following the cart into the square they elbowed their way to a spot where they could see everything. As before, the prisoners were unloaded and a French Army officer stepped forward to address the crowd. The first prisoner soon met his fate, but as he did it dawned on Evan the officer omitted mentioning Marcel Deschamps in his short speech. Evan could sense the puzzled look James was giving him, and he turned to acknowledge him, shrugging briefly before turning back to watch what was happening.

As the fourth victim met his end, the crowd looked expectantly at the remaining prisoner. The officer in charge made no move other than to look over at a knot of dignitaries cordoned off from the crowd by soldiers and sitting comfortably in chairs nearby. One of them in a French Navy officer's uniform finally rose and stalked forward, drawing everyone's attention.

To this point Captain Deschamps had remained slumped over on his knees, looking at the ground as he awaited his fate. On seeing the man's boots appear and stop in front of him, he raised his head. The officer standing before the prisoner spat on him before turning to face the crowd.

"Citizens," said Captain La Chance, his voice loud enough to carry around the square. "You see before you the worst sort of criminal. He is a naval officer sworn to protect the people of France and its colonies, yet he has betrayed you in the most heinous of ways. We have proof he is a spy for the British! He is a spymaster, sitting at the centre of a web of evil dedicated to defeating the will of the French people. Dedicated to defeating *your* will! He deserves the worst possible punishment. The guillotine is too swift and merciful an end for a swine such as this, but it will be his fate one day. I guarantee it! But it will not be today. We are not done with questioning him. I am sorry to deny him to you today, but we wanted to show you the scum we are defending you against. He will be back."

Turning to a pair of soldiers standing nearby he signaled them to come and take the prisoner away. Before they did the prisoner and his jailer stared at each other for a long moment, the hatred for each other burning on their faces unmistakable to everyone watching.

As the buggy and cart with Deschamps disappeared on its way back to the jail, James and Evan turned to stare in wonder at each other.

"Evan? What the Christ was this all about? Why didn't they do for him?"

"Damned if I know, but I don't care. We've got the opportunity we need after all. We are getting him out of there tomorrow night as planned."

Chapter Seven
March 1793
St. Lucia

By the afternoon of the next day Evan knew James was growing more and more frustrated with their inability to confirm whether or not Manon was in fact in the jail. Evan was too, but both knew little else could be done. Janine and her brother were still working to get more information without letup.

Despite their frustration Evan kept James busy with planning for the mission on the jail. Given it would be a night mission, they knew the men would have to familiarize themselves with possible routes to the jail and back to the ship. Once again they were expecting little in the way of moonlight so the knowledge of their route was critical. Evan decided to use only half of the men for the attack on the jail, keeping the other half to stand watch at the ship and be ready to leave in a hurry if they were pursued. Two guards were stationed at the far end of the dock area well away from where they were. But both men were seen to be falling asleep on duty and with numerous routes into the dock area Evan knew they wouldn't be a factor.

Evan set the attack for two hours into the middle watch, when he was certain few people would be on the streets. Even so, Evan knew he couldn't simply march through Castries with fifteen men at his back to the jail, so he decided to split them into four groups. An alley between two buildings not far from the main entrance to the jail became the agreed meeting point. Each group was to make their way to the rendezvous unseen. Evan was less concerned about once they were out of the jail and on their way back to the ship. If necessary, they would fight their way back to it.

Evan and James were finishing bringing the last of the small parties of sailors on the planned routes to the jail and back to the ship, while the remainder of the men finished offloading the last of the cargo, when it happened again. The same bustle of soldiers at the rear of the jail was the sign the guillotine would soon be doing its bloody work and the air around them filled with a buzz of anticipation, as the people on the street knew what it all meant too. Within a bare few minutes the crowds were streaming toward the main square.

Evan could only sigh as he watched it happening, a feeling of dread stealing over him. He knew James was staring at him and Evan was certain he also knew what he was going to say.

"Evan? They couldn't possibly drag him out here two days in a row, could they?"

Evan sighed. "Christ, I hope not. There won't be anything we can do about it."

Even as he spoke the first of the prisoners finally appeared. There were only three of them this time and all were men. Evan was relieved to see none of them was Marcel Deschamps, but he sensed James give a start beside him and stiffen at what they were seeing. As James uttered a stream of curses under his breath Evan finally recognized one of the men.

The last time Evan saw Paddy Shannon was during his trip to St. Lucia to see Marcel Deschamps two years ago. The genial old former Navy purser, who retired to St. Lucia after losing his leg years before, was a key conduit of intelligence information for years. Were it not for his telltale missing limb Evan wouldn't have recognized him. His features were drawn and grey, and he seemed shockingly thin. The old man was obviously tortured and beaten badly, as the same ugly bruising Marcel Deschamps bore the day before was marring Paddy's face. With his hands tied behind him the guards were forced to haul him bodily out to the cart.

Evan put his hand on James's shoulder for a moment as he murmured in his ear low enough no one could overhear them. "There is nothing we can do, James. But, by God, if there is a way to make whoever is responsible for this pay, then we will find it."

"My God, Evan," said James, too overcome by what was happening to say more.

With a feeling of dread and resignation, Evan led the small party of men automatically to a spot they could watch once again. An officer pronounced the sentence for the first two men, who were quickly dispatched with efficiency. When they were ready for the next prisoner the naval officer who addressed the crowd the day before stepped forward, after stopping to confer with a distinguished looking, older man dressed in a French Army uniform first.

"Citizens!" said the officer, as he stood before the slumped form of Paddy at his feet and scanned the crowd. "You all know me. I am Captain La Chance and I have been diligently serving as your temporary leader defending the Revolution for several weeks now from the reactionary forces seeking to take us backwards in time. I am pleased to tell you General Rochambeau has now arrived on St. Lucia, with orders to assume his new role as Governour of St. Lucia."

With a flourish La Chance pointed to the man in the Army uniform. "Citizens, I present to you General Rochambeau."

The man rose and took a lingering few bows to the crowd in all directions. The crowd responded with dutiful, enthusiastic applause and the General finally sat back down.

"Citizens, those of you who were here yesterday know I denied you opportunity to watch a traitorous spy meet his well deserved end. As I told you, the day will come when this will happen. I am mindful of your disappointment, though, so today I am going to make it up to you. This man you see before you is also a spy! We know he was one of the people serving the spymaster I presented to you yesterday. This man gathered information from a network of informers we are even now hunting down. We will not rest until they have all been found and brought here before you to pay the price for their traitorous actions."

La Chance paused to spread his arms wide for a few seconds. "Citizens. My brothers and sisters! I have dedicated myself to your defence. As soon as we have finished dealing with the scum you saw yesterday I will leave you in the capable hands of General Rochambeau and be off to Martinique to carry the Revolution forward to our brothers and sisters there too. I am proud to have served you."

La Chance took a long bow as the crowd

erupted with a sustained, lengthy round of cheering and applause. La Chance was forced to take several more before finally waving and returning to his seat beside the General. As he sat he signaled to the officer in charge of the execution to proceed.

After the blade's work was done once again Evan and James turned to look at each other. "I don't know what to say, James. I know you were good friends."

James stared back, his eyes cold and steady, but the heat in his voice was scorching. "Well, I *do* know what to say. I don't understand what the hell is going on. If both Manon and Paddy were being held for the same reason, why wasn't she losing her head today, too? And if they do have her, why in God's name can't we find out for certain she's in the jail? Something else is going on here and I don't like it."

"I don't know, James, but by God we are going to find out."

"Yes, we will. And Evan? I would ask a favour of you."

"Name it."

"This son of a bitch La Chance?" he replied, jerking his thumb over his shoulder in the direction of the guillotine. "I don't know if we will have opportunity to deal with him, but if we do I want him. I want to carve this bastard into a thousand pieces. Please?"

Evan reached out to James and the two men gripped each other hard by the forearm. "He's yours. And if we find Manon and someone has hurt her, I promise you I will be right there helping you carve up whoever this someone is. Let's get back to the ship."

***

They were finishing details of the raid on the jail when the American Captain came into the wardroom where they were sitting and staring at the map one last time.

"Commander?" said Captain Wild. "They have just offloaded the last of the cargo and are busy loading the rum I bought. I've got my fee and we will be done soon. We've pulled this off so far, but we need to be on our way or at least look like we're going to leave real soon. If we don't, someone might start asking questions I don't have answers for. Can we leave *now*, please?"

"Soon, Captain, soon," said Evan. "We will be doing what we came here for tonight. You should be ready to leave at a moment's notice. If anyone asks just make up some story. Tell them you might try a deal tomorrow to buy some excess French wine or maybe some brandy a local merchant can't sell due to prices being so high here. Tell them your men deserve a night off and a run through the local brothels to keep them happy. If we have to I will detail a few of them for this purpose."

"I sure hope you know what you're doing," said the Captain before stalking away.

James drew Evan's attention back once the man was out of earshot. "Right, let me see if I can summarize this. I confirmed last night there was only one guard on duty at the main entrance, as we were told would be the case, but we have to plan for the possibility of two. So if there is only one guard, I will approach with one of the men and distract him. If there are two we double the number of men, two to each guard. Everyone will have belaying pins on hand to get the job done quietly. I will also use my garrote if necessary. If the French have been stupid enough to let the guard have a key to the entrance we use it and drag him inside out of sight. As we are doing this the rest of the men come forward. We use the hand signals we've agreed on. The man with me strips him of his uniform and we find someone who fits the clothes to keep anyone passing by from being suspicious."

Evan nodded agreement. "So if he doesn't have a key, Hopkins and Wishart will do their job to get us inside fast and quiet, right? What do you propose doing with the guard's body?"

"Nothing for it, but to drag him out of sight in the alley as fast as possible. The hand signals will tell you what we need. We may have to think on our feet if someone comes by at an inopportune moment. If we have to take them out too we do so and deal with whatever else comes our way."

"All right, so now we are inside and we deal with the rest of the guards. You are going to lead a party to do this while I take the others into the cells below. You are also going to search the upper floor."

"Yes. I will try to distract the guards by speaking French so we get close enough to take them out without a disturbance. If the guard outside the rear entrance hears anything we deal with him, too, but I can make this decision when the time comes. So in addition to the belaying pins the men will all be armed with knives and a cutlass. No pistols, as we discussed. Once we have the job done we travel back to the ship in one group, unless there is pursuit, in which case you will lead one party with the prisoners back to the ship while I fight a rearguard action. If necessary, you leave without us."

Evan sighed and remained silent for a few seconds. James looked at him and spoke once again.

"Evan, I know what you're thinking. You don't like it, but we both know we have to plan for the possibility something goes wrong. I'm the expendable Lieutenant here and you are the senior officer. Look, I know this town like the back of my hand now. If we get cut off and you have to leave without us, I'm the one best placed to hide the men and get them to our fallback pickup location on La Toc Beach."

"Yes, you are right. But there is one other thing we haven't discussed and we should. I think it likely there are other prisoners in the jail."

"I know. I've been chewing on that issue in my mind for a while, Evan. What are we going to do?"

"Our orders are specific. Get in and get Marcel Deschamps out of here. Of course, once we knew maybe Paddy and Manon could be in there it was obvious they would be included in the rescue. We didn't know for certain he was in jail, but I guess we should have put the question of refugees to Sir James Standish. Even so, I'm not sure he would have an answer for us."

"So the questions are who are they, how many of them are there, and what kind of shape are they in?"

"Exactly. I think there are more Royalist families in there. How many, well, who knows? We know what kind of shape they will be in because we've seen prisoners being brought out. Whoever we rescue is going to slow us down and the more people we get out of there the more it is likely to slow us."

"I don't know what to say Evan. The thought of leaving people guilty only of supporting the wrong side in a conflict behind galls me. And let's remember, this is a jail. There may well be real criminals who deserve to be in there mixed in with the royalists and Captain Deschamps."

Evan sat back in his chair, deep in thought and searching his heart for answers, before he came to a decision and looked over at James. As an officer Evan knew a day could come in his career when the lives of civilians could be at stake, hanging on a decision only he could make. His hope was always he would never have to face such a day.

"The decision is we take the royalists, if we can, and if it does not jeopardize our primary mission. I am going to rely on Captain Deschamps to tell us whom to bring. If a decision has to be made to bring only some then I, and I alone, will make it. No one else will bear responsibility."

James rose from his seat. "I will ensure the men know what we want."

***

As expected, the quarter moon was beginning to make its presence known, but they got minimal light from it. High clouds drifting past obscured it completely every few minutes and Evan was grateful the men were familiar with their destination. Everyone was wearing the darkest possible clothing available as they started leaving the ship in staggered groups ten minutes before the appointed time. Lights were out in most buildings and at this late hour the majority of the town was asleep. Evan knew a few bars in the town remained open until almost dawn and could hold patrons, but this was a risk he could do little about.

Evan and his party were the first to the rendezvous, but the others soon appeared and were all accounted for. Evan checked both entrances to confirm the number of guards. As hoped for, only one man guarded each entrance. Evan made certain everyone was ready and signaled in silence to James to begin the raid.

After ensuring no one was about in either direction James and the sailor selected for the task went forward as quiet as they could, staying in the deep shadows of the street as long as possible. The guard appeared oblivious to their approach until they were less than ten feet away. Evan could see the man finally turn toward them and focus on James, who was pointing further down the street to distract the man. The sailor with James was already shifting to position himself behind the guard and in the second the man turned to look in the direction James pointed, the sailor struck hard. The belaying pin hammered into the man's skull with a crunch loud enough to be heard even where Evan and the rest of the men were in hiding. James grabbed him as he crumpled forward, easing him to the ground to ensure as little noise as possible was made.

Evan quickly scanned up and down the street for signs of anyone coming to investigate, but nothing stirred. James was giving the pockets of the unconscious guard a thorough search and he pulled out a small ring of keys, which he held up for Evan to see. Evan signaled for half of the men to come with him as he moved forward to join James. But even as they arrived the sound of a muted commotion in the distance signaled potential disaster.

Everyone froze where they were as Evan hissed out his command. "Still!"

Within seconds Evan and James knew trouble was coming their way. The sound of several raucous male voices, some attempting a ribald, drunken song, was soon followed by the light of a torch appearing in the distance a little over a block away. To Evan's dismay, unless they turned away soon, they would pass right by the entrance to the jail. The possibility this was a troop of soldiers out drinking and about to return to their barracks was all too real.

Evan cursed softly as he ran through the possibilities open to him, but with no time to do anything options were limited. Stripping the man of his uniform and replacing him with one of his own men would take too long. Taking the unconscious guard with them was a possibility, but he would slow them down and they could be seen. Evan knew he was left with no choice.

"Abort!" he hissed. "Get back to the rendezvous, now! James, put the keys back in his pocket in case they are missed."

The crowd of sailors needed no further urging and James hastily did as Evan ordered. As they all melted away into the darkness Evan heard a muffled curse behind him and he paused his flight, realizing James was stopped several paces behind him. James was looking back toward the jail, directing a stream of steady curses in as low a voice as possible at a sailor still lingering at the entrance to the jail. Whoever the man was moved the guard's body to a different position on the entrance steps. Pulling something Evan couldn't see out of his pocket the sailor waved it several times over the guard. Finally dropping whatever was in his hand on the unconscious man the sailor turned and scrabbled as fast as he could back to the rendezvous, running low to the ground in order not to be seen.

James grabbed him by the scruff of his collar the second they reached safety and got out of sight. Evan knew James was furious. Slamming the man against the building wall hard, James brought his face to within an inch of the sailor's.

"Hopkins, you imbecile," said James, his voice full of menace. "Did God give you any brains? Disobeying me is a bad idea. You know, I'm sure you've been introduced to the lash before. It must have been a long time ago, so maybe its time I introduced you to it again."

"James," said Evan, calling him over in a low, urgent voice as he watched the entrance to the jail. "Deal with him later. Get the men back to the ship. I'm going to see what happens here."

"Sirs, permission to speak. Please, sirs?" said Hopkins. The desperation in his plaintive voice was obvious and both officers turned to him, even as the sound of boots and the singing drew ever closer.

"*What*, goddamn it?" said Evan. "Speak fast."

"Sir," said Hopkins, his voice rushed. "There

was no time. I moved the body to make it look like the guard fell and hit his head on the step. I was carrying a flask of some French brandy on me, so I splashed a bunch of it all over the guard and then I left it on him. I'm hoping whoever finds him will think he was drunk and nothing more."

James groaned quietly while Evan raised a hand to his forehead as if feeling a sudden headache. But a sudden cry of alarm from down the street made the still drunken, raucous voices change to cries of alarm.

Evan looked at James. "No time. Get the men out of here. I think those are soldiers. I am staying behind to see what happens."

Evan could see the concern written all over James's face, but he nodded and signaled for the men to follow him. After watching them disappear toward the opposite end of the darkened alley Evan turned back and strained to listen to what was going on.

There were ten of them and they were indeed soldiers. One of them was more senior than the rest, made obvious by the deference they paid as he ordered them to stand aside. Bending on one knee over the guard he recoiled at the smell of the brandy. Reaching over he picked up the flask and sniffed at it, recoiling once again. After dropping the flask he lifted the guard's head to examine the man's crushed skull and the blood staining the edge of the step.

Evan breathed as huge sigh of relief as the man finally stood and spoke loud enough for Evan to hear. The guard was dead, but the soldier attributed it to being drunk and falling hard enough to smash his skull. One of the soldiers asked if a search of the area was needed, but the man shook his head even as he swayed drunkenly on his feet. He waved an arm around and asked if anyone could see anything. The rest of the soldiers looked around, but they all shook their heads. The soldier in charge began pounding on the door of the jail for a long minute before it finally opened a face peered out. As soon as the new guard appeared the soldier began berating him, asking if he too was drunk on duty.

Evan knew he needed to leave. As he made his way back to the ship he thought through the implications and by the time he stepped on board his decision was made. A cluster of faces was waiting for him, with James in the middle and Hopkins nearby. Evan went straight over to the sailor and shook his head. The man stiffened as he awaited his fate.

"Hopkins," said Evan. "I have to say, I am torn. I don't know whether to kick you in the arse for having somehow hidden liquor on you or to pat you on the back for your quick thinking, so I'm going to call it a draw and do neither. As near as I can tell your ruse worked. Those soldiers were all too drunk to see anything other than what you wanted them to see."

The relief on the man's face was clear. "Thank you, sir. I'm glad it worked."

"Yes, well, just remember you are escaping punishment *this* time. I expect the Lieutenants here will be watching you closer in future."

"Count on it," growled James.

"Commander?" said the American Captain, the hint of nervousness in his voice obvious. "Can we please get out of here now?"

"No, we are staying tonight."

"Sir, you said we would leave. You and your men came rushing back here and may have attracted attention. I don't know how we will explain being here another day. Look, I could expose you and—"

Evan grabbed the man by his shirtfront and pulled him close to his face. "Listen to me, you arsehole. I told you we are staying. Our mission is not done and we aren't leaving until it is. Lieutenant Cooke, I want this man watched at all times. He is to leave the ship only if absolutely necessary. If he does leave it I want you attached at the hip to this fool. If he shows any sign of giving us away you are to stick a knife in his heart immediately."

Evan shoved the Captain roughly away. "We will need to gauge the reaction tomorrow and see if they change the number of guards, both day and nighttime. If it looks like they have fallen for this ploy then we are going in again tomorrow night."

"Sir?" said James. "What if it turns out the jail has added more guards anyway?"

Evan sighed, because this was an all too real possibility, but he knew what his answer would be. He looked at the hard, stone-faced men standing around him and knew he needed to be straight with them.

"It doesn't matter. Captain Wild *is* right about the fact we can't stay here too long. The mission is we go in and get our people out. We are going in tomorrow night, regardless of what happens."

Chapter Eight
March 1793
St. Lucia

Captain La Chance stalked up the gangplank of *La Felicite* and went straight for his cabin in the stern of the ship. The crew knew at once something was wrong from the look on his features and almost as one they turned away to look busy at some task, in the hope his wrath would not fall on them. But the Captain didn't stop until he was able to slump into his chair, throwing his hat across the room in his frustration. He sat staring out the stern windows for a long minute before calling for his cabin steward. As the man knocked and entered, the Captain said only one word.

"Brandy."

The steward was well trained and needed no further orders. Within less than a minute the man was back, placing a large, half full snifter glass on the desk before the Captain. Another curt order to leave followed and within moments the Captain was alone with his thoughts. He sighed as he took a big sip from the glass.

His meeting with General Rochambeau did not go well. The amiable persona and grateful respect the man displayed on first arriving in St. Lucia to assume his new role was gone, replaced by the personality of a demanding, unhappy tyrant. The Captain ground his teeth in frustration, cursing Marcel Deschamps for yet again being the source of his problem. And this problem was now huge.

The Captain knew his prisoner deserved

credit for being astute enough to see the direction matters were going in and, along with the former Governour Colonel Gimat, taking steps to hinder the progress of the new French administration's goals in the Caribbean. The government became suspicious when more and more rumours slowly came to their attention about the Army in St. Lucia and the local workers not being paid properly. The clerks sympathetic to the Revolution managing it all were the first to surreptitiously sound the alarm.

At first everyone's pay was reduced by small amounts, beginning in 1791. Over time as the situation worsened, the reductions were increased to exorbitant levels. The Governour claimed tax revenues from tolls and excise duties were lower than needed due to price inflation and the poor economy. The Governour apparently knew every good lie contains an element of truth and for a time this worked. But despite efforts to keep the numbers to himself his clerks knew better.

The dark suspicion Governour de Gimat was withholding the resources of the colony for future Royalist purposes in the Caribbean came to the fore as he continued with bland assurances to questions about it all. His pleading he was doing the best he could while failing to make any tax remittances to the homeland also raised warning flags. For a time the Governour even blamed it all on lax record keeping by the same clerks who were sounding the alarm. Knowing the need to act, the French administration sent their agents Montdenoix and Linger to turn the tide in their favour. Once the two agents took control of St. Lucia they tried finding out exactly how much was siphoned away without success, although they knew the sum could only be enormous.

The failure of the two agents to pry the secret of where the money was hidden from Marcel Deschamps was how the problem for Captain La Chance started. With the brutal honesty of hindsight, the Captain also admitted to himself he owned it fully. His first mistake was to let the two agents off the hook for their failure to achieve this part of their mission. Overconfidence he could succeed where the agents failed was his second. Marcel Deschamps was proving far too resilient and the gap in the man's armour was still not apparent. Even his attempt to weaken the man's resolve by having him dragged out to the guillotine failed.

Captain La Chance sensed the General's concern, seeing numerous small warning signs emanating from the man. Knowing the need to address them he decided to send Paddy Shannon to the guillotine, believing the man bore no further secrets of value. La Chance was convinced the old man really was what he claimed to be, a small piece of the spy network on St. Lucia whose only real job was to pass the information on. He was also convinced Marcel Deschamps was the recipient of this information.

Sending an unimportant old man to the guillotine didn't work, though, and General Rochambeau made it crystal clear he wasn't going to botch the task of getting the money back in the same way. Captain La Chance would be fully and publicly held to account for dereliction of his duty unless results were achieved soon. The Captain's orders were indeed as he announced to the crowd the day before to carry the Revolution and the will of the administration further into the Caribbean. Martinique was to be his next challenge, but the General made it clear he held the authority to change this.

The Captain would be stripped of his authority at a minimum, and left to sit while the General sought direction from Paris as to what to do with him. The frightening part was the General's insinuation people who failed in their duty to the government could find their fate to be the ultimate penalty.

The thought of being dragged out to the same guillotine he had installed, hair shorn and hands tied behind his back, was a nightmare the Captain wanted no part of. He toyed with his glass for several minutes longer thinking through his plan. Doing so helped him to calm down, but the frustration remained. As he decided his next steps he knew he was fortunate he could combine his course of action with a way to ease his frustration.

La Chance remembered the day the soldiers brought Paddy and Manon into the interrogation room in the jail for the first time. As soon as he saw her he ordered her separated from her father and sent to his ship to be held in chains while awaiting his arrival. They beat Paddy for hours the same day to get answers, but in the back of his mind La Chance was savoring the possibilities of what he could do with the lithe young black woman when he got her alone.

She was defiant at first, but he slapped her hard a number of times and threatened to have her father sent to the guillotine if she didn't cooperate. This threat was what finally made her compliant. He raped her three times the first night and she was everything he imagined in his fantasies during the day. Even simply thinking about it stirred his blood once again. A fresh round of questions and another bout of slaking his desires would be a good start to solving his problem. The fact her father was already dead was a detail she didn't need to know, at least not yet.

He called for his steward, and the Captain smiled for the first time in several hours as the man appeared for his orders.

"Have the girl brought to me."

***

Manon's heart sank as she realized from the sound of the steps growing closer they were coming for her once again. But she sighed and looked into her heart to find the strength she knew she would need to endure. The unaccustomed light the two men brought with them hurt her eyes as she waited in submission while they unlocked the chain binding and chafing her ankle. She was given no time to rub it or enjoy the freedom as they hauled her with rough hands to her feet and marched her out of the hold serving as her prison. She felt no need to ask what was happening, already certain of where she was being taken.

She glared at the Captain in mute anger as he ordered the two grinning sailors to leave his cabin. She thought the ritual would be the same as he called for the steward, but the Captain surprised her by ordering the man to bring a tray of food and gesturing for her to sit. When the steward returned and placed the tray on the desk between them the Captain returned to form by ordering him to bring in towels, soap, and a bucket of warm water. The servant was soon back with everything ordered and after leaving for the final time the Captain waved a hand at it all.

"Well? What are you waiting for?"

Manon sat glaring at him, forcing away the overwhelming desire to leap across the desk and claw his eyes out. But she closed her eyes to find her strength, as she thought it through once again and concluded the possibility of fighting her way out didn't exist.

"Look, woman, I've brought you good food to eat. If you prefer the slop they feed you in the hold then this is your business. You are welcome to keep eating it. But I will have you clean yourself up. You stink of the ship's hold and you are filthy. Or perhaps you would prefer I bring my men in to do the job?"

Manon sighed, unable to resist pulling the tray of food closer. The fish was still steaming from the grill and the smell was tantalizing. Fresh cooked bread and cheese filled the remainder of the plate. The Captain sat in silence watching her as she ate her fill, unable to hide how ravenous she was at first. When she finally finished he smiled and nodded toward the bucket of water.

Manon stared at it and sighed once again before wordlessly standing to pull her torn and stained dress over her head, leaving her naked before him. She slowly sponged and soaped herself with deliberate, thorough movements, which she knew were merely delaying the inevitable. The animal watching her in silence was obviously enjoying the fact she was taking her time and she knew it. She considered doing the job much faster, but knew it would serve little purpose and the feeling of being clean again was wonderful. The problem was she knew it wouldn't last. As she finished toweling herself off the Captain stood and came out from behind the desk. He grabbed the towel from her hands and flung it across the room.

After he finished raping her once again she lay on his cot, feeling soiled and violated. As the tears streamed down her face she heard the Captain cross the room to a side cabinet. She finally forced herself to swing her legs over to the floor and sit up. Aware the questions would be coming next, she watched as the Captain pulled a bottle from the cabinet and refilled his brandy snifter.

"So, Manon. Your father sends his regards and his fervent hope you will finally give me what I want. I've told you I will be generous if you do. You and your father can simply go back to your lives and all will be well. Doesn't this sound good?"

Manon could only stare at him. "Bastard. We both know you are a liar, so why keep up the pretense?"

La Chance shrugged. "We all do what we must to survive in this world, don't we? Look, I'm convinced you have the information I want. You are a spy for the British. Your father has already told me the two of you have gathered information for years for them. But you were both just small fish before you left the island. I found it interesting you moved to Antigua and, you know, I'm not stupid. If there are any British spies about, Antigua is likely where they would be based. And what do I find when we finally raid your father's bar? I find *you*, back here again."

La Chance paused to sip at his drink. "You see, the thing is he claimed you were involved with nothing after you left St. Lucia, but I don't believe him. And you know what? He may be telling me the truth, at least as he knows it. I think I've got everything out of him I'm going to get, so really, you know, he is expendable at this point."

Manon grew cold as he finished, feeling desperation and fear surge through her. "For God's sake, he's an old man. Can't you just leave him alone if you've got what you want from him?"

"Sorry, I can't do that. At least not until you cooperate. I think you know what I want."

"My God, you bastard," said Manon, unable to keep the heat from her voice. "I've *told* you everything I know. I told you I did hear from my father of this man Deschamps you keep talking about and that I think he was the contact my father gave the information he collected to. And, I told you I don't know anything else about him. Look, if I really don't know what you want, how am I to convince you of this?"

"Yes, well, it is a problem, but I still think you are lying. And you are going to have to stop doing it soon, because I have my own problem, you see. The new man in charge here in St. Lucia is unhappy that I haven't been successful in finding where your friend Marcel Deschamps has hidden what we are looking for. If I don't succeed soon it may well be my own head that rolls some day. Since I would prefer to keep my head where it is, that means either you tell me where it is or your father will go to the guillotine."

Manon couldn't keep the tears from streaming down her face as she screamed out her response, the pent up frustration and desperation boiling over. "But I don't even *know* what it is this man has hidden! My God, how can you do this? I don't know what to tell you."

"God, do you think I'm stupid, woman? We both know its money he's hidden. The entire resources of the colony were stolen, and we want it back."

"I'm sorry, I *don't* know," said Manon, as she sobbed. "This is the first I have heard of this."

As she watched the Captain consider what she said for a second she felt a tiny spark of hope he might at last believe her. But the hope died as he spoke.

"You know, you are very convincing. But I really do think you have been keeping company with British spies and I believe they have trained you well. No matter, I still have a little time and perhaps this is what you need to consider your own position. I think I'm going to pay another visit to Captain Deschamps and your father now. You can think about this and perhaps when I return you will see it's better to just give me what I want. You are a very beautiful woman, the kind I have a weakness for, and I hate the idea of sending a beautiful woman to the guillotine. We could work out some arrangement for you, I'm sure. *If* you cooperate. Yes, think about it for now and we will talk again when I come back later. I am going to want answers."

As he finished he rose and came over to stand in front of her. She knew from the way he reached out to run his hand through her hair what was coming next. Fresh tears fell from her eyes.

"But before I go, I believe I have ample time to have some fun with you again."

***

Captain Deschamps heard the soldiers coming as he lay on one of the cots, too weak to stand for long. The rest of the prisoners sharing the cell with him shrank back toward the walls fearfully, in a futile attempt to remain unnoticed. His spirit sank, as the probability was good they were coming for him yet again, but the struggle to find the strength to resist was harder and harder. His body was a mass of steady, throbbing pain from previous beatings. A cut opened right above his hairline in a previous session was particularly sore, stubborn in its refusal to heal. One of the other prisoners with some medical training examined it as best he could and expressed concern the wound was festering badly. He was also worried at how feverish the Captain looked.

This time there were four of them. They stopped outside the cell he was in and unlocked the door. Captain Deschamps briefly registered the thought the number of guards was unusual before they came in. To his surprise they went straight to a young couple brought only days before to the jail. The man was the recent inheritor of his father's plantation courtesy of the guillotine. He and his young wife were caught trying to slip away to sea via the port of Soufriere further south of Castries with as much of their gold and jewelry as they could carry. Neither had suffered any interrogation to this point and the stark fear of what might be coming was written on their faces.

Two of the guards tied the two young prisoners hands securely behind them while the other two cut their hair short with rough slashes from their knives. For a brief moment the Captain thought his turn would come another day, but they came for him too. As this was the second time he was being taken out with other people at the same time it was a whole new experience and with it came the fear. He tried to discern whether what he was seeing fit a previous pattern of guard behaviour to no avail. In past some of the guards were particularly sadistic and enjoyed ensuring everyone in the jail knew exactly what was about to happen to the people they were taking away. None of those people were ever brought back. Knowing it unlikely he would be dragged out to the guillotine only to be denied to the waiting crowd a second time, the Captain's heart fell and he felt certain his time was up.

But the guards were silent this time as they dragged the three inmates out of the cell. As it became clear their destination was in fact the second floor interrogation room once again, Captain Deschamps realized he was at a point where he felt nothing either way. He was resigned to whatever was coming, be it yet another beating or to finally meet his end.

Captain La Chance was waiting for them, staring out the open window of the room. He motioned to the soldiers to put Captain Deschamps in a chair beside the table in the middle of the room. The two young prisoners were put in chairs with their backs against the wall and tied to them in a position they could watch what was happening. The four soldiers were told to remain as La Chance pulled up his own chair and sat down.

"Marcel, how pleasant to see you again. I doubt you have changed your mind, but I suppose I should ask before we proceed. Well?"

"You are wasting time, Jean, you pig," said Deschamps, his voice feeling strangely thick. "You know the answer."

"Well, you are right I cannot afford to waste any more time. I want to get on with my mission, but our new Governour is insisting I get answers from you, to the point he is practically threatening me. I sent the old man collaborating with you to the guillotine yesterday to keep the man happy, but I'm afraid it failed to mollify him. Yes, the old man implicated you fully, but I already knew you were guilty. So I'm sure you believe your situation couldn't possibly get worse, but I guarantee you it certainly could and will."

"Sir?" said the young plantation owner, with a pleading, desperate look on his face. "My wife and I would like to make you an offer. We will sign over the deed to our entire plantation if you would be so kind as to let us leave. We won't be any trouble."

La Chance turned in annoyance as the man spoke, before bursting out with a harsh laugh as the man finished. "You don't understand, do you? I'm afraid the time is long past for any such options. Your plantation is already forfeit."

He ordered the guards to gag both of them to ensure no further interruptions and as they did La Chance looked back at Deschamps. "So, Marcel, I'm curious. We don't have an exact tally of how much money you and Governour de Gimat stole. The least you could do is give me this."

Deschamps wearily shook his head. "Jean, how stupid do you think I am? I know all the strategies. Wear the prisoner down to a point where he is so weak he unthinkingly agrees to give his inquisitor a tiny bit of information. After a while, another bit is wormed out. And slowly it becomes a flood and it all comes out because the prisoner is relieved his torment is going to end one way or another."

"Marcel, none of this changes the fact you and the Governour are thieves. You have stolen money belonging to the government of your homeland, right when it is at war and has the greatest need. This makes the two of you traitors to your people. I can't believe you don't see this. Look, you and I hate each other for our own reasons. But even I have to admit you are a patriot. You just backed the wrong side. The time has come to look past this and recognize the money belongs to the people of France and its colonies, and they need it. Can you not see you must be true to your principles and be the patriot the people need you to be?"

"*Principles*?" said Deschamps, unable to resist responding. "I heard from the good people you have tied up behind me there is a rumour you maniacs have sent the King to the guillotine. What kind of crazy principles demand that? Listen, you bastard.

Governour de Gimat and I are the real patriots here. Both of us were happy to support reforms. We knew they were needed. But not like this! Chopping people's heads off is not a solution to anything. So yes, I hid your money and you'll not get the secret of where it is from me. It will go to where it is needed most, which is to defeat you and all the other lunatics like you."

"Well, I thought trying to be nice about this one last time might work, but obviously not," said La Chance, before sitting forward and staring hard into Captain Deschamps's eyes. "So, Marcel, I've been thinking. You were stationed here a long time, weren't you? And you were always one for the ladies. I'll bet you have someone special to you here, someone to keep you happy every night. I wonder who she is?"

Captain Deschamps did his best to keep his face bland, but the beatings and the months spent in jail carried an enormous toll and a vision of Simone's loving face filled his mind. For the briefest of moments as it did, he was unable to stop the surprise and fear sparked by what La Chance said from flickering across his face before he could master himself once again. His heart sank as he saw La Chance's glee on realizing the question struck home.

"I see I am right. I am surprised I didn't think of this sooner. I must be getting old. So, Marcel, it is only a matter of time before I find out her name and you will, of course, cooperate when she is brought here. Why don't you just spare her and tell me what I want to know?"

"I don't know what you are talking about."

"Hmm," said La Chance, appearing lost in thought. "I wonder?"

La Chance sat thinking for a moment, before smiling and turning to one of the guards. "Go to my ship and get the girl. Bring her here to me while I continue asking this stubborn imbecile more questions."

***

Manon was trembling with fear as she was taken from the ship. With hands tied behind her back she was marched to the jail. She was still deeply afraid as she was dragged into the interrogation room she and her father were taken to when she was first arrested. Her spirit sank as she saw La Chance standing in the middle of the room beating a man unfamiliar to her with a two-foot long club. La Chance stopped what he was doing as she was brought in. He ordered the guards to bring her a chair to sit beside the unknown man, who seemed only barely conscious of his surroundings. Her mind quickly registered two other people new to her, gagged and bound to chairs against the far wall.

"Ah, Manon. I thought I would have you join us. You do remember your old friend, I trust?" said La Chance, as he gestured toward the man he was beating only moments before. Reaching for a nearby jug of water he threw a copious amount into the man's face to bring him back to consciousness.

She looked at the man who was now struggling to focus on his surroundings. A puzzled look crossed his face as he saw the young woman sitting unexpectedly beside him. He returned her stare with a blank look. Manon turned back to La Chance, perplexed and worried.

"Am I supposed to know this man?"

La Chance turned to look at Deschamps, who shook his head.

"I have no idea who this is, you bastard."

La Chance stepped back, studying both of their faces before he finally spoke. "You are either both very good actors or you really don't know each other. But this, you see, is the trouble with being spies. One can never be completely sure of the truth, especially when I am certain you are both good at what you do. Well, no matter."

"Manon," said La Chance. "In case you really aren't lying to me, permit me to introduce you to your good friend Captain Marcel Deschamps. And Captain, I'd like you to meet Manon Shannon. She is one of your spies and the daughter of Paddy Shannon. Oh, sorry, I should have said the *late* Paddy Shannon."

Manon went cold from head to toe as he spoke. She stared in disbelief, willing him to be lying, but she could see the cruel smile on his face telling the story.

"Yes, I really must apologize, Manon. I believe I mentioned earlier today he was still alive, but I was confused. It's what happens when you get a little older. I sent him to the guillotine yesterday. You know, I see from the look on your face you are hoping I am lying to you. Well, I can prove I'm not. I'll be right back."

She couldn't hold the tears back any longer and she sobbed in her misery, unable to focus on anything. But La Chance returned within a minute and as he sat down he threw a bag on the table in front of them. With a flourish he dumped its horrific contents on the table. A severed human hand fell out, along with a wooden peg leg. The hand wore the wedding ring Paddy always refused to take off even after Manon's mother passed away. Manon recognized it all instantly as belonging to her father and she screamed her anguish. The two gagged prisoners watching from the other side of the room both gave muffled cries. Marcel Deschamps gave a soft groan, too, as he shook his head in dismay.

"Manon is your name, is it?" said Captain Deschamps. "He spoke of you while he was in jail with us. Your father loved you dearly. They took him away yesterday after they cut his hair short. They told us he was going to the guillotine. None of the people they've done that to have ever been brought back."

Manon sat slumped, still sobbing out her anguish and crying. La Chance waited for her to stop, but when she showed no signs of letting up he reached across the table and slapped her hard on the face.

"So, this is a lesson for both of you. As you can see, I am prepared to do *anything* necessary to get what I want. Do either of you have anything you want to tell me?"

Deschamps shook his head slowly, but Manon struggled to regain her composure. After a few long seconds she looked up with pure hatred in her eyes.

"You son of a bitch," she said, her voice a cutting hiss. "You are a dead man. I guarantee you are not going to die an old man. They will carve you into little pieces and feed them all to the sharks."

"Really? And who is it that's going to do this? Your British spy friends, perhaps? Oh, *my*, I'm terribly scared. Listen, you bitch. This traitor sitting here beside you has some bitch of his own somewhere on this island. Who knows, he may even have spawned some traitorous brat children along the way. I think you know who she is. As I told you before, you can save yourself if you just tell me what I want. So maybe I believe you when you say you don't know where he hid the money. I'm not going to believe you don't know him or the whore he is keeping. Just tell me and I will set you free, right now."

Manon could only shake her head, unable to keep more tears from forming and falling down her face in frustration. "You ignorant fool, I don't know what you are talking about. I *don't* know!"

La Chance sat back in his chair, looking from one to the other of his prisoners before finally sighing. "Fine, I'll just have to do this the hard way. But perhaps a little more incentive will help you two change your minds."

La Chance turned to look at the four impassive guards who were watching it all, patiently awaiting their orders. La Chance pointed to Captain Deschamps and Manon.

"First, I want you to bind these two to their chairs and gag them. I don't want them talking to each other. I'm going out for a bit, but I'll be back. I have a few things to organize. I *do* want them to watch what you are going to do to these two, though."

La Chance eyed the two fearful looking

young people sitting in their chairs against the wall and laughed. "Sorry. As I told you, your plantation is forfeit. I suppose I should have mentioned your lives are forfeit, too."

He looked around and smiled at Deschamps and Manon as the two young people stared at him back in horror. He ignored the muffled cries of their shock. "Marcel, I hope you and Manon enjoy the show, although if you decide to cooperate I could be enticed to be merciful. If you choose not to save their lives I'll have more for you to watch when I get back. I have to go get their execution organized and while I'm at it I think I'll have a few enquiries made. I'll bet there are plenty of people in town here who know you by sight and have seen you around. Someone will have seen you with your woman. I'll find out and when I do, she will be in here with you. You can sit and watch as we do the same to her as what is going to happen here. Enjoy!"

La Chance turned to the guards and rapped out his orders, pointing towards the two young prisoners. "After you finish gagging those other two someone needs to beat him to a pulp, but keep him alive enough to enjoy watching as you all take turns raping the woman. She's a pretty one, so I'm sure you'll have fun. I'll be back in thirty minutes or so. If he decides to talk come and get me."

"For God's sake, Jean!" said Deschamps, his voice hard to understand as he croaked out a plea. "They're too young to suffer this fate. You've already made their fathers pay the price. Why not just send them away?"

"Send them away?" said La Chance with a

laugh. "Has captivity made you soft in your head? They would just go join the rest of the enemies arrayed against us and probably spawn even more enemies along the way."

Manon was appalled. She looked at Deschamps in dismay as they were bound tightly to their chairs and gagged by two of the guards. The young prisoners muffled screams began even before La Chance left the room.

***

The Captain returned almost an hour later carrying a drink in his hand. As he walked in he checked to see if his orders were carried out. The young plantation owner's head was slumped to the side, with only his bonds to hold him in place in the chair. His face was a bloody mass of bruises and he appeared barely conscious. His shirt was ripped away and his entire upper body was covered with welts. His wife fared no better. Slumped in a piteous, sobbing heap on the floor, her dress was torn into little more than shreds and her face was badly bruised.

La Chance nodded to the guards. "Well done. Three of you can take them out and have them put on the cart for the guillotine. They are ready for us outside, but wait until I arrive before taking them to the square. One of you remains here with me. I need to have another conversation with these other two."

He stalked over to his seat at the table as three of the guards did his bidding. He took a sip from the mug as he sat down in front of Manon and Captain Deschamps once again. After taking a moment to make himself comfortable he smiled. The rich smell of strong French brandy wafted across the table.

"Terribly sorry to be late. I felt the need of some refreshment. This is such tiring work, you understand. Well, I wonder if you are ready to talk? Let's find out."

Manon glared at him with eyes cold as ice while the guards removed the gags, but left them both bound tightly to their chairs.

"You sadistic bastard," she said, the second the gag was off. "I hope when they come to carve you up they do it little pieces at a time, so you suffer too. How do you live with yourself, knowing you are a monster?"

La Chance shrugged and held his hands wide. "This is just a matter of perspective. To you I am a monster, but to others I am a hero. Who is right? In just a short while, you see, I will be outside presiding over more executions. The people in the crowd all think I'm defending them and are treating me like a hero. So I do what I must. But I have now answered your question, while you have not answered mine."

"Give me a knife and watch me cut your balls off for your answer."

"Captain, how about you? It's not too late to save your woman, you know."

Deschamps shook his head and made no reply. Manon's eyes narrowed as she watched Captain Deschamps, who appeared to be struggling to find the energy to even move his head.

"No? I'll bet you think you have been clever, Marcel. You think you covered your tracks and no one knew where you were going or whom you were seeing. I've already got some people asking around, but perhaps we will ask questions of some of your former shipmates too, Marcel. I'm sure someone is going to remember what their former Captain's habits were. Where he liked to spend his off duty time or perhaps his mention of someone inadvertently. Yes, I see the fear in your eyes. Still have nothing to say to me? If I find her there will be no mercy. Perhaps I shall let the men have their way with her just like today."

"You sick animal," hissed Manon, unable to hold back any longer. "Can't you see the man isn't well? You won't get answers out of a dead man."

La Chance remained staring at Captain Deschamps in silence. Manon could see a hint of doubt on their tormentors face, but she also realized he was thinking furiously. The feverish look on Captain Deschamps's face was indeed worse and she was certain he was no longer fully aware of where he was. After almost a minute La Chance appeared to make a decision as he downed the remainder of his drink and stood up.

"You may be right, my pretty one. He does look sick, but this is his own fault for being uncooperative. On the other hand, he is an accomplished spy. This may well be an act to buy respite while he pins his hopes on my not finding his woman. He is wrong, though, because I will find his woman. And I'm even willing to let him die because I'll bet *she* knows where the money is too. You *hear* me, Marcel, you bastard!"

Captain Deschamps brought his head up to

stare at La Chance with glassy eyes, but made no response. La Chance shook his head and waved the remaining guard over.

"They are waiting for me downstairs. Put the gags back on these two and move them over to the window. Make sure they watch the entertainment, even if you have to hold their heads every second of it. When its done have him taken back to the cells downstairs and have her taken back to *La Felicite*."

As the guard began tying the gag over Marcel Deschamps mouth once again La Chance turned to Manon. Without warning he slid a hand down the front of her dress to grasp one of her breasts. She tried to bite his arm, but he merely grabbed a fistful of hair and pulled her away.

"You know," said La Chance, wearing a cold smile on his face while tightening his grip on her hair. "I actually prefer it when a woman fights back a bit. You *are* a fighter, aren't you? And you seem to be getting far less cooperative. I am quite looking forward to tonight."

Chapter Nine
March 1793
St. Lucia

Evan and his crew spent their day marking time and doing their best not to attract attention. To his enormous relief no hue and cry ensued over the attack on the guard at the jail. As the morning wore on he took two men with him on a roundabout route through Castries, eventually passing by the jail. As before two guards were posted at either entrance. Given their bored looks Evan was certain no one was expecting extra vigilance of them. None of the other soldiers on the streets appeared on edge either.

He was surprised when he returned to the ship to find the crew preparing to take a load of small casks of different sizes on board. The load wasn't large, but enough was there it would take the men a couple of hours to complete the job. Seeing Lieutenant Cooke standing with Captain Wild supervising the operation Evan made his way over to them, not bothering to speak as he let the question appear on his face. As he strode up Captain Wild held up a hand to forestall him from asking.

"Yes, yes, I know I wasn't going to acquire anything else, but there was no choice. Some arsehole claiming to represent the harbour master came by with a soldier in tow and complained we were taking up valuable space on the dock. He wanted an exorbitant fee for us to continue staying where we were if we weren't going to be doing any business. I used the fallback plan to get him to leave."

"Fallback plan?" said Evan, as he looked at

Lieutenant Cooke for confirmation of what the man was saying. The Lieutenant nodded, so Evan pointed to the casks and looked back at the Captain.

"I assume these casks are the result?"

"Correct. I figured they were going to come and be a pain in the arse sooner or later, so I told one of the locals I was thinking about buying some of his excess stock of brandy and cognac. Remember? You were the one that told me to make up some story. I just decided to actually do it to make it look good. Of course, you realize I do expect you to pay me for this. I *am* cooperating with you, you know."

Evan laughed. "Christ, how stupid do you think I am? You're going to turn around and flog this for a tidy profit when you get back home."

"What profit?" said the Captain, a scowl on his face. "You may know what the Navy is all about, but you know nothing about business. The price I paid was ridiculous and I can prove it to you."

Evan rolled his eyes. "Fine, whatever, we shall discuss this when we get back to Antigua. I may perhaps cover *some* of this if you can actually prove what you are saying. Who knows, I may even buy some of it for myself, as long as what you charge me isn't as ridiculous as you claim. Do carry on."

"Sir?" said Lieutenant Cooke, forestalling Evan from leaving. "He also told the fellow we would be underway and gone come dawn."

Evan gave them a cold smile. "Well, he's right on that point. We are going to accomplish our mission and get out of here, hopefully long before dawn arrives."

***

After going over the details once again with James, Evan made only two changes to the plan. This time they would try the rear entrance to the building. With it set back from the street because of the courtyard, the small stables, and the fence, the likelihood was slim anyone would pass by in the dark and notice an altercation. The problem was anyone approaching this guard unexpectedly would automatically be deemed suspicious and the chance of him sounding the alarm was infinitely greater. They also knew of the possibility the guard on station inside would be much closer to the rear door. The darkness was their friend, though, and the minimal moonlight gave them the luxury of a slow, stealthy approach.

The other change was to their rendezvous location, yet again an alley, but this time closer to the rear entrance. Evan smiled on hearing only one guard was posted at each of the entrances. Once Evan confirmed everyone arrived without problems he gave the signal for the raid to begin. Four men detached themselves from the group and crept from their position in silence. One of them took a torturous route, using every shadow he could find, to make his way to the corner of the far side of the jail out of sight of the guard. James was in the lead with the other party, and Evan watched as they stopped beside the other corner of the building.

James slowly poked his head above the low stone fence, clearly gauging the situation. James waved one of his men forward and pointed toward the guard. Evan thought he could see the faint outline of the man on the far side of the building creeping slowly forward and hugging the wall, the same as the man James sent forward was doing.

The guard was oblivious to what was happening. Evan watched as the man's head nodded to the side as he leaned against the wall, struggling to remain awake. Despite watching and listening with care, a moment later Evan was surprised to realize the guard was no longer standing there. Evan blinked as he looked around him, straining his senses for any sign of an alarm being raised, but nothing happened. Evan looked again, but the guard was definitely gone and he knew the men had succeeded in taking down the guard without any noise. James and the remaining sailor slithered over the wall and strode forward, no longer attempting to hide what they were doing. As James got to the entrance he turned and gave Evan the prearranged signal to join him.

Within moments Evan and the rest of the men were crowded around the rear entrance. The guard's body was hauled off to the side and stuffed under a bush to keep it out of sight. The man's jacket was removed and some of the excess blood he shed was roughly dried. Even as one of the sailors pulled the jacket on another sailor came over to James. Evan could see the man grin in the dim moonlight as he held up a key. James took it from him and signaled to the man wearing the uniform jacket to join him. James was about to insert it into the lock when Smith stopped him.

"Sir," said Smith, his voice low and insistent. "Let Tommy Wishart do it. He's very good with locks and keys. He can do it real quiet like and buy us a second or two."

Wishart stepped forward to accept the key from James and he knelt to inspect the lock closely. He examined both the lock and the key back and forth several times before gently inserting it into the slot. After slowly testing it a few times Evan finally heard a barely audible click as the lock mechanism accepted the key.

Wishart stood up and spoke in a low voice. "Sir, the door is unlocked, but I think it impossible to open this door in silence. I recommend go in fast."

James nodded to the man before reaching out and yanking the door open as fast as he could. The sailor in the uniform jacket strode inside with James close behind. Evan followed, his knife at the ready. The sleepy French soldier sitting in the room they found themselves in looked up from the table he was slumped over, his head on his arms. Evan saw his eyes register puzzlement as he focused on the jacket and the man wearing it. By the time the guard realized the danger he was in the hands of Evan's sailor were already around his throat in a death grip. Evan dimly registered another of his men slipping past him and plunging a knife into the guard's back.

Evan and another sailor were side by side as they followed James further into the interior of the building, striving to make as little noise as possible. Evan saw James take quick looks into various small side rooms they passed, but they were clearly unoccupied. A light shone under the door to a room at the front of the building, however, and as they got closer the door opened. This time, the guard appearing in the doorway was fully awake and he saw his danger right away. Seeing he was outnumbered, he turned and fled for a door on the opposite side of the room.

As the man reached the door and turned the handle to open it, trying to call a warning, James was upon him. The garrote cut his voice off as he got the first word out. James pulled him backwards hard at the same time as he twisted the garrote handles to tighten the grip and they both fell backwards to the floor. The guard clawed with desperate, futile effort at the constraint around his neck, but James maintained his position behind him. As the guard began thrashing about like a speared fish Evan stabbed him in the heart to put a stop to it.

But even as he did Evan's mind registered the door the guard had run for was opening and another guard was now peering inside. To Evan's horror it was the front entrance door and this man was the sole guard outside. But before the guard could register shock or surprise another of Evan's men grabbed the guard by the throat with one hand. As the stunned guard's look turned to one of terror and he dropped his musket to claw at the crushing hand on his throat, the sailor plunged his knife deep into the man's chest and dragged him inside.

Evan went to the door and stepped outside, hoping fervently no one saw what happened. He closed the door behind him without latching it, allowing his eyes to adjust to the night once again. He stood still for a long minute, doing his best to pretend he was a tired guard slouching against the wall. The sailor who attacked the front door guard hissed a low query to him through the door, but Evan told him to wait a moment longer. Finally satisfied no one was about or sounding an alarm, Evan heaved a sigh of relief and stepped back inside. The sailor slipped on one of the dead guard's jackets and taking the dropped musket, he stepped outside to stand guard in the man's place.

"So far, so good. No one appears to have seen anything," said Evan in a low voice, seeing the question on James's face.

James nodded. "All quiet in here, too. I thought we made enough noise to wake the dead in here, but maybe this was it for the guards or perhaps we weren't as noisy as I thought. I'll take my party upstairs and I'll find out soon enough."

"Right, I'm going to the cells. Hopefully one of these bastards we've done for here has the keys."

Evan turned to go, but James forestalled him. "Evan?"

He turned back to find a desperate, pleading look on James's face. "Please find her."

Evan sheathed his knife and gripped James's shoulder hard for a quick moment. "I promise you, if she's here she is the first one out. Let's go."

***

The room at the rear of the building was filled with a crowd of men anxiously awaiting orders. James signaled to the small party of men they planned would join him for the search upstairs to follow him. Creeping slowly up the stairs in single file, James peered with care in both directions when he reached the top. No lights were on and the hall was dark. Fortunately, some of the doors to the various rooms were open and a little moonlight streamed in to give them at least something to find their way with.

The rooms all proved empty except for one. This one was pitch dark, but the door was ajar. James held a warning hand up as he slid through the door slowly, striving hard to make as little noise as possible. As he entered he could hear the sound of low snoring coming from one of the corners of the room. The smell of stale brandy assaulted his nose. A floorboard creaked a tiny bit and James stopped moving, waiting in silence. Nothing stirred and the snoring continued.

James sighed inwardly, knowing of no way to tell if anyone else was in the room beside the snoring guard. He strained every sense he could to no avail. Looking behind him he signaled to the sailor following him he was going to deal with the snoring man. The room was so dark he couldn't even be certain the sailor saw his signal, but there were no other options.

James crept ever closer and after a long minute he knew he was right beside the bed. Striking fast he grabbed at where he thought the man's head was, hoping to get his hands on the man's throat. He was off slightly, and the man's snoring changed to a garbled cry of surprise before being cut off. Even as he struggled to crush the man's windpipe he heard a startled cry behind him. James was surprised as someone pulled a curtain back and dim moonlight flooded the room. He looked over his shoulder in time to see a second guard already held a sword in his hand and was struggling to his feet.

James's heart sank, knowing he wouldn't have time to react before the guard would strike, but whoever followed James into the room cut the guard off. The belaying pin hammered onto the man's skull with a brutal crunching sound dropped him to the floor like a stone, allowing James to turn his full attention to his own victim. As James released his grip unexpectedly the man gasped to draw breath once again, but it became his last as James plunged his knife into the man's heart.

James stood up and focused on the sounds around him, wanting to ensure there were no other sounds of fighting about before he looked to see who saved him. Hopkins was the sailor who followed him in and he grinned back at James in the moonlight. The two men stared at each other for a moment before James finally smiled in a way he knew could easily be interpreted as a grimace.

"When I catch you drinking on duty, do me a favour and don't go thinking this incident is going to save you."

The sailor's grin widened. "I won't, sir."

***

Evan opened the door to the cells with slow care in case there were yet more guards. The fetid, stench filled air assaulted Evan's senses the second the door opened. He could see steps leading down to the cells disappearing into a stygian darkness, although as he knelt to peer in he thought he could see small, faint sources of weak light towards the distant walls. Given the darkness and the stench, Evan felt certain there weren't any guards. Evan crept slowly down the stone stairs, senses on alert for an unexpected attack.

Reaching the bottom he stood for a long few seconds to be certain. The faint sound of snoring came from a distant corner of the darkness, while a soft groan sounded from a different spot. Certain there were no guards, he turned to the man silently following him down the stairs and ordered him to pass the word for someone to find a few torches. As he stood waiting his eyes finally adjusted to the darkness enough to realize the faint dim light coming into the cells was from small, two-foot long, thin slits in the walls, spaced in regular intervals around the entire enclosure. From what he could see of the nearest slit a man would have difficulty putting his arm through it to the outside world. Evan was appalled these were the primary source of light and air for the prisoners. Despite how small the openings were, Evan knew light from the torches would be visible to people passing by outside. While it might attract unwanted attention, little could be done about it other than get in and out of the jail as fast as possible.

The sound of their voices awakened one of the prisoners. A groggy, fearful, female voice speaking French came out of the dark, asking who was there. Although the torches were still being prepared, Evan decided to risk a response.

"We are not your jailers. Are there any guards down here? We have come to find someone."

"My God, no, there are none down here! Who are you?" said the woman, sounding fearful and fully awake.

The sound of her voice awoke others and more querulous voices came from the darkness around him. Even as they spoke, though, a pool of light appeared at the top of the stairs and soon three men holding torches were standing beside Evan. One of the men held up a large ring with keys on it.

"Sir? We found this upstairs. The guard we did for after we got in was carrying them."

"Excellent. Let's hope they work. Right, first we find the Captain."

Evan was appalled at the conditions in the jail. The cells were dank and dirty. He could see a total of ten separate cells, some of which held several people. Buckets of human excrement were overflowing in a couple of them. To his disgust there were even a few young children in the cells. The prisoners were all fully wide-awake now and many staggered over to clutch at the bars confining them, reaching out imploring hands for attention. A barrage of voices growing ever louder vying for his attention made Evan realize he needed to gain control of them.

"Silence!" he shouted, barely loud enough to be overheard, while waving his arm in urgent need to have them calm down. After what seemed an eternity the voices died down, allowing him to speak.

"Listen, all of you, please. We are British Royal Navy. We are looking for some friends. Is Captain Marcel Deschamps here?"

"Sir? He's over here," said a male voice.

Evan walked over to the man who spoke and found he was pointing to a cot in the cell he was in. Marcel Deschamps lay on it, appearing dead to the world.

"God Almighty, is he alive?" asked Evan.

"Yes, but he is very sick. I fear for his life. He has moments where he is conscious and knows everyone, but they are fewer and fewer. They have sorely tried the poor man."

"Right, bring those keys and keep trying them until we find one to open this cell," said Evan over his shoulder to the sailor with the keys before looking back at the prisoner. "Who are you, sir?"

"I am Jeremie Pettit, sir," said the man, before gesturing toward a woman who came to stand beside him. "This is my wife Marie. We own a plantation on the north side of St. Lucia, or I should say, we did. We were told it is forfeit. We've been here for weeks now and are waiting to be sent to our doom."

As the sailor fervently tried different keys on the ring Evan quickly scanned the cells and did a rough estimate of the number of prisoners. With growing unease he realized he couldn't see Manon anywhere.

"Mr. Pettit, it looks to me like there are about twenty people here in total. Does this sound about right? Are you all supporters of the King here?"

"Yes, except for the men in the cell down at the very end. I believe they are all thieves or perhaps worse. Look, is the King still working to find a way to heal the divisions in our country? We heard rumour he was murdered. We have feared the worst, and now you are here. What is going on, sir?"

"The only thing your King is doing is growing cold in his grave, sir. He went to the guillotine at the end of January," replied Evan, as several of the prisoners gasped in shock. "Our countries are now at war as a result. I am here on a rescue mission for Captain Deschamps and one other. Listen, we have little time here. Have any of you seen a young black woman named Manon Shannon?"

The plantation owner responded by shaking his head and turning to give his wife a questioning look, but she showed no sign of recognizing the name either. The door finally clicked open and the sailor with the keys swung it open wide. The owner gave a sigh of relief.

"Thank God! Sir, you said you are on a rescue mission? Can you take us with you?"

Evan didn't respond to the man. He ordered the sailor to open all of the cells except for the one the owner specified was full of criminals. Evan took one of the torches and strode over to kneel beside Marcel Deschamps. The torchlight was enough to recall the Captain from unconsciousness and as he opened his eyes he focused without comprehension on Evan's face before finally speaking.

"My God, am I having a hallucination? Is it really you, Commander Ross? Have they captured you, too?"

"No, Captain," replied Evan, allowing relief to flood through him. "I am here to get you out of this hellhole."

The Captain stared at Evan unspeaking before finally closing his eyes, only to open them once again. He finally nodded and, his voice thick with emotion, he reached out to grasp Evan's hand.

"You really aren't a dream, are you? I prayed help would come. I fear you may be too late, Commander. You must save these good people here with me, though. For myself, I have little strength left."

Evan could see the feverish look on his face

and knew the man was right. The Captain held his hand with no more strength than a baby. Evan could see he wanted to say more, but he forestalled the Captain.

"We will see about this, Captain. For now, you must save your strength. We have to get you out of here and back to our ship immediately. We will talk more when we are on our way to Antigua. I must organize our escape."

As he stood and turned back to the others he found James standing behind him. The frantic look on his Lieutenant's face showed James had already realized Manon was not in the jail. Evan knew he needed to dispel any hope. He reached out his hand and put it on James's shoulder.

"She's not here, James. I'm sorry. No one seems to have seen her."

James closed his eyes and took a deep breath, clearly trying to master his emotions. Evan could see he was clenching his fists hard. He finally opened his eyes and spoke.

"I can't leave her, Evan. You've got to get the Captain out of here. I understand this. But give me leave to stay behind. Please?"

"Christ, I need time to think, and I don't have any. But you're going to stay behind regardless of anything I say anyway, aren't you? Look, we have to complete our mission and to my mind this means helping these poor people get out too. Help me get these people back to the ship and I will think on the way."

The anxious sailors moved fast as Evan began issuing a stream of orders. With the cells all opened except for one, several prisoners were anxiously milling about, desperate to get away. Evan divided his men into small parties of twos and threes, knowing they couldn't return en masse to the ship without someone wondering at such a large crowd of people wandering through the dark streets in the middle of the night. Each group was tasked with taking two or three of the prisoners and making their way back to the ship, with a party to leave every thirty seconds. Like Captain Deschamps, some of the prisoners were so weak they would have to be practically carried back with arms around a sailor on either side. Evan gave instructions to have them pretend to be drunks carrying a comrade insensible from imbibing too much if they ran into trouble.

As the groups began leaving Evan stalked over to the five men still locked in the remaining cell. All of them were standing, clutching at the bars of the their cell and watching Evan with fearful eyes. Four of the men were black and one was white. Evan stopped and looked at each of them in turn before speaking.

"I'm told you are criminals. What are your crimes?"

The lone white man was a deserter from the French Army, while three of the four black men confessed to being thieves. The last man hung his head and confessed to having killed a French soldier. Evan shook his head.

"I have no interest whatsoever in taking you with me. However, I confess I am loathe to leave anyone in a hellhole like this, even thieves, deserters, or murderers. If you give me your word you will not sound the alarm the second we leave here, we will give you the keys to your cell as we go. If you get out and sound an alarm, I guarantee we will make time to come back and kill you."

All of them nodded acceptance except for the man who confessed to killing the soldier. He appeared a little younger than Evan, perhaps in his mid twenties. He got down on one knee and raised his hands in supplication to Evan as he spoke.

"Sir? I beg you, please take me with you. I was a house slave on the Thomas plantation. My master was a good, good man and when they came for him and his family I was afraid. They tried to rape his wife on the spot and I couldn't bear it. I killed the soldier, but they caught me. If you free me from here and they catch me again, I will simply be put back in here. I have nothing left to return to. Eventually they will send me out to have my head cut off, just like my master."

Evan was doubtful, although the man did appear sincere. Feeling harried and anxious to get away Evan was going to deny the man, but a feminine voice came from behind him.

"Sir," said the female prisoner, forestalling the sailor who was escorting her out of the next cell over. "I know of this slave. My husband and I owned the plantation next door. This man was well regarded by his owners. I wasn't there when they came for his owners so I can't confirm the truth of what he is saying, but I think you should consider the possibility."

Evan nodded to the woman and she left with the sailor. Knowing the need to make a decision,

Evan called for the keys and pulled out his knife to ensure none of them made a move to escape once the door was open. The sailor with the ring of keys opened the door on Evan's signal and pulled the man out before slamming it shut once again.

Before the prisoner could say anything Evan looked him in the eyes. After putting his knife away he grabbed the man by his shirtfront and pulled him close.

"I'm taking a chance on you. Fail me and you are a dead man. What is your name?"

"Sir, I am your man. My name is Baptiste."

Looking around, Evan saw the cells were empty and they were the last ones remaining. "Right, let's get the hell out of here."

The four remaining prisoners began to clamor for the keys as the three men walked away, but Evan told them to shut up. Taking the ring of keys from the sailor Evan ordered the other two men to wait on the steps with the torch. He threw the keys hard across the room and they landed right outside the cell, skittering along the floor and through the bars to the waiting men. Satisfied, Evan pointed to the upper floor and the three men left the prison as it returned to darkness. Evan knew the prisoners would eventually figure out which key would open their cell, but it would take them longer in the dark.

By the time they got to the upper floor he found only one party remaining to depart. They put out the torches and called the sentry in from the front door. As they left by the rear entrance they gathered the remaining sailor still standing on guard and, keeping to the shadows, they carefully made their way through the darkened streets. Evan was relieved to find no sense of alarm anywhere. As they stole closer to safety a part of Evan's mind focused on his next problem. He pushed his worry over the fate of Manon from his mind in the rush to get the prisoners away, but he knew he would have to make a decision. James would remain behind, as he knew one more effort for her sake was necessary. Even if James succeeded in finding and freeing her, the problem was getting them off the island when the time came.

All was quiet on the docks as Evan and his party finally reached the ship. Evan was thankful for the still minimal moonlight, as even with small parties of people it would be suspicious to see several of them appear and board the ship in a steady stream. But no one challenged them as they crossed the open dock area and boarded the ship. The second he got on deck he issued a stream of orders to get *The Ocean Mist* underway as fast as possible. As he finished he turned to James, who was standing patiently at his side.

"Right, it's not within the scope of my orders to come back here again, but I don't think Sir James Standish will have a problem. I don't think Captain Laforey will either, so I plan to be back here in a week. We will bring the *Alice* this time, as I'm sure they will have it ready. If not, I'm going to drive them hard so it will be. You will have to watch for us. We will come in after dark and pretend to be Yankees. You will need to have either freed her or have figured out where she is. If we need to fight to get her out we will. If you haven't tracked her down you're going to have to make a decision, James. We can't keep doing this."

James nodded. "I know. I'm going to turn this bloody town upside down. I'll find her."

The two friends gripped each other's forearm hard once again.

"Stay safe and watch for us," said Evan.

James nodded and left the ship, disappearing into the shadows of the docks within seconds. As soon as he was off the gangplank was hauled up. Not wasting any time, they cut the lines tethering them to the dock and got underway. As they slowly sailed out of the harbour a few faces standing watch on the warships turned their way out of curiosity, but no alarm was raised. They were free.

***

An hour later Evan was finally able to disentangle himself from the constant series of decisions to be made. The freed prisoners were all in varying degrees of distress in different ways. For most of them he was heartened to see the effect of simple, proper food and fresh water on them. Within minutes of finishing the hastily prepared meals many curled up where they lay on deck with blankets provided by the sailors. All of them were unwilling to go below to face what seemed yet more confinement.

A number of medical problems ranging from infected wounds to a broken arm not set properly and serious bruises from previous beatings by the guards demanded attention. Evan and Captain Wild were the only ones with the rough skills to deal with it all, but the lack of resources and training gave them few options. Seeing them struggle, the slave Baptiste stepped forward to offer his help. Evan gave him a questioning look as he made the offer, but the man seemed sincere and soon proved his worth. One part of his plantation duties was to help with injured slaves and he demonstrated his skill effectively.

Captain Deschamps proved the greatest challenge. The sickest prisoners were all moved to below deck and made comfortable in the main quarters where the crew would normally have slung their hammocks. Evan was watching as Baptiste examined the festering wound, sucking in his breath in dismay at its condition. He did his best to clean it and wash the Captain well before spooning some broth into the sick man's throat as he held the Captain's head up to receive it. The Captain responded to his ministrations, growing lucid enough to forestall the slave from giving him more. The Captain looked over at Evan and raised a hand enough to signal him to come closer.

As Evan passed Baptiste he paused and gave the slave a questioning look. The man gave a small, negative shake of his head in return when he was certain Captain Deschamps wouldn't see him. Evan nodded and went to kneel beside the cot set up for the Captain. Despite being lucid, the Captain still appeared badly feverish.

"I see you did as I asked, Commander," said the Captain, hearing the moans of other sick people around him. "Bless you for bringing these people. I feared the King's supporters would face persecution and this is why I remained behind. I hoped to find a way to get them all out after Governour de Gimat fled, but the bastards moved too fast on me."

"I'm sorry not to have gotten to you sooner,

Captain. Sir James didn't know of your fate and by the time we grew concerned much time was passed. But you are free now and can continue the fight with these people once you are on Antigua and are better."

The Captain coughed and closed his eyes for few seconds before opening them again. "I think my fight may be over, Commander. I feel my strength gone and this is why I must tell you of the money."

"The money?"

Evan pulled a stool over to sit on and sat listening in shock as Captain Deschamps explained what he and the former Governour did. "We simply couldn't bear the thought of any money simply being handed to the pack of scoundrels we knew them to be, you see. I was going to take it all with me along with the people."

"Good Lord, how much is there, Captain?"

"Plenty, Commander, enough to make it worth your while to go back to St. Lucia and get it. In truth, I don't know exactly how much there is, but consider the Governour was siphoning off funds for almost two years. So all I ask is for it to be given to royalist refugees like these poor people you have saved to help them rebuild their lives and, even better, mount a campaign to defeat these bastards. Can you promise me this, Commander?"

"Good God, Captain. You know I can't do that. I *can* promise I will take this up with Sir James, but the outcome? Not possible to guarantee. But I am going to have to go back to St. Lucia as I have another missing agent there. Your contact Paddy Shannon was taken along with his daughter. We know he went to the guillotine, but we haven't been able to find her. So if you want me to get this hoard of money I can certainly try."

The Captain was silent for a moment. "I guess this is the best I can hope for. Please do try with Sir James, Commander. But you mention Paddy's daughter? The son of a bitch I should have killed years ago interrogated her at the same time as me earlier today."

"God Almighty! Where is she, Captain? We've been searching everywhere."

"La Chance has her, Commander. He made the two of us watch the executions and then he sent her back to his ship, the frigate named *La Felicite*. Unfortunately, I think he decided right from the start to take advantage of her."

"*Damn* me, I should have thought of this. Thank you Captain, at least now we know. James and I will cut a path through to him and cut his balls off."

"Before you do it, get the money. And while you are about it, I have one last thing to ask of you. Do you remember, Commander, the place we went to eat just before you sailed home after our last adventures here in Castries?"

"The place just outside town with the stunning view of the entrance to the harbour and the town? What was the—oh, I remember! It was on La Toc Road. I couldn't possibly forget the wonderful dinner we enjoyed."

"The woman running it is *my* woman, Commander. Her name is Simone and she's another of the reasons I've stayed on here all these years. We have a daughter who I don't think I'm going to be able to watch grow up. Simone has it all hidden away. All you need do is go to her, tell her whom you are, and tell her I sent you. She will not tell you anything, though, until you tell her the secret password we agreed upon. It is the letters J, A, and D in sequence. They stand for Jolie Anne Deschamps, which also happens to be the name of our daughter. Simone and I knew the day might come where I could be in trouble, so we decided upon this to prepare for any eventuality. Commander, I beg you, please take both of them away with you. The pig La Chance has figured out I have kept a woman somewhere and he believes, correctly, she knows where the money is. I have been very careful to cover my tracks, but I fear someone may have noticed I spent a lot of time there. Promise me, please? They are everything to me."

Evan grasped the Captains weak hand and gave it a squeeze. "I will try, sir. We owe you that at the very least. And I want you to stop talking now. You will get better and we will talk more then."

Captain Deschamps nodded and let his hand slump back to the cot. "Bless you, Commander. And now I must rest. I have no strength."

Evan rose and saluted the tired, fevered looking man lying before him. The Captain acknowledged him with one last tiny nod and closed his eyes.

Two days later Evan was standing on the quarterdeck with Captain Wild, preparing to tack and wrestle with the entrance to English Harbour once again, when Baptiste came up to him and requested permission to speak.

"Sir? The fellow you've been concerned about, your Captain Deschamps? He's gone, sir. I'm sorry, there was nothing I could do."

Evan hung his head for a moment on hearing the news, before recalling himself to thank Baptiste and dismiss him. He turned and walked over to the rail to face out to the open ocean before speaking to no one but the wind and the waves.

"And so passes a brave man."

Chapter Ten
March 1793
Antigua and St. Lucia

The immediate problem on docking in English Harbour was the royalist refugees. Food, shelter, and medical care all needed to be organized. With no where else to house them in comfort Evan left them on board the ship while he spent the next several hours arranging to meet their needs. Word of their presence soon spread, however, and Evan was bombarded with a host of questions from officers on the ships in harbour about their mission. In the midst of it all Captain Laforey sent for Evan to make his report, and with a sigh, Evan temporarily dismissed the crowd of people looking for orders from him.

Evan saluted and came to attention as he came into the Captain's cabin. The Captain looked up and smiled, before waving a hand at the chair in front of his desk.

"Rumour has it you have reappeared with a bunch of civilians on board. I expect you have an interesting story for me, but I'm also sure you have your hands full dealing with them. Is there anything I need to know immediately or can it wait until you have time to write a full report?"

"The mission was only partly successful, sir. We got the man we wanted out of prison, along with all of the people we brought back, but our agent suffered severe torture and died on the passage back. The number and type of warships in Castries harbour remains unchanged from my prior visit. The main thing you need to know is I must to go back, sir.

Lieutenant Wilton is still on St. Lucia and another of my agents is still being held prisoner there. Also, I have information on the whereabouts of a significant amount of money the royalist supporters secreted away from the radicals. The money is at risk, and we will want to attempt to secure this and deny these funds to them."

Captain Laforey's face lit and he sat forward at the mention of the money. "A *significant* amount, you say? How much, sir?"

"Our source didn't know for certain," confessed Evan. "But he did assure me it would be worth our while to make the attempt to capture it. Captain? I believe I have the makings of a plan to do achieve this."

"Do you, now?" said the Captain, sitting back in his chair and wearing a contemplative look on his face.

"Yes, sir. I need a little time to fully think it through, but I am fairly certain it could work. We need to act fast, though, and it will require the help of you and your people to succeed."

Captain Laforey smiled. "Well. I'm really looking forward to this report of yours. Please go do what you must, but get me your report as soon as you can. I will need some time to think about your proposal, of course. You are dismissed, sir."

Evan was thankful by the time he returned to the Dockyard a response to his message to Governour Woodley seeking help with housing the refugees was awaiting his arrival. Evan was grateful to find the Governour was already organizing efforts to deal with them and all Evan needed to do was arrange for their transport to St. John's. As he supervised their loading on to the four carriages rounded up for the purpose, several of them stopped to express their fervent thanks for saving their lives. The women all stepped forward to give him long, grateful hugs of appreciation.

Time to enjoy their thanks was a luxury he didn't have, though. As soon as the last of them were on their way he went in search of the Dockyard Shipwright. The news was not what he was hoping for, as the *Alice* was still not ready for sea. Fortunately, the work was not far from being completed. After two hours of cajoling and negotiations, Evan finally secured agreement from the man to focus on getting the *Alice* done within the next two days. Several other ship captains waiting on work would be unhappy their own needed work was being delayed, but knowing Captain Laforey's interest in the money, Evan was certain the complaints would soon be deflected. Evan's men were also going to find themselves assigned the task of helping with the effort.

By the end of the day Evan was exhausted and he once again stumbled home. Alice's happy smile on seeing him quickly vanished as she saw how tired he was. Evan gave her a terse summary of what happened as he wolfed down a hastily prepared hot meal. He knew how desperately worried Alice was from the look on her face, but he could offer little comfort.

"I'm sorry, my love," said Evan, as he wrapped his arm around her. "Our wedding will have to wait a bit longer."

After washing up for the night he fell into bed and was asleep within moments.

***

Feeling refreshed despite rising before the dawn Evan did the same as the night before, washing up hurriedly and this time devouring a cold breakfast. In the Dockyard he found a harried looking Lieutenant Cooke already prodding the men to get on with the task at hand. Satisfied everything was well in hand despite the seeming chaos surrounding the *Alice*, Evan made his way to his office and shut the door. With a sigh he stared at the small mountain of unopened correspondence and reports. After ordering a clerk to brew some tea, he sat down to deal with it.

Fortunately, most of the paperwork was routine enough it could wait. After dealing with a few urgent pieces he set about his first task for the day, which was to get his reports done. Two hours later he finished his report and set about making copies. After sending one off to Governour Woodley and another to Sir James in Barbados, he walked out to the Captain Laforey's frigate and handed a third copy to the duty officer for the Captain.

Back in his office Evan shoved the still waiting pile of paperwork to the side after reaching for a pen and paper. He pulled a map of St Lucia out of a cabinet behind him and unfolded this on his desk too, before taking out a small booklet of tables of the moon from a desk drawer. Evan sat deep in thought for the next two hours, occasionally scratching away at the blank paper before him, sometimes striking out what he put down and starting again. As he finished he rose and stretched, rubbing his eyes. He was about to sit down again when the expected knock on his door came. A Marine from Captain Laforey's ship entered and Evan held up his hand to forestall the man.

"I know. The Captain wants to see me. Please let the duty officer know I will be there shortly."

He pulled out a fresh sheet of paper and did a hurried, basic sketch of Castries harbour and its surroundings. After adding in the locations of the docked warships Evan folded the map and took it with him.

Captain Laforey bade him to be seated once again as he stared at Evan's report on the desk in front of him. "Well, Commander, you did have an interesting mission, didn't you? It is unfortunate you weren't able to secure the money before you left."

"Captain Deschamps never made mention of what they were doing in his reports to Sir James Standish, sir. If he had told us, it may be this would have ended differently."

"In any case, I do see the need to act with speed, Commander. You mentioned you have a plan?"

"Sir, I do."

"Excellent. Let's enjoy a little glass of wine while we contemplate this."

As the Captain called to his servant and ordered glasses to be fetched Evan reached into his pocket, pulling out the map and putting it on the table. The two men pored over it for almost an hour, discussing the various elements of it in detail. Evan was glad the Captain was there to ask questions as the man pointed out a couple of small, but critical elements not accounted for. Fortunately, the Captain saw no flaws to prevent the plan from working. As they finally sat back and looked at each other, the Captain rubbed his chin in thought. Evan was apprehensive, knowing what remained was for the Captain to make his decision. The Captain didn't keep him waiting.

"Commander Ross, I confess I like this. You haven't needed a lot of help from me to put this together. I see opportunity for some mischief here along with a chance to make ourselves somewhat richer than we are now. My only concern is the timing. We both know this is tight and there are a host of things which can go wrong, but there is nothing for it. But yes, you have my support. Well, perhaps I am also concerned about what exactly happens if things don't go to plan and you must leave your agent or even your Lieutenant Wilton in St. Lucia again. You do realize if this happens mounting yet another rescue would be suicidal, right?"

"I understand this, Captain. I know my people will understand it, too. The risks are obvious when sailing into a hostile harbour. We simply have to succeed."

"Exactly. I have some things to organize on my end here. Let me know as soon as your ship is ready to depart. I will be ready on my end."

Looking down at their glasses, the Captain saw they both held a mouthful left for each man. He picked up his and Evan took his cue to do the same. The Captain smiled as he raised it to clink with Evan's.

"To success, Commander. To success and confusion to the French!"

***

Evan chafed at every delay and made himself a nuisance to the crews working on the *Alice*, but by early afternoon two days later they were ready for sea. Despite the worry for his friends and how anxious he was to get on with the mission, he couldn't help the flush of pleasure at standing on the quarterdeck of the *Alice* taking her out of English Harbour. This wasn't the first such time he was standing on her deck as she left harbour, having sailed on her as a passenger years before, but this was the first time he was sailing her out under his own command.

As soon as they were free of the bonds of the harbour Evan called for Lieutenant Cooke. Evan smiled when the young Lieutenant came over to the weather side of the quarterdeck and saluted.

"Lieutenant? I recall you and Lieutenant Wilton assured me these men were experienced sailors. I'd like to do a few drills with the sails to see how well they do. Give them a few tasks and let's watch what happens. I'd also like to see how good they are with weapons. I suspect none of them have enjoyed any real practice for a while now and I think they could be rusty. Given we may be needing those skills soon I think we should do some live fire exercises."

Lieutenant Cooke grinned cheerfully. "Sir, I was hoping you would suggest this. I confess it's been a long time since I have practiced myself."

Evan kept close watch on their progress as

the men went through the sail exercises the Lieutenant set for them. With an eye on his watch Evan maintained a bland face, but he smiled inwardly on realizing the men were as skilled at what they did as he hoped. He was pleased to see the three men he acquired from Barbados were all serving aloft, too. While they weren't as efficient as the others, they were trying and Evan knew they would learn.

The live fire exercises took longer to make him happy, as the men were indeed out of practice. The men were slower than they should be between firing each weapon, but toward the end of the exercise they were showing improvement. Evan was still not certain whether he was happy about the changes the Shipwright suggested were necessary, but they were done and he knew he must live with them. Instead of the six pound cannon he wanted the Shipwright convinced him carronades would serve him better as his primary armament. The *Alice* now carried three of these much smaller weapons on either side. Two swivel guns were his only other mounted and available weapons, one fore and one aft on the upper deck.

What the man said made sense, though. Speed and deception were his primary defence. With the *Alice* pretending to be a merchant vessel, her defences needed to look the part. The six-pound cannons Evan wanted mounted fore and aft, with more below on the gun deck, would not make sense. The guns were far too big and heavy, taking up valuable space an alleged merchant vessel would want for cargo. They would also require a much larger complement of men to fire them. Evan acknowledged the point was critical, as he was sailing with a far smaller complement of men than normal for a warship the size of *Alice*.

Evan knew the benefits of carronades. They were simpler to use, needing only two or three men to fire one. They could also accommodate a wider angle of fire because the slide they were mounted on wasn't as wide as a six-pound cannon and they were easier to shift about as they weighed far less. Like a six-pound cannon, they could be loaded with round shot, bar shot, grape, or canister shot. The downside was a much shorter range of accuracy, meaning they were best suited to close action. But the more Evan thought about it, he saw that close in, defensive action was the most likely scenario he would ever face with the *Alice*, especially as he simply didn't have enough men to actively pick a fight with anyone. Besides, the eighteen-pounder carronades the *Alice* now carried were larger than the twelve-pounder carronades most merchant vessels or warships of a size similar to *Alice* would have, if any. The *Alice* would still pack a heavy punch.

Knowing there were also more options and what they could do as a result helped allay his concerns. Hidden deep in the hold were two more carronades available to be hoisted out and brought into service if needed, although these would take time to bring into play. To provide more immediate aid if required another eight swivel guns of various sizes were also hidden away. These were much easier to move about and could be quickly mounted wherever needed. Several crates of muskets and small arms along with the usual array of cutlasses and boarding pikes rounded out the tally of weapons at his disposal, along with ample ammunition for everything.

Soon after the starboard side carronades roared out for a final time Lieutenant Cooke appeared on deck and came to report. The smell of burnt gunpowder followed him as he saluted Evan.

"Sir? Did you wish to continue? It will be dusk soon."

"No. But we need to reduce sail. *Alice* is sailing faster than I expected, although I shouldn't be surprised at this. We will need to time our entry into Castries carefully. So have them secure the guns and deal with the sails. Also, it's time we took down our colours and replaced them with an American flag. From this point on we are an American merchant vessel and need to look the part. After that is all done, call all hands. I need to speak to them."

Several minutes later a crowd of faces stood in a semicircle around Evan waiting for him to begin. The individual faces were starting to become more familiar to Evan, but associating the names correctly with the faces would take more time. The one man he identified quickly as someone he felt he could rely on was the bosun, Wallace Mitchell. He was heavily muscled, without an ounce of fat on his oak tree like body. Despite Evan's suspicion the man was over thirty years old he could move as lithe as any top man. Evan tested him with various small tasks since first meeting him and agreed with Lieutenant Cooke's assessment of the man's professional competence. Evan wondered how any Captain would be willing to free up someone like this, but he filed the thought away for later. Either his former Captain would call on Evan for a favour at some point in the future as a result or some reason would come to the fore as to why Mitchell was made available.

Recalling himself Evan realized everyone was waiting for him. "My Lieutenants assured me you are all experienced and competent sailors. I'm glad to say I can see they have not failed me, as with the exception of a few new hands whose inexperience is understandable I agree with their judgment. Your gunnery needs work, especially as our lives depend on it, but we can fix this. You all know we are off to St. Lucia yet again and you know the basics of our mission. There is one thing I would like to ensure you understand, however. Our Lieutenant Wilton is still on St. Lucia. The reason for this is we have an agent, someone who has helped our cause many times, who is being held against her will by the goddamn Frog Captain of *La Felicite*, the frigate you saw in harbour the last time we were there. We have only just learned of this. Why I'm telling you this is the agent is also Lieutenant Wilton's woman. God only knows what this bastard Frog is doing to this poor young woman, but Lieutenant Wilton wants to carve this pig into little pieces and he is counting on us to help him."

Several faces darkened as Evan spoke and a ripple of muted anger surged through the men. Evan raised his hand to quiet them before continuing.

"Yes, I wanted you to know what is at stake. Among other things, we are going to cut our way onto that frigate and free her. Yes, there is also the possibility of realizing gains with prize money. So be ready. You are dismissed. Lieutenant Cooke, the men have worked hard today and done well. You know what to do."

Lieutenant Cooke grinned as he saluted and turned to the nearest man with orders to fetch the rum ration.

***

The following day was uneventful, as St. Lucia grew ever closer. Lieutenant Cooke made adjustments to ensure the men weren't standing long watches and were given plenty of rest, knowing it would be a long night ahead of them. Evan deliberately sailed on a course away from the usual routes ships would use and was grateful to find no sails on the horizon as a result. Even so, he found himself waiting longer than he otherwise would have to make his final tack before running direct to Castries, as the *Alice* and the wind were conspiring together to get him to his destination sooner than he wanted.

Midnight was when he made his final course change for the harbour entrance. The plan was to be docked by one in the morning, at two bells of the middle watch. They would have two hours to accomplish the mission before all hell would break loose in Castries harbour. The moon was a quarter full, but fortunately the high cloud Evan was hoping for materialized to mask what they were doing to the maximum extent possible.

As they slipped through the harbour entrance Evan gave thanks yet again the French were derelict in putting a battery on either point of land guarding the entrance. The Morne Fortune fort with its large battery was certainly well within range of the entrance to the harbour, but being sited on top of a nearby hill a considerable distance away meant the fort's weakness was the inability to communicate quickly with it.

Evan gave orders to reduce more sail, leaving barely enough canvas to maneuver to the dock. The port and the town were quiet, with few lights showing anywhere. As they got closer Evan realized there were only two warships in the harbour and with a sinking heart he cursed the French Captain La Chance out loud, praying the man was still in St. Lucia. Evan quickly realized from the shape one of them was the same corvette from before, but it took longer to identify which of the two frigates remained. Lieutenant Cooke saw the problem too, and the two officers stood side by side with their night glasses trying to make out for certain which ship was still in port. The young Lieutenant was the first to identify it for certain.

"Thank God, Sir, I'm certain it is *La Felicite*. I don't see Captain Deschamps's old ship the *Marie-Anne* anywhere."

Evan took a long few moments extra to be absolutely certain for himself, but he finally sighed in relief. "Yes, you are right. I wish I knew where the other goddamn frigate is, but this does make our task tonight much easier. Even better, there is a spot now available at the dock not far from *La Felicite* and away from the corvette. Take us in and dock us there, Lieutenant. And bring those American sailors to the quarterdeck as planned. Even with it being the middle of the night I expect we'll be enjoying some company here soon."

As they got ever closer to the dock Evan kept a close eye on the two French warships for any sign of alarm. He could see French Marines stationed as guards on the dock at the gangplanks leading to both ships and he thought he saw movement on the deck of *La Felicite*, but it was difficult to know for certain. As the men aloft furled the sails while others made lines fast to the shore, Evan looked to where he knew the Customs men maintained their office on the far side of the dock. As he did he saw a guard by the office door knocking to alert whoever was on duty. Someone stuck his head out the door of the office for a moment and disappeared back inside. All remained quiet for a few minutes until finally a party of three men emerged from the building and made their way toward the *Alice*, bringing the duty guard with them. Evan quickly realized two of them were Customs officers who were obviously unready to have to do anything, as both men were hastily pulling on their uniforms and tucking in their shirts as they walked. The other two men with them were soldiers.

Evan knew this was a critical point for the mission. This time they didn't have Captain Wild, with his experience and his American accent to help with their cover, which was why the two American sailors Evan recruited were to stand in. While they were fully briefed on what Evan wanted, how well they would perform was another matter. The discussion between Evan and Lieutenant Cooke surrounded the possibility of pretending to be Americans themselves, but they rejected the idea knowing neither could adequately fake the necessary accent. Another concern was some of the Customs men might be ones able to recognize them both from before. The problem was if things went wrong one of them needed to be nearby to deal with it. Evan decided he would have to risk being the one to do it, since his dealings with them had been so limited.

As the four men came on board one of the Customs men stumbled and almost fell off the gangplank. He was grabbed by his coat and hauled back by the soldier behind him. The man turned and scowled at the soldier, brushing himself off as if he was soiled somehow by the touch before resuming his unsteady climb to the deck. Evan quickly realized the man was drunk and his hopes soared at the possibility the others were in the same state too. The other Customs officer soon revealed he was as inebriated as his colleague, as he gained the deck and loudly slurred a demand to speak to the Captain. The two soldiers, however, appeared wide awake and sober, standing impassively to the side as the Customs men began talking to the sailor Evan designated would perform the role of Captain. His sailor, a man named Webber, was already dressed for the part in better clothing of the sort a merchant Captain would normally wear.

As Evan shifted his position to get a better look in the moonlight he groaned inwardly when he realized the second Customs man to board was one he encountered before on his first trip to St. Lucia. He couldn't abruptly leave the deck without attracting attention, so he tried to move slowly into the shadows in the hope the man was too drunk to remember him.

"Who are you fools?" demanded the first Customs officer. "Don't you know you are not to enter our harbour in the middle of the night? We could have sent word to have you blown out of the water."

The man paused for a moment before turning to his colleague while bursting out in laughter. "We *should* have them blown out of the water for disturbing us. I was just about to take her dress off."

"We know we are causing a problem, sir, and we apologize for any inconvenience," said Webber, bringing the two drunks attention back to him by launching into the story Evan provided for him to use. "We needed to reach harbour soon as our water supply is tainted. We didn't realize it until a number of the men grew ill. When I checked our remaining supplies I found they were all gone bad. I'm sure the men will all recover, but we must have clean water, sir."

Webber paused and stepped a little closer to the two Customs officers. "We've not been to this particular island before, but with the war on now we would like to be more regular visitors and we really don't want to be any trouble to you. We will certainly pay any necessary fees. I assume you can help us with this?"

The two men looked at each other and smiled, before the second Customs man responded. "Why, yes, we certainly can. Things like this are best sorted out in private. Perhaps we can discuss this in your cabin?"

"Ah— certainly," said Webber, after a moment of hesitation. "This way, please."

Evan cursed himself, as this was an

eventuality they weren't prepared for. He knew Webber would require help to get out of the unexpected jam he was in. To this point the man was doing well, but the sailor gave Evan a quick, nervous glance as they passed by. The Customs man Evan knew from before followed his glance and looked directly at Evan, slowing to a halt and staring in puzzlement.

"Say, I recognize you. Why do I recognize you?" he said, as he peered closer at Evan. Yes, you are the man with the one arm—"

As the man began speaking Evan knew the game was up and he needed to give the signal. He put his hand on top of his head and made as if he was about to respond to the Customs officer while plastering an innocent look on his face. Before he could even get a word out his men were in action. As Evan watched a hand appeared from behind the Customs officer and covered his mouth. The man's eyes bulged for a millisecond in fear and shock before he was dragged into the shadows of the deck. The sounds of the scuffle were muted. Evan heard more muffled thumps as other bodies hit the deck, but no other sounds came.

"Right. Lieutenant Cooke? Find someone to clean the blood off and slip on one of those soldier's uniforms. Have him pretend to stand guard by the gangplank on the dock and look as bored as possible."

"Sir?" said Webber, as he came to stand before Evan with a downcast look on his face. "I apologize, sir. I think I gave it away when I looked at you there. I wasn't sure what I was going to do when we got into your cabin."

"Not your fault, Webber," said Evan, clapping his hand on the man's shoulder. "It's this dead fool's problem he recognized me. You did well and I shall remember it."

"Thank you, sir," said Webber, the relief obvious on his face.

As Evan waited for the fake guard to assume his position on the dock he took a long, careful look around the harbour for any signs of alarm or trouble. Evan hoped the appearance of the guard would allay the suspicions of any other soldiers or officials in the area. He also fervently desired the four men to be the only ones on duty this late at night. So far, at least, nothing was stirring on the docks. Once the sailor marched down the gangplank to take up his position Evan waited a long minute, but nothing happened. With a deep breath he made his decision to proceed and he turned to Lieutenant Cooke.

"Everyone stays on board for now. I need to show myself for Lieutenant Wilton."

"Let me know if you see anything," said Evan once he got to the sailor. He stood beside the sailor on the dock, slowly scanning the immediate area while hoping he didn't have long to wait.

"Sir, on your right. Something moved in the shadows over there."

Even as the sailor spoke James stepped into the weak moonlight and strode quickly over to where they stood. Evan signaled for him to follow and within moments they were back in the shadows on the quarterdeck of the *Alice*. Evan could see the lines of worry etched into James's face as he stood before him to report.

"Christ, am I glad to see you, sir. It got real interesting around here after you left. They turned the goddamn place upside down looking for the prisoners, because they weren't completely sure they escaped on your ship. But I haven't met with any luck in finding her, damn it all. The best I've got is a vague bit from a server in one of the bars the officers of both the Army and the Navy frequent. There was a table of officers from both services talking about going to a local brothel one night. Then she heard one of them say not everyone needed to do that and they all laughed. I'm wondering if there is a military prison somewhere she might be in?"

"James," said Evan, putting his hand up to forestall him and pointing toward *La Felicite*. "I have information, too, and what you are saying tallies with what I know. I believe she is being held on that frigate, or at least, she was. I am hoping she is still there."

James stiffened and turned his head to glare at the frigate further down the dock before looking back at Evan. His face was frozen and with his eyes turned to ice, he raised an eyebrow in question. As Evan explained everything he learned from Captain Deschamps he could see James clenching his fists in silent rage. Evan was afraid James was going to explode with anger, but he remained in control with obvious effort.

"Permission to lead the boarding party, sir?"

"I can't think of anyone better for the job. You're going to have to wait just a little longer, though. I'd like to be there when you kill this bastard

La Chance, but I have my own task to perform."

Although Lieutenant Cooke already knew the situation and what they planned, he signaled for him to join them as Evan quickly outlined the details for James's benefit. "So I am going to leave immediately to find the Captain's woman and the money. I'll take Mitchell and nine other men with me in case we run into trouble. Hmm, I'll take Wishart and Hopkins too in case we have to break in. It won't take us more than fifteen minutes to march there. If I can I'm going to steal a horse and buggy along the way because we might need it. I plan to be back before the fun starts here, but in case I am not I want you both to understand you are *not* to send parties out after us. Your mission is to wait for the signal and then board the frigate. You know what to do. If I am not back by the time you complete your mission you get the hell out of here. James, if I survive and have to go into hiding I will try to communicate via the fishing boats. Any questions?"

"Sir?" said Lieutenant Cooke. "Lieutenant Wilton doesn't know about the armbands."

"Yes, with the moon behind those high clouds I think we should use them. Have to distinguish friend from foe somehow, so the boarding party will all use them. Right, I will leave you two so you can brief your men. Good luck."

Evan left the two officers talking and strode over the bosun. "Mitchell, you are to detail nine other men to join me. Cutlasses are in order here, but if the men want to bring other weapons they can. No muskets or pistols, because we do not want to draw attention to our presence. Be ready in five minutes."

As the man nodded and stalked away Evan studied the dock area and the other warships in the distance for signs of alarm once again, but all was still calm and he smiled at the action to come.

***

Evan and his men slipped easily into the shadows as they left the ship with no alarm being sounded. The *Alice* was tied up toward the far end of the docks, fortunately close to the turn off for their destination. High clouds continued to dim the moonlight, making it difficult to find La Toc Road at first. But even with the passage of four years since Evan was there last he recognized the route when they crossed it. Hugging the shadows at the side of the road in single file they tramped along making good time. But being unused to the need for stealth they also made far too much noise.

"Best effort not to sound like a goddamn herd of elephants, please," said Evan over his shoulder to the men following him, ensuring his frustration was clear from the tone of his voice.

The incline of the road gradually steepened as it followed the line of the ridge. Evan relaxed a little as there were no homes nearby along this part of the road due to the rising landscape. But ten minutes into their journey the road began to level off and homes began appearing on either side of the road. Evan kept an eye out for a buggy and cart to steal, but no opportunities arose. No lights were on in any of the buildings they passed.

As they reached the crest of the ridge and the ground leveled off, Evan saw the tavern as he remembered it right on the highest point of the ridge.

As they got closer they could see no lights were on in the tavern itself, but the dim light of a lantern came from what Evan recalled would be the kitchen area. Evan signaled to the men to stop while he scanned the area to ensure no one was about or watching from the shadows, searching his mind for other details of the place he visited four years ago. With it came memories of a much more peaceful, pleasant evening and the wonderful dinner he and Captain Deschamps enjoyed.

Satisfied they were undetected he led them as close as he dared, before signaling a halt once again. Creeping over to a window through which the dim light streamed out he slowly peered over the ledge to look inside.

Evan's memory was correct. At the far end of the kitchen a young, beautiful white woman was tidying up and putting dishes away. No one else was about. He knew she was too young to be Captain Deschamps mistress, but he hoped she could be a source of information. He thought about simply tapping on the window shutters to draw her attention, but he knew he couldn't risk her sounding an alarm. Evan signaled for Wishart and Hopkins to come forward and pointed to a rear door leading into the kitchen area. After explaining what he wanted, the two men nodded and moved to the door. In less than two minutes Evan saw Hopkins come into view in the kitchen and, moving with cat like stealth, he stalked after the young woman. Evan admired the man's patience as he waited for her to put away some plates she held in her hands before he struck.

With the sailor's hand clamped hard over her

mouth the woman was unable to scream. Hopkins used his other hand around her body and her arms to pull her back to him as he braced himself with his back against the wall. He also wrapped one of his legs around one of hers, pinning her with no options to struggle and get away. She wriggled in desperate fright at first, but Hopkins was whispering something in her ear.

By the time Evan crept inside she was calm enough to stop fighting Hopkins, realizing he wasn't hurting her. But terror and puzzlement showed in her eyes as Evan stepped softly toward her. He hesitated for a moment, trying to decide what to say to her, before realizing that despite her feminine features she was nonetheless familiar.

"Your name is Jolie Anne, isn't it?" said Evan.

The girl’s eyes widened, this time in surprise. She took her own few seconds to make a decision before giving Evan a tiny, wary nod.

"My name is Commander Evan Ross, British Royal Navy. I sincerely apologize for having frightened you like this. I didn't know who you were and I couldn't risk you sounding an alarm. Look, I need your help. I am going to order this man to release you. Your father told us where to find you. You and your mother are in grave danger and we are here to rescue you. We must move quickly. We could just search the building, but I don't want to frighten your mother too. Please go to her and bring her to me, quickly."

As he finished Evan nodded to Hopkins and he freed the girl. She stepped away from the two men and looked from one to the other for a hesitant few seconds, biting her lip in obvious fear they were lying. As she saw they were in earnest she mastered herself, before disappearing through a doorway in the rear of the kitchen. Within minutes she returned, leading a woman who appeared middle aged over to Evan. From the similarity of her features Evan knew instantly she was Jolie's mother.

Evan introduced himself and asked if she was Simone. The woman nodded and before Evan could speak again a tear slid down her face.

"He's gone, isn't he, Commander? I can see it on your face."

"I am very sorry for your loss, madam. We were able to free him, but he was weakened and died of an infection before we reached Antigua."

Jolie gave a heart-rending sob and hugged her mother hard, but Simone simply stood there with a stream of tears falling down her face. Evan was about to continue when a young, sleepy looking black man came into the kitchen.

"I heard voices and oh! —" He turned to run back the way he came, but found it blocked by Hopkins.

"Joseph! Stop! These men are friends," said Simone. "Commander, he is a servant and a friend."

Evan nodded. "Is there anyone else in the building we should deal with? We absolutely do not want an alarm raised."

"No, Commander," she replied, wiping her face with the sleeve of her nightgown. "We knew Marcel was taken and we heard of the jailbreak. They were searching everywhere. We've been so worried, but we hoped he was among those freed and would survive. But sir, why are you here now?"

"I think you know why, madam. The code is J, A, D. We are here for both you and your daughter and the money. We must leave immediately, madam. Captain Deschamps feared his captors learned of you and your daughter and have been searching for you."

"We know, Commander. They posted a reward for information. Fortunately, they do not have enough specifics to identify us, at least so far."

From the corner of his eye Evan saw the young servant wore a shocked look on his face and they all turned as one to look at him.

"You are the ones!" said the servant, eyes wide. He turned and shoved Hopkins hard as he dashed out the doorway he entered by. Hopkins fell in a heap as Evan swore and ran after the man. He got through the door in time to see the man burst through another door leading outside, which Evan knew was on the opposite side of the building from where the rest of his men waited. Cursing himself for not surrounding the building Evan ran outside too, pulling his knife from his belt as he did. As he got outside and saw the length of the man's head start, Evan realized he would have only one chance. Taking careful aim in the dim moonlight Evan threw the knife as hard as he could at the man's back.

The long hours of practice paid off as the knife struck the man below his left shoulder. He crashed to the ground, but to Evan's dismay it appeared the knife was not sunk deep. The servant clawed at the knife and flung it away as he stumbled back to his feet and kept going. The ground gained on the man was lost in an instant when Evan tripped on a protruding tree root in the darkness. By the time Evan got to where his knife lay the man had already disappeared into the dark brush. Evan swore to himself yet again and went back inside.

"My God, I can't believe he has run to betray us. I thought we could trust him," said Simone. Her daughter appeared equally stunned at the man's disloyalty.

"This man is going to sound the alarm, madam. We must leave, *now*. Show us where the money is and then if you have any belongings you simply must take with you get them fast. Only what you can carry, please. Have you a buggy and horse we can use?"

"Yes, Commander, we do. It will serve to transport the money and my daughter and I. But sir, did Marcel not tell you of the others?"

"Others? No, he did not. What others?" Evan groaned inwardly as he spoke.

"Sir, there are nine others who must come with us."

"Nine? Oh, God. Let's sit here at this table," said Evan, holding a hand to his forehead as he sat down. "Tell me what I need to know."

Chapter Eleven
March 1793
St. Lucia

Simone took time to brush away the tears, trying to master her emotions better before she spoke again.

"Commander, Marcel made many friends here on the island. Some of them owned plantations in more remote areas with no suitable harbours nearby. When he realized what was happening he sent word to two families of dear friends in just this situation to come here. His plan was to keep them in hiding here until he could arrange passage elsewhere for them. But he was taken before he could do it and we didn't know whom his contacts were who would help them get away. With the situation worsening there was no choice but to keep them hidden and hope for deliverance. Commander, I beg you. They must come with us."

"God Almighty, this is stretching my orders, but we will try. Where are they?"

"Thank you, Commander," said Simone, the relief clear on her face. "You know, Marcel told me of you. He told me you were a good man and he respected you very much. Sir, we have been hiding them in a nearby home on the seaward side of the ridge. It's not far. Jolie can go with your men and explain what has happened. They will be only too happy to leave."

"Hopkins, go get Mitchell and have him come in here," said Evan. "Where is the money madam?"

"Underneath your feet, sir."

"Eh?" said Evan, knowing a puzzled look was on his face as he looked down at the floor.

"Your men will need to move this table and lift some floor boards, sir. You will definitely need the horse and buggy we have too, because there are four chests filled with money and they are heavy. I watched Marcel store it here and it was almost beyond his strength to wrestle it all in."

As she finished Hopkins and Mitchell returned. Evan ordered Mitchell to take half of the men and go with Jolie to collect the other refugees while sending the others inside to him. While he waited Evan moved the table to the side and studied the floor closely. Simone came to stand beside him and pointed at several board joints.

"Marcel was clever, Commander. He didn't cut any of the floorboards into an obvious pattern. He lifted the boards and made random sized cuts to make it look more normal. Once they were back in place the only way to tell anything was beneath them is by looking at the joints themselves. See how there isn't much dust and grit is between these ones, whereas over here the joints are full?"

"I do," said Evan, turning as the rest of his men came in. Evan gave them their orders and, using a pry bar Simone produced, they soon pulled up the boards. Beneath it all was a cavity in the floor barely large enough for four closed wooden chests all of the same size. Evan judged them to be roughly two feet long with almost the same width, but no more than one foot in depth. Each chest took the effort of two men to haul it out of the cavity in the floor. As the first was placed on the table in front of Evan, Simone stepped over and grasped the lid.

"They aren't locked, Commander," she said, lifting the lid. "As you can see, your trip is worth the effort."

Evan quickly realized she was right, as the chest she opened was filled to the brim with coins. Most were silver of varying denominations, but sprinkled throughout were larger gold coins. He turned to Simone with a question in his eyes.

"Good God, how much is in these chests?"

"I don't know, Commander. Marcel never told me and I never asked."

Evan shook his head in wonder. He expected it to be a substantial sum, but once converted to English funds this was likely to be several thousand pounds. The sight of the hoard incited an immediate buzz of excited conversation among the men, which Evan knew he needed to stop.

"Don't get ideas, any of you. You're all going to be searched when you get back to the ship. Right, close the chest and keep it closed. Madam, are you and your daughter ready to get out of here? We must leave, immediately."

"First let me show one of your men our buggy. Then I will need two minutes and both of us will be ready."

Evan fretted as he waited outside with time wearing on, pulling out his pocket watch every so often in hope less time was gone than he feared. He knew he was already at the outer limit of what he deemed would be acceptable time for the mission in the tavern and any more delay before returning to the ship was courting disaster. But the men soon drew up the horse and buggy, and the money was quickly loaded on to it. As they were finishing Mitchell appeared with another horse and buggy and several more people. Two women with a small child each were riding in the buggy, while the remaining five males were walking beside it. One of the children was a newborn.

"Sir," said Mitchell. "All present and accounted for. Sorry it took longer than we thought. They convinced me bringing a buggy would be worth the extra few minutes. The mother of the newborn is still very weak and would be quite slow if it was necessary for her to walk."

"Very good, Mitchell," said Evan, sighing to himself at the delay nonetheless.

But his worry disappeared when Simone and her daughter finally came outside moments later, both carrying a small satchel of belongings each. Evan breathed a sigh of relief as he turned to his men.

"Right, two men to each buggy. The buggies stay in the rear. The rest of you are with me. Stay sharp and as quiet as possible. Best effort for haste, please, everyone. I fear we have been too long here and we may be in for trouble. Let's go."

As they moved out doing as steady a pace as could be managed in the dark Evan knew they were making more noise than he wanted, but with little point in badgering them into doing better he held his tongue. Instead, he called Hopkins to join him at the point of the column. As the man came to his side Evan kept his head on a swivel, watching for any sign of danger, while talking to Hopkins from the side of his mouth.

"Hopkins, you did well back there. I am thinking you and your mate Wishart are better than any of us at moving with any kind of stealth. I need you to take him with you and hurry ahead of us. I'd like to be optimistic, but I am afraid we will have company soon. If there is a party on the way to confront us I need to know how far away they are, how many there are, and what kind of weapons they are bearing. If you do encounter anyone send Wishart back so I can arrange an ambush. If you can, stay behind in hiding and then follow them. Once I spring the trap take as many as you can from behind as quiet as possible. If you don't meet anyone rejoin us at the bottom of the hill. Can you do all this?"

Even in the dark Evan could see Hopkins grinning. "Tommy and I like a good fight, sir. I'll get him and be on our way."

Evan watched as the two men passed him and disappeared into the dark road ahead doing a steady jog. Several minutes passed and Evan was beginning to think they would make it without incident when Wishart came loping out of the darkness. Evan raised a hand to halt the column and hissed a warning to the men behind him as Wishart came up to him, his chest heaving from the exertion of climbing up the hill.

"Company, sir. There are five soldiers and a fellow with them Hopkins thinks is the one you stuck a knife into. We think one of the soldiers might be an officer. We were surprised there are so few coming, but Hopkins believes the bastard that got away from you didn't have the full picture. He only saw the men inside the kitchen, right? He didn't know the rest of our men were outside waiting. The soldiers all have muskets, but we don't know if they are loaded and ready. Hopkins is at the turnoff to the dock at the bottom of the hill. We spotted them coming our way and I stayed as long as I dared to make sure they were in fact heading for us. Hopkins said he would follow the plan you laid out. They are no more than a minute or two at best behind me, I think."

"God damn it," said Evan, rubbing his forehead in frustration.

***

James made his way over to the shadows where the lookouts waited with Lieutenant Cooke. The four men watching the direction of the harbour entrance were the youngest, with the best eyes among the crew. Another two men were aloft. More were vying to be the first to spot the sign they were waiting for by using night glasses. James was checking in with them every few minutes, but the answer was the same each time. James stared hard into the gloom of the harbour, cursing the fact the moon was still masked so much by the high clouds and willing for the wait to be over. But he knew the murk of the night was also a blessing, as when the time came the darkness would help.

His pocket watch was not his friend, however. He checked it yet again and cursed to see the time to act was upon them. Evan's orders were the attack was to begin at three in the morning and James gritted his teeth in frustration. Evan and his party were supposed to have been back on board already.

"Curse it," said James, as he stalked over to Lieutenant Cooke yet again. "Lieutenant, what does your watch say?"

"Umm, perhaps a minute or so before three? What are your orders, sir?"

Even in the pitch dark, James could see the grim look on the young officer's face. Both men knew the consequences of beginning the attack and what it might mean for Evan. They also knew their orders. James cursed aloud once more.

"And we still have no sign of our friends in the harbour?"

"Not as yet, sir. They are late, too. Do we delay, sir?"

James stood clenching his fists in growing frustration and anger once again, biting his lip as he thought the implications through. An overwhelming urge to simply grab his cutlass and lead the men on to *La Felicite* came over him, but he fought it back with effort. James damned himself for his weakness in giving in, even for a moment, to the emotions roiling through his body. A cool mind and a new plan was what he needed. After several seconds of thought he finally replied to Lieutenant Cooke.

"Yes and no, Lieutenant. We can delay, but only a little. We have less than ten minutes and all hell is going to break loose whether our friends are here or not. Nothing else is going to schedule here, but I'm quite sure the Captain's surprise will be on time. So we need to buy a little time for our friends to get here and hope they show soon. If not, we are going to have a major fight on our hands."

"Sir? How can I help?"

James stared at the young officer, looking him up and down before striding over to where the dead French Customs officers and soldiers were hidden out of sight. After studying them for a few seconds he stepped over to the railing closest to the dock to peer out at *La Felicite* and the dock area around it. With a quiet hiss he called the Lieutenant over.

As the young officer joined him in peering over the railing James explained his plan. "I am going to put on the uniform of this dead soldier over there quickly. I thought one of them would be a fit for you, but I don't see it working, so it will have to be me. I was planning on leading the men onto the ship anyway. I want you to organize the men and have them make their way using the shadows over to the shed you see there closest to the gangplank of *La Felicite*. I am going to march off the ship here and join the man we already have on guard at our ship. The two of us will pretend to be French soldiers coming over to have a chat with our unsuspecting colleague standing guard over there. We will wait until our men are in place before we make our move. The men are to await my signal to attack. I am hoping we can take him out without anyone on board realizing it, so when we board it will be with complete surprise. I'm taking the flare gun with me and will give the signal as soon as I can."

James paused a moment to study *La Felicite* one more time. "There doesn't appear to be much activity on deck, but I can see light in the stern cabin. If the Captain is in there, the son of a bitch is mine. You will remain behind here with the men we have designated to stay behind. Your orders are to wait no longer than necessary. If it becomes clear we have failed to take *La Felicite* you are to leave, regardless of whether Commander Ross is back. Is this clear?"

"Sir, it is. Permission to use the swivels to clear a path on the ship just before you board?"

"You can kill as many of these bastard Frogs as your heart desires when the time comes, Lieutenant. Just make sure you send our real colours aloft before you do. Now get the men going, sir. We have no more time to waste."

James pulled off his own clothes and stripped the dead soldier of enough of his uniform to pull off the deception while Lieutenant Cooke organized the men. A steady file of them crept off the ship and dashed into the shadows of a nearby building. As James finished pulling on the dead man's clothes and was about to leave Lieutenant Cooke dashed across the deck to him.

"Sir!" said the Lieutenant, his excitement clear in his voice. "They're coming!"

Seeing the Lieutenant pointing behind him to the harbour entrance, James gave him a savage grin. "Excellent. Good timing, because I've had all I can take of this waiting around."

James grasped the young man's hand hard as he turned to go. "Confusion to the French, sir!"

Before making his way down the gangplank James grabbed a cutlass to take with him and stuffed the flare pistol into a pocket of the uniform coat, hoping it wouldn't be too noticeable. He knew the French sailor standing guard over *La Felicite* might see and recognize the weapons, but it wouldn't matter soon as all James needed was enough time to get close to the man. With grim determination James signaled to the sailor standing guard over the *Alice* to join him and together they began walking toward *La Felicite*.

"I'll be talking French to this bastard right up to when we get close to throw him off. I'd like to take him as quietly as possible so we can get on board without an alarm being sounded."

But even as the man nodded the faint sound of a pistol report came from not far away. Both men turned to the source and as they did, James realized the shot came from the direction Evan had gone to get the money.

"Sir?" said the sailor with him, a hint of uncertainty in his voice.

"We stay with the plan, God *damn* it," said James, his voice low as they drew ever closer to the man. He could see the man was staring off into the darkness, trying to discern what was happening and where the shot came from. Sensing their approach the French sailor turned to look directly at them, obvious puzzlement on his face. James allowed himself one last inward curse before he began speaking to the sailor in French.

***

Evan rubbed his chin in furious thought as he quickly scanned the area around him, trying to decide if it would suit for an ambush. Realizing it would, he quickly formed a plan and turned to his waiting men.

"Wishart, well done. Right, I want two of you to stay behind, one to each buggy. Turn them around and take them back up the road till you are out of sight, quickly. I want half of the rest of you in the bush a little further down the road and the other half with me over here. No prisoners. Everyone waits till I break cover and then you do what you have to. Whatever we do, we need to make sure these bastards don't get a chance to fire their weapons and bring more attention down on us."

Fortunately, a bend in the road was not far back and it took only moments for the buggies to disappear out of sight around it. Evan and his men secreted themselves with only moments to spare, crouching in the brush and small trees along one side of the road. As silence descended the crunch of several pairs of boots on the ground came to their ears. Evan positioned himself in a spot the furthest away from the direction their adversaries were coming from. He expected they were coming in single file, which meant ensuring they were level with him before springing the trap. This ensured his men lined along the road could spring from hiding and pick a man to attack without running into anyone else.

They weren't in single file, however. The darkness made it hard to be certain, but there looked to be two men leading a group of four tramping behind them in a shambling, incoherent mass. Evan knew it wouldn't matter, though, and raising his cutlass as he stood he gave the signal and moved forward. He hoped to make as little noise as possible to get even closer to his victims as he sensed his men doing the same beside him. But as he began moving he stumbled on an unseen root, almost falling flat on his face. With a curse he steadied himself, readying for the fight once again. The momentary stumble was all it took for his men to bypass him and get to their victims first.

All around him the night exploded with the sounds of struggle. Several of the French soldiers gave cries of surprise, some of which were cut short as the cutlasses did their work. The sailor nearest Evan when he stumbled moved into the lead of the attack on the two men at the front of the column. The sudden, loud report of a pistol was followed by a curse from the sailor, but the man kept going and he slashed the life from the traitorous servant who alerted the French. He lost his own life in the process, as a second later the officer with the pistol took him high in the chest with the point of his sword.

The French officer was left with no time to enjoy his small victory as Evan came after him with a devastating slash. The man was fortunate to survive with a desperate, last second parry. Evan soon realized the man was as skilled a swordsman as himself. The two men struggled back and forth, slashing hard at each other. Had the fight been between the two of them alone, pitting his officer's sword against the much cruder, heavier naval cutlass, the French officer might even have come out the winner. But his fight was ended by the crushing impact of another cutlass slashing from behind on to the point where his neck met his shoulders. As the man crashed to the ground Evan looked around and realized he was the last of their foes standing.

"Let's hope this bastard hasn't called even more attention to us with that shot he fired, damn it all. Right, someone go and get the buggies. The rest of you shove these bodies out of the way. How is that man that was with me?"

"Jones is dead, sir," said one of the sailors.

Evan sighed. "He comes with us. They'll just have to make room on one of the buggies."

The men guarding the buggies were ready for the order and they appeared within moments of getting word to move out. As they drove up the distant sound of shouting was followed by the unmistakable bark of at least one larger calibre weapon coming from the direction of the port, making everyone turn their heads. Evan swore at the sound.

"*Damn* that bastard with the pistol," he said, before turning to the waiting group of men and singling out four of them. "Right. You four men, you are with the buggies. Your job is to get these people and the money on board the *Alice* at best speed. I don't care what else may be happening in the port, you are not to let anything stop you. Once you get done ask Lieutenant Cooke for orders."

Even as he finished the sounds of distant fighting increased and grew in intensity. Occasional popping sounds told of more pistols being brought into the fray, but the swivel guns stayed silent. Evan shook his head and turned to the remaining men.

"The rest of you are with me. We are going to do a light jog ahead of the buggies to clear the way if necessary. If there is no one opposing their path to the *Alice* we will join in support of Lieutenant Wilton in whatever the Christ is going on down there. Let's go."

***

"You!" said James, as he spoke in French

while getting ever closer to the still puzzled looking guard at the foot of the gangplank to *La Felicite*. "Yes, you, *damn* you. I saw you drinking on duty. You're on report for this."

The sailor's jaw fell open, surprised at the tone of command James employed so effectively to throw him off, but he recovered with a quick reply. "But— I wasn't drinking! Who are you? It sounded like a pistol—"

The sailor never finished his sentence as the sailor with James plunged his knife into the man's heart and grabbed the man before he could hit the ground. James looked around to see if an alarm was being sounded as he pulled the flare pistol out and fired it. The flare soared aloft over the ship in the direction of the water and burst, bathing the ship in a garish red light for the few brief seconds it lit the sky. Within seconds, the querulous voice of an officer came from the deck of the ship. The sailor was still holding the dead guard in his grip as James turned to see a French Lieutenant glaring down at them.

"What the hell is going on out here? Who shot that goddamn flare? And what's wrong with him?"

"The man's completely drunk, sir. He can't even stand on his own. We'll have to bring him on board."

"Very well. But where did the damn flare come from and what the hell was the sound we heard just before it? I thought it was a pistol shot."

"We don't know anything about all of that, sir," said James, with a quick nod to the sailor with him. "We'll get this man aboard and then go look if you wish."

"Fine, I—" said the officer, before he turned sharply to look behind him, taking a few hesitant steps away from the railing. "What the hell—"

James heard several loud thumps coming from the far side of the ship and knew they were boarding grapnels, meaning his signal to the raiders coming in support to cut out the frigate succeeded. A bare second later two swivel guns mounted on the stern railing of the *Alice* barked, cutting a devastating swathe with the small grapeshot they were loaded with. The French Lieutenant was swatted away like a twig in a hurricane, disappearing from view.

Shoving the dead French guard away, James pulled out his cutlass and charged up the gangplank, screaming over his shoulder for the men to follow him. As he gained the deck he saw a stream of confused looking French sailors pouring on deck, coming up from the stairs to the lower decks. The long days and hours of pent up frustration released, as James slashed three of them down while the rest fell back in fear of his determined attack. Within seconds the cluster of men from the *Alice* joined him in the fray. But even as they did yet more French sailors came boiling up from below. The desperate French found themselves fighting on two fronts, as the sailors from Captain Laforey's frigate gained the deck and joined the fight. Using three of the frigate's boats, they had sailed into the harbour without lights and boarded from the starboard side of *La Felicite,* exactly as Evan planned. Seeing there were enough men to deal with the situation, James fell back and began working his way aft.

He found a scene of carnage as he reached the quarterdeck. Only four men were on deck along with the dead officer, but they all suffered the blast of the swivel guns. No other Frenchmen were making their way to the quarterdeck, but coming from the other side of the ship a British Lieutenant stalked toward James, his sword at the ready and murder in his eyes. James knew he was being treated as a foe because of the uniform he was wearing, despite the French blood staining it. He held up his hands to forestall the officer.

"I am James Wilton of *HMS Alice*. I am in disguise." As he spoke he pulled off the uniform coat he wore.

"Thank you, sir," said the officer, coming closer and dropping his sword from the ready. "I didn't recognize you at first. What is the situation?"

"Commander Ross is late, but I am hopeful he will arrive soon. I suggest take charge on deck. I'm going to take a couple of my men and go after our missing agent and the bastard Captain of this ship."

The Lieutenant nodded and ran to join the chaotic, raging fight. James pulled two of his men to the side and signaled for them to follow him. Dashing for a hatchway with stairs leading below they took them in a rush. They were attacked the second they got below deck by a party of French Marines struggling to join the fight. James killed the first man who came at him by sidestepping the thrust aimed at his heart and stabbing his assailant with the point of his cutlass. Shoving him aside James parried the blade already coming at him and kicked his opponent in the groin. The two sailors following him joined in and took over, slashing at the Marines hard despite the cramped quarters.

James shouted orders to his men as he turned to go aft, knowing the Captain's cabin was nearby. "Deal with these bastards! I'm going after the Captain!"

Despite the unfamiliar surroundings he found his way there within moments. A young French Marine waited, guarding the entrance with his sword. Despite looking nervous he raised his sword in defiance as James dashed toward him. As he did, a muffled scream coming from inside the cabin was cut short. Even though the sound was brief and muffled, James knew in an instant the scream came from a woman, and worse, he knew the voice was Manon's.

With a bellow of anguish James attacked the French Marine, unstoppable rage lending strength to his sword arm. The man quailed in terror and tried to run, but James cut him down with a devastating slash and shoved him to the side. The door was locked, but James wasn't going to be denied. With overwhelming force James threw his entire body at the door. The flimsy hinges and lock was no match for the power in his attack. They crumpled and bent, splinters showing where the wood was ruptured all around them. James raised his cutlass and kicked the door hard with one final thrust even as another scream came from inside the cabin. This time, the scream was one of pure agony.

***

Evan and the five men with him reached the bottom of the hill and turned off La Toc Road to head for the port within a minute of leaving the buggies.

The sounds of fighting and screams of dying men grew ever louder the closer they got. As they finally got close enough to see what was happening Evan was relieved at first to find the way was clear to the *Alice*. But even as the thought came he saw a party of French soldiers streaming out of what Evan knew was one of the many local taverns close to the docks. Evan swore to himself as he counted his opponents and realized they outnumbered his own party by more than double his own strength.

Even as he watched he saw one of them notice his party and point straight at Evan, doing the same as he was. He knew the man could see they were carrying weapons, too. The French soldier was gesturing wildly with his hands and the others all turned to look at Evan. Almost as one they pulled out their swords and headed for Evan and his men. Evan swore to himself, but the refugees and the buggies appeared behind him heading for the *Alice*. Furiously grasping for something to even the odds against him, Evan gave orders to his men to do the only thing coming to mind.

"Right, let's go, men. Steady walk toward the crowd coming toward us. Keep your swords in your hands, but not at the ready. They may be uncertain as to who we are and what we are doing, so we take advantage of this. I will talk to them in French and try to keep them uncertain. Once we get within ten feet we rush them."

As they got closer Evan spoke up while doing his best to look puzzled. "Say, do any of you know what is going on? We heard what we thought was a pistol shot and then we heard a heavy weapon.

Does anyone need help?"

The ruse worked well enough to get the Frenchmen to lower their swords. A couple of them looked at each other, wondering what to do. Evan realized what was saving him was the lack of an officer to give them direction, so he added to the deception.

"Have any of you seen any officers? It would be better if someone could tell us what to do."

As he finished speaking he screamed to his own men and rushed forward. "Now!'

The French soldiers were taken aback by the sudden change in tactic even as the first of them died from Evan's blade. For the first long few moments the surprise favoured Evan and his men and they pushed their adversaries back, but the larger numbers began to tell. The French were angered at the deception and began slashing with desperate fury. Men were screaming all around Evan as he cut and parried with increasing desperation. Five of the French soldiers were already down and out of the fight, but the rest were pressing Evan and his men hard. From the corner of his eye he saw one of his men was on the ground, bleeding profusely from a fatal cut. Another was desperately holding his side, blood seeping through his fingers, while trying to fend off the French soldier who delivered the cut.

A part of Evan's mind was fervently trying to think of a way to turn the tide while another part was focused on defending himself. Beside him, the injured sailor finally succumbed to a thrust from his foe and he too fell to the ground. With his man down the French soldier paired up with the man attacking

Evan, who needed every ounce of his skill to beat them back. He knew it couldn't last and he resolved to take at least one of them with him.

Even as the thought crossed his mind a party of sailors from the *Alice* crashed into the French soldiers from behind, screaming a collective howl of fighting lust. Within seconds several of the French soldiers were dead on the ground, unaware of what hit them. The remainder found the tables fully turned, as they were now the ones surrounded and fighting for their lives. One by one they fell, their lifeblood seeping slowly into the dust. As the last of them was cut down Evan looked around to gauge the situation.

The two buggies were empty of their loads, standing derelict to the side on the dock. The remaining refugees were being helped on board and he could see the four chests stacked on the dock, waiting to be carried on board too. Evan saw Lieutenant Cooke standing on the quarterdeck of the *Alice* and as the two men looked at each other Evan raised his sword in salute for the help. The Lieutenant raised his own sword in acknowledgement before using it to point to a spot near Evan. Evan turned to look and swore at what he saw.

"Christ, how many Frog soldiers are there in this goddamn town?" said Evan, as he saw yet another file of soldiers appear on the dock. As he stood trying to discern their intentions, the final surprise Evan planned came into play. Even muffled by the ridge sheltering the harbour entrance, the full broadside barrage from Captain Laforey's frigate was still loud enough to make every man in sight stop and stare in the direction it came from. They couldn't see the shots as they flew by, but the scream of the broadside tore the air as it went past over their heads. A series of distant thuds far up the hill toward the fort on Morne Fortune told them what the target was. Evan looked over at the new party of French soldiers, who were taken aback by the sound of the broadside. Many were milling about, uncertain of what to do, but a cluster of them pointed at Evan's group and began moving in his direction fast, with weapons at the ready.

"Right, enough of this. Time to get the hell out of here. Fall back on the *Alice*!"

Chapter Twelve
March 1793
St. Lucia

Manon gritted her teeth in pain and frustration as La Chance grunted and strained over her, raping her for the second time in as many hours. She had tried to claw his eyes before he began, also for the second time, but he merely grabbed her hand and twisted it hard behind her back to a point it brought tears to her eyes. As she felt her arm was on the point of breaking he finally released her. In her relief she let down her guard to grasp her sore arm and he used the opportunity to slap her hard enough on the face to send her reeling into the cabin wall. As he roughly shoved her on to his cot she tried once again to scratch the side of his face, unwilling to submit. A second, more powerful slap ended her will to resist and all she could do was try to find the strength to endure. Pinning her arms to the side he had forced himself on her. With tears running down her face she wondered yet again how she would find the strength, as each new time he abused her she felt she was reaching a point where no more tears could possibly be left to cry. Deep inside, she felt her reserve of strength to resist was dwindling too.

As La Chance began moaning ever more frequently Manon could only close her eyes, desperately wanting him to be done. But despite willing herself to draw inward and ignore what was happening, other sounds began to intrude insistently on her consciousness. With effort she focused on them and, as sudden insight stole over her, she realized the sounds were those of the alarm being raised. As she focused closer to be certain she distinctly heard the sound of several voices raised in fear. She couldn't stop a part of her from daring to hope and even as she bit her lip, allowing a tiny flame to grow inside her, the muffled report of the swivel guns came from outside.

She opened her eyes and saw La Chance still straining over her, oblivious to everything except what he was doing. With a sudden, deep groan of pleasure he reached climax. As he did Manon leaned forward as far as she could and spat in his face. He responded by grasping one of her breasts hard enough to make her scream as he finished.

"You're a real bitch, aren't you?" said La Chance, breathing hard from his exertions while kneading her breast with cruel strength, enough to bring more tears to Manon's eyes. "You're one of the best fighters I've ever enjoyed."

To Manon's amazement, the Captain still seemed oblivious to the continuing sounds of the fighting outside. Despite her pain she smiled for the first time in what seemed an eternity. As La Chance saw her smiling, his flushed grin was replaced by a look of puzzlement.

"I may be a bitch, but you are a *dead* man," she said with a hiss. "I told you they would come for me, but you didn't believe it. *God*, I hope James kills you slowly."

As she spoke he slid off her and stood up, listening to the sounds from above. His puzzled look changed in an instant to one of horror. But as he turned to reach for his uniform Manon kicked out hard, aiming for his groin with all the power she could muster. The pent up anger at the days and weeks of abuse lent extra strength to her effort, but he was moving and she missed the target. La Chance didn't escape completely, though, as her mistimed kick took him solidly in his lower abdomen. La Chance gave a sharp grunt in agony, as the strike left him winded and doubled him over. In desperation Manon scrambled off the cot, searching for a weapon she could use. With little at hand, she resorted to clawing at his face as he finally straightened up. She drew blood with both hands as she raked her nails down the side of his head and he screamed in pain, but it failed to stop him. His punch to her stomach was hard enough to fling her back against the wall of the cabin, leaving her in a crumpled mass of pain.

Manon clutched at her stomach, gasping in desperation to overcome the agony and regain her wind. La Chance was rushing about the cabin, struggling to get into his clothes and find his sword as fast as he could. But she knew the Captain had been drinking when he began tormenting her almost two hours before and she could see he was still unsteady as a result. Part of her wanted to simply lie there and pray for help to come, but the anger boiling up moments before still held her in its grip. La Chance finished strapping on his dirk and was rushing across the cabin to reach for his sword, unmindful of Manon as she struggled to her feet.

All she wanted in the haze of her anger was to hurt him and make him pay. La Chance was reaching out to grasp his sword as she deftly tripped him from behind. He stumbled and wavered for a brief second, trying to keep his balance without success, before crashing face first hard into the floor. Fearing he would recover fast Manon tried to reach past him to grab the sword for herself, but he repaid her in kind by grasping one of her ankles and pulling hard. She lost her balance and screamed as she fell into the wall. She could feel her left shoulder was injured bad, but she needed to avoid La Chance getting the upper hand again. Drawing on reserves of strength she didn't know were there, she began struggling to her feet by leaning on the wall for support. An inarticulate, muffled howl of anger and anguish came from outside the door as she rallied her strength.

Her heart sank as she saw La Chance get to his feet first. The Captain's nose was broken from smashing into the floor and blood was streaming down his face, mingling with the blood oozing from the scratches she inflicted on him earlier. He reached a hand up to his nose and after pulling it away he stared in horror at all the blood in his hand. His face flushed in rage as he looked at her, even as someone outside hammered the cabin door hard enough the sound of it splintering was obvious. The sounds of fighting all around them grew more intense and the broadside from Captain Laforey's frigate howled overhead. But La Chance seemed insensible to the danger and he pulled his dirk from his belt.

"Goddamn bitch!" he swore, plunging the dirk with all of his strength to the hilt fast and deep into Manon's belly before withdrawing it.

Manon screamed at the blinding pain and clutched at her belly as she slid back down to the floor, ending in a crumpled heap propped against the wall. She watched the rush of blood seeping through her fingers in shock for a brief moment before the door to the cabin was smashed off its hinges and flung across the room by James. He rushed inside and took in the scene in an instant.

"Nooo!" he screamed, his face torn by his anger and anguish at what he saw.

***

Evan shoved at a few of his men who lingered, clearly spoiling for a fight with the oncoming group of French soldiers.

"Are you all fools? Get going! We have a mission to accomplish still," shouted Evan, watching the soldiers getting even closer.

He joined the remaining few in a steady run back to the ship, knowing it would be a race. But the four sailors who lingered weren't in as good a shape as Evan, who quickly realized he was outpacing his men. In dismay Evan saw the leading French soldiers would likely catch up to them. With only a hundred feet to go to reach the gangplank Evan gave a curse and went for the element of surprise again, stopping in his tracks and howling an order to stand and fight. The three leading French soldiers were taken aback at the sudden change and weren't able to react in time. The first soldier ran straight onto Evan's thrust and was still crumpling to the ground even as Evan engaged the next man and almost decapitated him with a high slash at his neck.

Evan knew they were in trouble, though. This party of French soldiers outnumbered him once again and those following the leaders were fully prepared to face him. But Lieutenant Cooke and the crew of the *Alice* came to his defence. Seeing what was happening, the men had reacted quickly by mounting two swivels on to the railings where they could be used. The swivels barked out within a second of each other and the grapeshot from one of the weapons blazed past Evan right over his head. Men fell in a wide swathe as it plowed into the dense pack of French soldiers converging on the fleeing sailors.

"Christ! Not so close, goddamn it!" shouted Evan, as he parried a slash from a frightened French soldier.

Evan could see the man he faced knew the initiative was no longer theirs and realizing he was almost alone in facing their foes he turned and ran. One of Evan's sailors made to go after him, his blood lust for the fight still upon him.

"Back, you imbecile! Get on board, all of you! Now!" shouted Evan.

Even as the last of them streamed on board the French soldiers on shore were already regrouping. Several found positions using whatever cover they could find and began sniping at anyone who moved on board the *Alice*. The two swivels barked out yet again, making them duck for cover. A few seemed to be shooting at *La Felicite* too, but given the risk of hitting one of their own men most were directing their fire toward the *Alice*.

A musket ball tore splinters from the railing beside Evan as he ran to where Lieutenant Cooke was directing fire at the French. A third swivel was being brought into play and it spoke as Evan got to him.

Adding to the chaos another salvo from Captain Laforey's frigate screamed overhead.

"Sir, welcome back," said the Lieutenant, a huge grin splitting his face. "I gather you met with success?"

"Yes, and thank you for your timely help, sir. We were delayed, but I'll explain later. Right now, its time to make sail and get out of here. Have them toss the gangplank away and cut the lines to shore. I don't want them to get the idea to rush us. What is the situation with *La Felicite*?"

"Sir, I can't tell. I think Captain Laforey's men have the upper hand, but there is clearly still some fighting going on both on deck and I believe below. I haven't seen the signal yet to confirm the fight is over."

Evan strained hard to see what was happening on *La Felicite* without success. "Any sign of Lieutenant Wilton?"

"None, sir. He led our party on board after the flare went up and the fight started. I haven't seen him since. It's too dark."

Evan grimaced, worried for the fate of his friends. "Right, let's stand off into the harbour. If we have to we can hook onto *La Felicite* and support Captain Laforey's men. If nothing else it will make it even harder for those bastards shooting at us."

Lieutenant Wilton stepped away and began issuing a stream of orders to the men and within moments the main sail fell even as the lines were cut. The ship came slowly alive with the touch of the light wind as the distance between them and the dock grew ever greater. Evan heaved a sigh of relief, but even as he did the sound of yet another swivel gun firing came from a different direction and this time, the shot was from further away. The two officers looked at each other before turning to the direction the sound came from.

"Sir?" said Lieutenant Cooke, using his night glass and staring further down the line of the wharf to where the French corvette was still tethered to the dock on the other side of *La Felicite*. "I think the shot came from the corvette."

"Damn," said Evan. As he finished speaking the fort on Morne Fortune finally responded to the attack on it. The muzzle flash of cannons in the battery lit the top of the mountain with a garish stab of light and a second later the heavy balls screamed overhead, followed by the thunderous roar of the barrage echoing around the hills. Within seconds the din of yet another response from Captain Laforey's frigate came from out at sea, except this time no shot flew overhead. Evan knew this was strange, but no time to think about why this was so was left to him as the French corvette took another shot with their swivel at *La Felicite*.

"Commander Ross! We have the signal from *La Felicite*. Our colours are aloft! But sir, I think they are looking for assistance from us. Yes, I can see Captain Laforey's Lieutenant waving at us and pointing to the corvette."

"No sign of Lieutenant Wilton, still?"

"None, sir."

"Well, then. Let's give them a hand, Lieutenant," said Evan, although his jaw tightened with worry for the fate of James and Manon.

***

James's heart fell at the sight of Manon's nakedness and the blood seeping through her hand. Seeing the dirk covered with blood he realized at once La Chance was the cause. A towering rage came over him as he locked eyes with La Chance and James screamed as he rushed forward to slash at his foe.

"Bastard!"

La Chance quailed with obvious fear, but in desperation he used his dirk to deflect the heavy cutlass enough to the side with only a bare inch to spare. The force behind the strike was still enough to twist his wrist, numbing his hand and forcing him to drop the dirk. James threw the heavy cutlass to the side, as it couldn't be wielded effectively in the confined quarters of the cabin anyway. He grabbed La Chance with both hands by his shirtfront and before the man could react James pulled him off his feet and threw him hard across the cabin. The Captain tried to protect himself, but it was to no avail and he crashed into the far wall.

James was back on him in an instant, pulling out his own dirk as he rushed over, but fear lent the Captain new strength and he kicked at James's leg hard enough to drop him to the floor. The Captain leapt on top and grabbed for the dirk, striving to rip it from his grip. The two men rolled back and forth on the floor, struggling with all their might to gain the upper hand. But James knew the strength gained from long weeks of training would win out and, as his eyes bored into those of his enemy, James could see the man was weakening. James pressed his advantage and, pinning the Captain with his body, he used every ounce of his strength to push the dirk steadily toward the man's head. James could see real fear appear on the Captain's face.

"*Yes*. You are dead and you know it, you bastard. Enjoy roasting in hell!"

With a final push James brought the dirk with overwhelming strength to the side of his foe's head. But as James made a final push to drive the dirk home Captain La Chance brought a last reserve of strength to his hands and managed to deflect the strike once again. This time, though, he didn't escape fully. The dirk slashed down the side of his face from above his hairline, barely missing his ear, but slicing deep into his flesh all the way to the base of his jaw. The Captain howled in pain and shoved James hard.

James fell backwards, but still gripped the dirk as the two men struggled to their feet. The Captain tried to run for the open door, but James caught him easily with a hand on his shoulder and spun him around. As he did he plunged the dirk deep into the Captain's heart and, knowing the man was finished, James left it there. Using both hands he grabbed La Chance and flung him hard once again across the cabin. With chest heaving from the effort, James bent over double for a moment trying to recover before turning to Manon.

"Manon!" he said, rushing to kneel at her side.

"Hello, lover," she replied, her voice strained and weak. "I knew you would come."

"God Almighty, what has this animal done to you?"

Slipping his arms underneath her he picked her up as gently as he could. She groaned, deep in pain, as he did. By the time he put her down on La Chance's cot he saw yet more blood was running through her fingers. Pulling her hand away with care he sucked in his breath at the sight of the damage.

"My God, we have to stop this bleeding," said James, as he turned to desperately search for something to bind the wound with. He ripped a shirt from the Captain's wardrobe closet and balled it up into a compress he put in her hand.

"Hold this to your wound, my love. I'm going to see if I can find the ship's surgeon."

"Don't leave me, James, please?" said Manon, holding him back with a weak hand. "I'm afraid. I don't want to die."

"You're not going to die, damn it. Stay with me!" said James, kneeling beside the cot.

As he spoke a sailor came into the cabin. James realized he was one of the men from the *Alice* who stormed aboard with him, in what now seemed hours before. The man's cutlass was dark with stained blood.

"Sir? The Lieutenant from Captain Laforey's ship sent me to check on you. He said to tell you the ship is now secured. We are under fire from the corvette, but we are about to cut loose and stand out from the harbour. Any orders, sir?"

"God, yes. If there is a surgeon on board find him and bring him here, fast. The French may have one on board."

"Sir, I think there is. Someone said the wounded were being taken to the orlop deck to be treated. I'll go at once."

As the sailor left James turned back to Manon. "Hang on, my love. We'll get you help. God, I'm so sorry we couldn't get here sooner."

"I don't feel good, lover," said Manon. "I'm cold."

James grasped one of her hands, noticing right away how cold it felt, and cursed himself inwardly. Looking about in desperation he found a blanket within moments and covered her. He grasped her hand once again as he finished.

"There, is this better?"

"A little, but I still don't feel good. It hurts bad, James."

"Don't worry, I'm sure the surgeon will be here soon and he will help. You are going to get better and when you do, I want you to marry me. Will you marry me?"

Manon gave him a weak smile as a tear ran down her face. "I know you do. You have for a long time, but you just haven't been ready. And yes, I will marry you, lover."

James leaned forward and gave her a long kiss, his own tears mingling with hers on her face. As they kissed, James felt and heard the sudden shift as *La Felicite* came alive. They were no longer tethered to the shore.

***

As the *Alice* drew further away from the dock Evan gained a better view of the situation. Ignoring the crackle of musket fire coming their way from the shore, he took a few moments to decide on a course of action. The corvette was a bare three hundred feet further down the wharves. He could see the entire town was alight, with everyone aroused from their beds by the din of the fighting. Evan smiled as he realized the attention of the officers on the corvette was fixed on *La Felicite* and they had yet to comprehend the role the *Alice* was playing in the situation. A second swivel was now set up on the stern rails of the corvette and several French Marines were shooting at anything moving on board *La Felicite*. More of the Marines were doing the same from the rigging. They also appeared about to cut their lines and make sail, too. Gauging his distances with care, Evan knew if he acted fast he could stop them and turn the tide of the fight.

His priority was to ease the pressure on the raiders on *La Felicite*. With the winds light and minimal canvas aloft Evan knew a little time was available for the plan forming in his mind. Taking command of the quarterdeck he issued orders to Lieutenant Cooke, who grinned once he understood what Evan wanted. He saluted and disappeared below after issuing his own orders to several sailors to join him. Evan strode over to the helmsman and explained what he was trying to do. As Evan fretted at the passing time he knew he was right to believe the tide and the wind were bringing the Alice slowly closer to the corvette.

"Just a touch to port," said Evan to the helmsman.

Evan was hoping to remain in the shadows of the harbour for as long as possible until they could fire at the corvette. He also wanted to fire at an angle. Firing straight into the bow or stern of a warship was always the preferred choice for any warship Captain, as the shot would barrel the length of the ship and cause major internal damage. The *Alice* was drifting into a position angled almost forty-five degrees from the length of the corvette, however, but Evan knew he could still do plenty of damage. As he watched the French ship he saw signs they finally understood what was happening. In a frenzied burst of activity the French readied their swivels once again and turned them toward the *Alice*.

Evan cursed aloud before shouting to the men around him. "Get down, now!"

Evan dropped to the deck along with the men around him and it proved not a moment too soon. Twin blasts of grapeshot ripped into everything around them. Splinters flew everywhere and a few men screamed as some found their mark. But even as Evan was getting to his feet the *Alice* replied. The lower deck carronades roared almost as one, bringing death and destruction to everything in their path.

Evan got to his feet and looked out at his foe. The stern of the corvette was mottled and pocked as if madmen with sledgehammers and axes had applied them to everything in sight. One of the swivels mounted on the stern was missing and while the other still hung on a crazy angle on what was left of the railing. No one could be seen standing.

"Excellent," said Evan, looking around at his men. Most were unscathed, but two of them received splinters big enough they would require careful attention to have them removed. Evan sent them below as a sailor came up the hatch and went straight to Evan.

"Sir, Lieutenant Cooke sent me for orders."

"Load the carronades with double shot. I want this corvette ripped to shreds. Two broadsides."

"Sir," said the sailor as he saluted and left, but Evan couldn't hear him as Morne Fortune sent yet another barrage screaming overhead out to sea. As Evan focused on what was happening outside the harbour the sound of another broadside came, but once again the fort wasn't the target. Evan frowned, knowing something wasn't going to plan. The suspicion was confirmed seconds later as the rumble of another broadside came echoing into the harbour from out at sea. Like the first one, this wasn't aimed at Morne Fortune either.

"*Damn*, what else is going to go wrong here?" swore Evan. But he knew whatever was happening wasn't his problem, at least not yet, as several shots from the Marines still in the rigging of the corvette flew past.

Evan glared at two sailors manning the nearest swivel. "Would someone *please* use the swivels and deal with those bastards aloft?"

"Sir," said one of the sailors, pointing at their foe. "They're about to fire on us."

"Oh, Christ," said Evan, as he saw the gun ports opening along the side of the corvette. Turning to the helmsman, he studied their position and ordered yet another slight shift, praying Lieutenant Cooke would fire first. Within moments his prayer was rewarded, as a second broadside bellowed from the *Alice*. This time the damage was to the hull on the stern half of the ship. The corvette rocked from the force of the pounding it took and muffled screams of pain came across the water. But several of the guns were run out on the fore half of the ship and Evan could see some of the cannon were being angled to point to the Alice. Evan knew not all of them would bear properly, but this was little comfort.

The swivel on the railing near Evan barked once again, a bare second before the French fired. The flash from the cannons bearing closest to the *Alice* was blinding and this time it was *Alice's* turn to reel from the punch. Evan heard the splinter of wood near the bow, but couldn't be certain how much damage was done. Muffled screams came from below and he hoped none of the refugees were hurt. But even as he cursed the *Alice* hit back once again, and this time she ended the fight. The much smaller carronades were far easier to maneuver to a different angle than the larger cannons on the corvette and were also much faster to reload. The forward gun ports of the corvette were the targets this time and they suffered badly.

As Evan surveyed the scene he saw the fight was gone from the stricken French corvette. The crackle of sporadic gunfire still came from shore, but the soldiers were shooting from hiding and gave no opportunities for targets. They were too far away and the darkness left them little hope of hitting anyone. Evan looked over at *La Felicite* and saw they now bore plenty of sail aloft and were well underway. The three ship's boats from Captain LaForey's frigate the raiding party used to sail into the harbour were also tied securely behind the stern of *La Felicite*. They passed the *Alice* within a hundred feet and Evan could see Captain Laforey's Lieutenant doff his hat briefly toward the *Alice* in appreciation for their help. He waved his sword in response, taking another moment to worry at why James wasn't on deck. But with unfinished business he brought his attention back to the injured foe before him. After ordering the men on deck to stand down from their weapons, Evan called one of them over.

"Go to Lieutenant Cooke, please. Orders are to keep using double shot for one last broadside. This time I want her hulled below the waterline."

While he waited Evan issued another stream of orders, sending a stream of men aloft to make full sail and follow *La Felicite* out of the harbour. As the rest of the sails were unfurled the final broadside roared out. The corvette reeled once again. As the *Alice* fell into line behind *La Felicite* leaving the harbour, Evan was certain he could see the French corvette was now riding at a strange angle on the water and he was certain of success.

Despite being finally able to turn his back on Castries, Evan realized the French of St. Lucia were not done with him yet. Yet another barrage from the fort overlooking the town blazed out and roared overhead, although to what target was the question. The sound of sporadic broadsides still came from out at sea. Evan realized how desperately tired he was, but he couldn't relax yet. What was happening outside the harbour entrance was a mystery, but he was soon going to find out.

***

James was frantic in his fear for Manon. Her breathing was shallower with every passing minute, yet no help arrived. She moaned in pain periodically, rocking her head back and forth on the pillow. James kept looking back and forth at the door, willing the surgeon to appear.

"Come on, sweetheart," begged James. "You know I love you. You must hang on for me."

As the frustration built to an unbearable level and James felt he could take it no longer, an older, grey haired man in civilian clothes James didn't recognize appeared in the doorway. He carried a small bag with him and he set it down as he knelt beside James.

"I'm the ship's surgeon of *La Felicite*," said the man, in answer to the mute question James knew was on his face.

He pulled back the blanket and, seeing the pool of blood on her abdomen, he gently pulled her hand and the bloodied shirt she held over her wound away. He sucked in his breath when he saw the damage.

"Get me some water and a dry, clean cloth. Preferably some clean linen. Fast, please," said the surgeon, not even looking up.

James rushed about and came back in moments with the water, grateful the dead occupant had kept a jug of it in his cabin. The surgeon was busy lifting her eyelids and James realized Manon must have slipped into unconsciousness. James rushed over to La Chance's wardrobe again and ripped out a linen shirt. When he got back the surgeon was gently washing away as much of the dried blood as he could. With slow, deliberate care the man probed around the wound, before pulling out a needle and sutures. After sewing the wound shut with deft movements he looked over to James and put out his hand for the linen shirt. The man deftly bound the wound, being careful to lift her as little as possible while running the cloth around her body before tying it off. Despite his efforts to be as gentle as possible, Manon moaned in pain each time he did something.

James couldn't bear it any longer. "Sir, will she be all right?"

The surgeon didn't reply. He grasped her hands and both of her feet for a few long seconds, before once again reaching up to pull one of her eyelids open. Her eye responded and focused on his hand, but didn't look elsewhere. The surgeon sighed and reached down to open his bag, pulling out a small bottle filled with liquid.

"Help me hold her head up, she must drink some of this."

As James held her head the man poured a portion of the bottle down her throat. Her immediate reaction was to gag, but the liquid stayed in her. The surgeon signaled James to keep holding her head as he reached for the water jug and poured a small mouthful of it down her throat too. Satisfied, he finally signaled to lay her back down on the cot. As James complied the surgeon pulled the blanket back over her and stood up.

James stood too, but he was worried by the bleak look on the man's face. The man didn't speak as he looked around the cabin and his gaze settled on the dead body crumpled on the floor. He walked over and using the toe of his boot turned him over to peer at his face before coming back to James. As the surgeon picked up his bag James could take no more.

"Sir! What is her situation? Why did you hold her feet?"

The surgeon signaled with his head for James to follow him outside the cabin. In the passageway outside he stopped and turned to face James.

"Sir, I don't think she can hear us, but I choose not to take the chance. I assume from the worry on your features she is important to you?"

"She is my woman, sir. We are going to be married when we get back to Antigua."

The surgeon sighed. Reaching out a hand he placed it on James's shoulder. "I'd like to tell you it will all be fine, but she is in God's hands, sir. I have done what I can and now she will either live or she will die."

He squeezed James's shoulder gently on seeing the devastation on James's face. "Sir, this is a very bad wound. I held her feet to see if they were cold and to some extent they are. This is a sign the body may be shutting down. Look, there is significant internal damage. The initial wound was a straight, deep thrust, but it appears the knife was removed in a slashing motion to the side. This means more possible internal damage than otherwise might have been the case. If any of her major organs were impacted it is doubtful she will live. Your only hope is the fact she is young. Were she as old as me I could guarantee she would die. The young have more strength to survive something like this. On the other hand, she was imprisoned for quite some time and, if I may, was in the clutches of a beast. Her strength was sorely tested."

The surgeon looked down at his feet and sighed before looking back up at James. "The way one human treats another human sometimes has turned me into a cynical old man and I fear for our collective future. I don't know who she is or what she was doing here. I heard a rumour she was perhaps a spy. But whatever she did, it was not deserving of the treatment she received from the monster calling himself my former Captain. Yes, I was aware he was abusing her, but what can you do? He was the Captain. He was a pig and if it was you who sent him to hell then you are to be thanked for ridding us of him."

The surgeon turned to go, but stopped himself and looked back at James. "You mentioned we are on our way to Antigua? I have more patients I must now go and attend to, but I will look in on her again before we reach our destination. I have given her something for the pain. The next twenty-four hours are critical for her. If she makes it past this point you may begin to hope. For now, you must pray."

As James watched the surgeon walk away he felt a tear fall and he reached up to brush his face. With a start he realized he must have been crying for some time without knowing it. He went back into the cabin and pulled over a stool to sit beside Manon. Her eyes were closed and her breathing was still shallow, although she was no longer moaning in pain. He bit his lip in worry for her and even as he did a fresh round of tears streamed from his eyes. This time he made no move to wipe them away and he took her hand in his instead.

"Come on, sweetheart," he whispered, bending close to her ear. "You can do it. We're going to get married. I didn't tell you, but I even bought a ring for you. Stay with me."

***

Evan was thankful enough moonlight was still about to make their way out of the narrow harbour entrance without difficulty. The passing minutes to reach the entrance seemed an eternity, but in reality the attack on the corvette ended less than a bare ten minutes before. His one remaining concern was whether the French would bring up weapons to fire at them from the shore, but in looking back over his shoulder Evan could see no sign of activity in the silhouette of the lights in town. With a start, Evan realized the Morne Fortune fort was finally silent. To that point their barrages were roughly four minutes apart, but they were well over this mark and with no one shooting at them any longer the French had stood down too. The ongoing sound of firing outside the harbour kept Evan anxious, though. As he stood watching, clenching his fist in frustration, Lieutenant Cooke returned from checking to ensure the refugees were unharmed while also looking for damage below.

"Commander," said the Lieutenant. "All is well below. No injuries among the people and the shots hit us above the waterline. Several were frightened, but I have reassured them we are safe, at least for now."

"Excellent," said Evan. "Mr. Cooke, I don't know what the hell is going on out here, but we need to be ready for anything. We may have to either fight or run. Have ten of the men stand to on the port side weapons. If we are running for it we will be tacking to the north as soon as we get out of harbour and if we are facing opposition it is the port side which will likely be in action, at least initially. You are to take command of them, while I remain on the quarterdeck."

"Sir," said the Lieutenant, as he turned to go below. But as he did a red flare soared high into the night from the deck of *La Felicite* as she passed through the narrow neck of the harbour entrance and moments later she sent a second aloft. Evan forestalled the Lieutenant from leaving.

"Belay my order for a moment, Lieutenant. That is the signal to Captain Laforey of our success. Perhaps its better you wait here to see what happens before you go below."

The *Alice* was only a bare minute behind *La Felicite* and as they too sailed out to open waters they were able to get a clear view of a similar red flare soaring aloft from another warship further out to sea. Evan expected this was going to happen and was ready with his own response. Within moments the *Alice* fired her own signal flares to warn Captain Laforey of her presence too.

"Sir!" said Lieutenant Cooke, unable to keep the excitement from his voice. "There's another warship out there, due east of the ship which just fired the flare."

"The one firing the flare is Captain Laforey's ship, Lieutenant. I don't know who this other bastard is, though."

Captain Laforey's ship was stationed directly

outside the harbour entrance, although much further out, and as they watched it fired yet another full broadside at the mystery ship. Using his night glass Evan studied the situation for a minute before lowering it and rubbing his chin. Beside him, Lieutenant Cooke pulled out his own glass and was doing the same.

"Sir!" said the Lieutenant, unable to contain his excitement. "Whoever it is taking on Captain Laforey is tacking inshore and coming closer to us. Perhaps it's a French warship which doesn't realize who we are?"

Evan brought his glass up for another look and even as the Lieutenant finished speaking Evan saw what was happening. Turning, he focused on for a moment on *La Felicite* and saw she was staying on course, heading directly for Captain Laforey's ship. But as he was about to lower his glass yet again, he saw the signs *La Felicite* was rounding up to present her side to the mysterious oncoming warship. Evan laughed as he finally put his glass away.

"Well, isn't he a clever one. We must remember to congratulate Captain Laforey's Lieutenant, Mr. Cooke. He has correctly assumed the Captain's foe is a French warship and he has also understood his opponent has no idea the ships sailing out of Castries are in fact under our control. His opponent thinks we could be more French warships coming to his aid, which is why he is coming closer to hand to join what he thinks are his friends. He is about to learn how wrong he is—ah, there we have it."

They couldn't see the broadside as the *Alice*

was to starboard of the port side guns firing from *La Felicite*, but it still lit the night with a brilliant flash to silhouette the warship for a brief moment. Evan raised his glass to watch the scene unfold once again for several moments.

"Sir? Did you still wish me to have the men stand to at the guns?"

Evan was silent for another second while still watching, before he finally lowered his glass. "No, there is no need. I got a good look just now at our opponent. I think this was the *Marie-Anne*, Captain Deschamps old ship. He must have been returning from somewhere and came upon the scene just in time to watch Captain Laforey dueling with Morne Fortune. He would have no idea we were cutting out *La Felicite*. Thank God he didn't return sooner. We might have been in far more trouble than we were if did. Well, he has turned tail and is running now, and we should do the same."

Evan peered at his watch in the dim light and gave a start as he realized it wasn't even five in the morning yet. He looked to the east and saw only the barest hint of the sunrise to come. He knew he was desperately tired, but he couldn't rest yet.

"Lieutenant, we are just coming up on two bells of the morning watch, believe it or not. We will now tack north to Antigua. The other ships won't be far behind us. Set enough men for a watch after we have tacked, and send the others to breakfast and some rest. Make sure our refugees get some breakfast, too. Somewhere in there, make time to feed yourself and rest, because you and the others will relieve myself and the men standing watch at eight bells."

Evan stopped the young man as he turned to go. "And Lieutenant? That was *well done*, sir."

The young man gave Evan a tired grin and saluted before turning away. Evan went to stand near the helmsman, who was watching the men aloft preparing to tack and waiting for the order to do his part. Evan stared over at where he knew *La Felicite* would be. As he did, he couldn't stop the worry for the fate of his friends from washing over him yet again.

Chapter Thirteen
April 1793
Antigua

The onset of spring in Antigua always brought a gradual rise in daily temperature, offering a taste of the hotter weather to come. James thought the temperature seemed higher than usual, but he knew the full dress uniform he wore was also the real likely reason a rivulet of sweat was running down his back. But he didn't care as his thoughts kept drifting back to the past few days.

The surgeon returned a few times during the voyage back, but each time he could do nothing to change the situation. Early in the morning before they reached the safety of English Harbour he came one final time. James was leaning against the wall of the cabin in a semi-conscious, dazed stupor, still sitting on the stool beside Manon. The surgeon gave him a gentle touch on his shoulder to wake him and as James returned to full consciousness he realized he was still holding Manon's hand. But her hand was cold as ice and her face held no sign of life.

With rising anguish James mutely willed the surgeon to tell him she was still alive. The man knelt by the bedside, but he didn't need long to assess her. He rose to his feet and turned to James, shaking his head. James flinched as if struck and his heart sank. As his tears fell once again the surgeon put his hand on James's shoulder for a brief moment once again.

"I'm sorry, young man. God has chosen to take her. I wish I could have done more for you. I will leave you now."

With a shake of his head James brought his attention back to the grave he was standing in front of, realizing everyone nearby was waiting for him. The coffin was already lowered into place and he stepped forward to throw the enormous handful of flowers he was holding onto it. He stood there for one final, silent moment with her before stepping back. This was the cue for the gravediggers to shuffle forward and begin shoveling dirt into the grave. As they did a party of sailors from the *Alice* stepped to the fore and raised their muskets, firing them as one in salute. The small group of people in attendance waited until the sound of the salute finished echoing before beginning to shuffle slowly away. Several stopped to give James a hug. But he felt wooden inside and was still unable to believe what was happening. Even the endless stream of tears shed since her death was at an end.

They arrived back in English Harbour in the morning of the day before. No time could be wasted in organizing the burial due to the heat. James cried his final tears as he placed the simple gold band he bought for her on Manon's cold finger right before they closed the lid on her coffin. Captain Laforey authorized her burial in the military cemetery and a military salute because of her service.

By the time the diggers finished their work and planted the humble wooden cross to mark her resting place only James, Alice, and Evan were left to watch. As the workers left Evan placed his hand on James's shoulder.

"I'm so sorry, James. I never should have allowed her to come with us."

"Evan, it's not your fault," said James. "We talked about this, remember? She wouldn't have taken no for an answer. It's my fault for not finding her sooner. I failed her, Evan."

"James, we *both* failed her. God, I don't know. I was naive to think she would somehow escape notice. We failed her father, too, damn it all. Paddy was a good man and I know he was your friend. James, I don't know what to say."

"Well, I do, James," said Alice. "Manon loved you and her father, and you must keep her in your memory always. She wanted to help and she knew the risks, so neither of you need beat yourselves up over what happened. She was a wonderful friend who loved all of us and I for one shall remember her with all my love. You both should too."

The two men stared at each other for a long moment before James finally nodded. "You are right, Alice. Bless you two for being the wonderful friends you are. We shall all keep her memory alive."

With a sigh, James took one final look at the fresh dirt covering the grave and turned to Evan, standing straighter as he did. "Evan, I need time. I need to get away for a little and deal with this. Sir, I request permission for a little time off."

"Permission granted. You will be back in time for the wedding, I trust?"

"Oh, yes. You couldn't possibly keep me away. I will be there and Manon will be with me in spirit."

"Do you need anything, James?" said Alice, placing a hand on his arm. "What will you do?"

James gave her a tiny smile and as he did he

realized he couldn't remember the last time his face wore one. Somehow, he was certain his last real smile had been when he was with Manon.

"Travel the island a bit," said James as he looked out to the sea in the distance. "Go fishing. Go for long walks. Get drunk. So don't worry about me, I will be all right. With you two as friends, how could I not be?"

The three friends hugged each other together as one, long and hard, before finally pulling apart.

"But for a start, let's go get out of these uniforms," said James. "I don't know about you, Evan, but I think I'm almost completely soaked in sweat. And maybe going to get drunk right now wouldn't be a bad idea either."

***

As they rode back to the home the three of them shared they passed several parties of sailors going to and from English Harbour. To a man the ones returning were so drunk it seemed a miracle they were able to keep to the road, while the ones leaving English Harbour were boisterous and loud, anxious for their turn to do the same. All of them cheered and waved at the two officers as they went by. Evan smiled and doffed his hat to each of them, knowing it would be a waste of time to remind any of them they should actually have been saluting him.

The party started the second the raiders set foot back in English Harbour. Many of the men involved in the raid on St. Lucia were younger sailors who knew of nothing but peace during their time in service. Having survived their first real action and been as successful as they were was as heady a potion as the rum they all wanted to celebrate with. Word of the potentially vast, unknown riches they successfully brought back spread like wind through the ranks. Speculation was rampant, but everyone was confident they would all soon have more wealth than they ever dreamed of.

After a quick wash up and change Evan found James was already done and waiting for them on the verandah of their house. Their dog Nelson had been tied up and lying in the shade when they first got back, but now he was playing fetch as James sat in a chair and tossed a stick for him to retrieve again and again. When he was younger and they first brought him to their home the dog would play for hours, but he was older now and tiring fast. As Evan came over to them the dog flopped down panting as he licked James's hand.

"At least I've still got you, Nelson," said James, as he pulled the water bowl over for him.

As Alice joined them Evan put his hand on James's shoulder. "You've got us, too."

"I know," he said, getting to his feet and gripping Evan's shoulder for a moment. "Let's tie him back up and head for the Inn. I don't think sitting around feeling sad is going to do me any good."

As the closest tavern to English Harbour and the only one not a decrepit shack, they expected the Dockyard Dog Inn would have a full house by evening. Even over two hundred feet from the entrance the din of loud, drunken voices were already assaulting their senses. From somewhere in the interior the sound of musicians struggling to be heard over the raucous crowd came to their ears and as

Evan walked in he saw a makeshift band set up against the far wall. Two sets of kettledrums backed up two men on violins and one other fellow playing what looked to be a flute. Several tables were roughly shoved together to the sides to create space for a small dance floor already crowded with drunken sailors and what Evan was certain were whores who had flocked to Falmouth Harbour the second word reached St. John's of the success of the raid.

Some of the men in the tavern were sailors from the *Alice*. A ripple of incoherent cheers went through the room as heads turned when they entered. Several mugs overflowing with ale and rum were raised in their direction. Evan could only laugh and wave his hand in acknowledgement.

As he waved he looked around for a table, but none were available as the tavern was packed. But the proprietors, Emma and Walton, appeared at their side and after giving James a long, welcoming hug they pointed to the verandah. As they got outside, Emma smiled and pointed to a table at the far end with chairs stacked on top of it.

"Thank God you're finally here," she said. "I've already hauled three groups of drunks away from it. They don't seem to understand the concept of having a table reserved for someone. When I told them who it was reserved for they all backed off meek as lambs, though. I saved this one for you as it's a nice spot with a view and, who knows, you might even be able to hear yourself think and talk to each other."

As the evening wore on James was mostly silent as they made small talk and enjoyed a delicious meal of fresh grilled fish and chowder along with bread. Alice's mother came out from the kitchen where she was helping out and gave James a crushing hug. Evan toyed with his mug of ale, debating having another, but he decided not to.

"I'd like to have another one of these, but I've got a meeting with Captain Laforey in the morning to go over my report. The Governour may be after me too, once he sees his copy."

"I'm going to make this my last one for tonight also, Evan. There are no answers in the bottom of a mug of ale. I'll be on my way in the morning."

"Are you going to be all right, James?"

"I'll be all right. And I *will* be back for next week."

***

Evan was grateful Captain Laforey's cabin was relatively cool, with a pleasant cross breeze blowing in through the open vent windows. Evan was wearing his uniform coat once again as this was a formal visit, but the Captain waved a hand at the uniform as he greeted Evan.

"Commander Ross, welcome. Have a seat and make yourself comfortable. You may take your coat off if you wish. I didn't even bother putting mine on this morning. It's getting too bloody hot again. Besides, we deserve to be comfortable while we contemplate our success. Drink?"

"Thank you, Captain, I will if you are having one. A *small* one, please."

The Captain poured them two small glasses of wine and they touched glasses before they sat down. "To success!"

"Well, thank you for your report, Commander," said the Captain, leaning back in his chair and relaxing. "As I once noted, you really didn't need much help from me, did you?"

"Sir? The raid would not have been successful without the capable work of you and your men. I know I mentioned it in the report, but I really do want to complement your Lieutenant in command of *La Felicite*, sir. That was brave and competent work on his part throughout the raid, and his quick thinking to have the men stand to the guns as he sailed out of the harbour checked the French warship perfectly."

"You are generous, sir, and I will ensure he is made aware of your thoughts. As it happens, I agree with you and I think the Admiralty will agree too. I expect he may find himself being promoted to command of *La Felicite*. And yes, I agree with your speculation the ship we were dueling with was the *Marie-Anne*. One of my lookouts has seen it before and he got a closer look at them than you. He seemed quite certain of it. Too bad we couldn't have captured her as well."

"Sir, I'm curious, if you don't mind my asking. Did you suffer any damage from the *Marie-Anne* or the fort? It didn't look like it from what I could see."

Captain Laforey laughed. "None, believe it or not. We *should* have, but we didn't. Those Frogs on the *Marie-Anne* must be ridiculously out of practice with their weapons. As it was they got fairly close to us before we spotted them and they opened fire, but it wasn't even close. Granted, we were maneuvering away pretty fast as they took their opening shots, but still. I like to think we did a little damage to them, though. But you know the problem with night actions. Once you fire your first broadside you're so blinded from the flash you have no idea what the hell you're shooting at from that point on. And as for Morne Fortune, well, God only knows *what* they were aiming at, because nothing got even close to us. I rather think they are somewhat out of practice too, although to be fair those poor fools likely had no idea what the hell was going on. During the day the fort would have figured it out, found our range, and sunk us in minutes. At night it's a whole other matter. Mind you, I dare say the broadsides we shot against the fort weren't any closer to them than what they fired at us. Even with our firing at maximum elevation I suspect all we managed was to blow up a few trees below their position. In any case, it gave you the diversion you wanted. Confusion to the French, Commander."

After the two men smiled and touched glasses once again in toast, Evan took a sip and replied.

"This is all good to hear, sir. The *Alice* got away fairly lightly with damage and injuries. I would like replacements for the three men I lost, if possible. I have several small injuries among the men, but they are all expected back at duty within the week. How did you fare with your men in the boats?"

The Captain shrugged. "Four men lost, three during the raid and one other that passed on today from his wounds. The rest will live. Frankly, the bill is low for such a resounding success, Commander, and everyone knows it. But I'm glad to hear your casualties were as low as ours. You and your men deserve plenty of praise too, sir."

The Captain paused to smirk at Evan. "Of course, I think our men with injuries are busy treating their wounds with *rum,* so it may be just a bit longer before they are back on duty than they would be otherwise. They all think they are rich beyond their wildest dreams. And who knows, by their reckoning it may be they actually are."

"Dare I ask, sir? Do we have a tally of how much we came away with?"

"Oh God, the clerks are still fussing over it all. It will take some time to sort out. We have coins of both silver and gold of various denominations mixed together and not all are of French origin. But I have been given a rough estimate and when you combine it with what I think we are going to realize from the prize court for *La Felicite*, plus a few pounds of head money for the French on board who surrendered, it comes to a nice, large number."

The Captain leaned forward for effect and grinned. "Does the sum of over two hundred thousand pounds sound good to you, sir?"

"Good Lord, Captain," said Evan, unable to keep his mouth from dropping open at mention of the sum.

"Yes, indeed, we have done well with this raid. As the two Captains involved in the capture I think each of us stands to realize a minimum of over twenty thousand pounds each. You are comfortably well off now, Commander. The Lieutenants will be happy, too. As for the ordinary sailors I think it possible they could end up with well over a hundred pounds each. Oh, yes, they have reason to celebrate. By the time the moneylenders get through with them it will be less, though. They will probably drink most of it away, but that's their problem."

"Sir? I made mention in my report of the wishes Captain Deschamps expressed to me for what would be done with the money. Is any consideration being given to diverting some of the funds to grant his wishes?"

"Good Lord, no," said Captain Laforey, waving his hand in dismissal of the idea. "At least, not that I'm aware of. This is not the way it works, Commander. The system of rewarding men putting their lives at risk by giving them shares in the spoils accruing from their efforts has enjoyed a long and successful history, sir. Anyone trying to monkey around with that would need their head examined, especially just as we are now back at war again. No, this is very much a matter for the prize courts."

"I understand, sir. Still, it seems a shame to me there are so many refugees in need of help. I talked to a few of the people we brought back from St. Lucia and they assured me there are many more who would dearly love to escape the guillotine. And it’s not just on St. Lucia, either. There are many royalists who have fled to Guadeloupe and Martinique, but I was made to understand matters are just as precarious there. Were we to give them support I think these people could be a wonderful resource for us in the fight against the madmen now in charge in Paris."

"Perhaps, Commander, perhaps. The Royal Navy is a rather good resource for us, too," said Captain Laforey, with a wry grin on his face. "Look, if you feel this strongly I think it is more a matter for you to take up with the Governour or even Sir James Standish when he arrives tomorrow."

"Sir James is coming? I didn't know."

"Yes, he knew the timing of the raid and wanted to be here to debrief everyone. You were rather busy with getting it all organized, so I took the liberty of informing him."

The Captain drank the remainder of the wine in his glass and put it down, a sign the meeting was over. Evan did the same, but the Captain forestalled him as he rose from his seat.

"By the way, Commander. You do realize, of course, your role in all of this isn't going to be mentioned in anything public, right?"

"Yes, sir," said Evan, allowing his own wry grin to appear on his face. "My colleagues and I have grown used to the idea over the years. Out of curiosity, will there be mention of the money?"

"Yes, I dare say I'll have to make a vague mention of it in the report that will make its way into The Naval Chronicle. Too many people know we came away with something, but I intend to downplay the estimated amount and, for that matter, the source. I think I'll just have it we found a certain amount of coin on the frigate and leave it vague. Perhaps a small pay chest or two for the French Army or something like that. People will be more interested to read of the daring cutting out raid and how our brave jack tars managed to pound a French corvette to matchsticks before they left the harbour on top of stealing a frigate from under the noses of the French. Yes, there will be many envious of my men and I. But it will give heart to everyone reading it, Commander, at a time when the nation needs it. Well done, sir."

Evan smiled and pulled on his uniform coat. "Thank you, Captain. I think it was a job well done all around."

"Commander? You know, I like people who help me, especially ones who make me a lot richer than I am. Please count on me as a friend if the need arises in future. And if you dream up any more plans like this one, *do* keep me in mind, eh?"

Evan laughed and saluted before turning and leaving the cabin.

***

Two days later Evan was going through the accumulated backlog of correspondence arriving while he was away and was pleased to find a letter from Captain Horatio Nelson mixed in with the rest. The Captain had written sporadically over the years since he departed Antigua, keeping Evan abreast of his circumstances. Evan was amazed such a capable officer was left ashore without a commission for so long, but with the advent of war he was certain this would change. Evan tore the letter open, hoping the situation was finally changed for the better for the officer who impacted his life in such a positive way.

The letter was shorter than usual, but it brought a wide smile to Evan's face as he scanned it. He was still grinning when a knock came on his door and Sir James Standish was ushered in to see him. Evan rose and saluted the Captain before they shook hands and sat down. Evan ordered drinks for them, which his clerk quickly served before departing.

"Commander Ross, it's good to see you again. But you were already smiling before I walked in the door. Good news, is it?"

"Ah, yes, sir," said Evan, pointing to the letter on the desk between them. "Captain Nelson has joined the fight. They finally saw fit to give him a ship at the end of January. Despite being on the beach all these years he has risen on the Captain's list and is now senior enough they gave him a 64 gun third rate, sir. It's the *HMS Agamemnon*. He was busy with provisioning when he wrote this, but he thinks it probable he will be sent to the Mediterranean. I'm amazed he even found time to write to me, but his first concern always was the people he led, so I guess I shouldn't be surprised. I confess I still find him inspiring."

"Excellent, this is good news. I knew they were thinking about giving him a ship. God knows I've badgered them often enough to try and get him to sea a lot sooner than this. Anyway, I'm sorry I haven't been to see you sooner, but the Governour wanted to see me the second I set foot on the island. However, it also gave me time to read your report. I am very sorry to hear of the loss of Manon Shannon. I know she was dear to Lieutenant Wilton. How is he taking it?"

"As hard as one might expect, sir. He is taking a little time off just now, but he will be back for this weekend. Will you attend the wedding, sir?"

"Wouldn't miss it. Well, we can debrief in more detail later, sir. I spoke with Captain Laforey yesterday, but it was brief and he wants to talk to me in more depth."

"Oh, sir? Did the Governour mention what was being done with the refugees at all?"

"Yes, we did discuss this and yes, I read about what Captain Deschamps wanted and your thoughts on the matter. Captain Laforey mentioned you raised the question with him, too. Commander, it is laudable you want to have the money directed to helping these poor people, but it won't work this way. Well, at least not directly. Please be assured the refugees you brought back with you will be cared for. But as for the rest, well. Even the princely sum you carried away from St. Lucia is a mere drop in the ocean, sir. Out here in the Caribbean the royalist refugees number in the hundreds. On the continent in Europe they number in the thousands. We are already giving homes to several thousand of them in England. Many more have chosen to find new homes in northern Italy or the Netherlands. Why, I heard the town of Koblenz in Germany is literally overrun with them. And yes, I know there are many more who may be in need out here. I expect more than a few are going to flee to America rather than to us."

Sir James stood and placed a reassuring hand on Evan's shoulder as he continued. "So do understand the government will do what it can for these people. We won't be able to save them all, though. This would be true even were the money Captain Deschamps and Governour de Gimat set aside a hundred times more than it is. It will especially be the case if the situation on St. Domingue continues to go downhill. A sizeable number of the plantation owners on St. Domingue aren't as crazy as some of their compatriots and they still hold allegiance to the French crown, even if their King is dead. I fear you will need to keep a weather eye on this island in the future, Commander. In any case, do enjoy the fruits of your efforts, sir. It is well deserved."

The Captain turned to go, but stopped and looked back at Evan with a twinkle in his eye. "Oh, I almost forgot. You know, most of the refugees in need of help both here and in Europe are minor nobles, wealthy plantation owners and business people. But not all of them are as well connected as the ones Simone Deschamps and you managed to save."

Sir James laughed as he saw the puzzled look on Evan's face. "You really don't know, do you? I guess she never told you. The people you saved have close family ties to our own King, sir. Apparently he even knows them reasonably well. Your role in this action will never see the light of day in the public's eye, but I can assure you Governour Woodley is already drafting a confidential report for His Majesty. He intends to give you and Lieutenants Wilton and Cooke the highest possible praise for your efforts. Who knows, the King may even write you."

Sir James laughed again, this time at the flushed look of embarrassment on Evan's face. "*Well done*, sir. Good day."

***

The small church Evan and Alice chose to be married in weeks before was packed with a curious mixture of people. Several Royal Navy officers from the warships in English Harbour were present in their dress uniforms along with the entire crew of the *Alice*. Sir James Standish and Captain Laforey were sitting in the front pews. Requests for new dress uniforms for the crew had swamped local tailors because of the newfound money available to spend. Mixed in with the Navy personnel was a sizeable component of the local congregation, most of whom were black. Many were slaves employed in small local businesses by their owners, although some were free like Alice. A number of them barely knew who Evan and Alice were, but the attraction of a Royal Navy officer marrying one of their own definitely wasn't an everyday occurrence and the event wasn't to be missed. Once the church was full the people began lining up at the open windowsills down the sides of the church.

Evan and Alice chose to be married late in the day right before sunset, hoping the little church wouldn't be stuffy. Fortunately, the moderate breeze appearing in time for the ceremony was strong enough to make it tolerable to wear a heavy dress uniform. As Evan stood beside James waiting for Alice to appear he looked at James, who grinned back at him. James reappeared the day before and both Evan and Alice were gladdened to see his spirits were much better. He seemed more deliberate and less carefree than his old self, but his smile and his sense of humour were back.

"Good plan to do this late in the day, Evan. If you'd done it too early in the day most of this lot wouldn't even have made it to dinnertime before they got drunk and passed out. But on the other hand, you wouldn't have to pay to feed any of them dinner if we were starting early."

Evan laughed. "Money isn't a problem anymore, though. Remember? Besides, the Dockyard Dog is a great place for a celebration party. I just hope Emma and Walton are ready for this. I know they have a feast of monumental proportions being prepared, but it's a big job. I mean, seriously, I'm worried that even the three roast pigs they're preparing might not be enough."

James laughed. "Yes, but don't forget the officer's party is on Captain Laforey's ship, so not everyone will be feasting at the Inn. There'll be plenty to go around at both events. I'm glad you mentioned the money, Evan, as I've been thinking. Both of us have plenty of resources now courtesy of Captain Deschamps. The home we've been leasing is nice, but you are going to need more space now, right? I think I'm going to find my own little place somewhere in Falmouth Harbour. Who knows, I may even have something built. Well, I don't want to rush things, so we'll see. Are you all right with this thought, though?"

"I am. I confess the idea of needing more space did cross my mind, although the thought of you having to move out wasn't a part of the plan. You are welcome to continue staying with us, you know. I was thinking of perhaps buying the place and fixing it up, adding more rooms and what not. But it's up to you, of course."

James rubbed his chin in thought. "Well, I appreciate this, Evan. I will give it more thought. I have to confess, though, I'm not real sure about having a squalling child around. I like my sleep undisturbed."

Evan laughed, but was forestalled from further conversation as the priest came to the altar beside them, signaling the wedding ceremony was about to start. Alice appeared at the entrance with her mother on her arm and Evan marveled his bride to be seemed more radiant than ever before. Her brilliant smile was like a stone dropped into a pond as the sight of it rippled through the crowd. Several people gave quiet gasps at her luminous glow in the fine, light pink gown Evan bought for her. But the sailors from the *Alice* at the rear of the church began applauding and cheering, which was soon taken up by the crowd, rising to watch her blush as she walked up the aisle to stand beside Evan. Emma looked beautiful too, as she came and stood beside Alice to serve as her bridesmaid.

Evan grinned at the thought Alice was showing a small, but noticeable bulge in her midsection, something everyone including the priest was ignoring. Fortunately, the stretch of nausea and morning sickness Alice had endured for several weeks prior seemed to be over.

They held hands as the priest went through the wedding service. After placing the gold wedding band on Alice's hand when the time came, Evan used his best quarterdeck voice to ensure even those outside knew his sentiments.

"I do!" he said, a huge smile on his face.

The priest pronounced them married and gave them a beatific smile. "Commander Ross, congratulations. You may now kiss your bride."

Evan made to give her a gentle kiss, but

Alice wasn't having it. She pulled him close and gave him a hard, full kiss that he quickly reciprocated. Evan wished the kiss would last forever as the crowd roared its approval. When they broke apart the priest raised his arms in celebration.

"Ladies and gentlemen, I give you Evan and Alice Ross!"

The roar of the crowd reached a deafening crescendo as they rose as one and began clapping, stamping their feet, and cheering. The tears finally came to Alice's eyes as she buried her face for a moment in Evan's chest. She turned to face the crowd with her arm around Evan at her side and as she did, she pulled James over with her other arm. She saw the single tear falling down his face and pulled both of her men together into one great, long hug with her. As they finally broke, she let go of James and smiled up at Evan.

"Let's go see what the future holds, my love."

The End

Author Notes

As with the two previous works in this series, the story of The Sugar Sacrifice has at its core a number of real events and people. Like any other historical fiction novel, the story deviates from reality where fictional characters become involved. As always, I made every effort overall to ensure the real events, people, and locations serving as a framework for the story are portrayed close to reality where possible.

The French Captain serving as inspiration for *The Sugar Sacrifice* was a real individual named Baron Jean Baptiste Raimond La Crosse, whose surname I changed to La Chance to make him the villain of this story. While my fictional character's behaviour contains several elements that mesh with those of the real man, it does deviate from the historical record of Captain La Crosse significantly at certain points. The real Captain did sail for St. Lucia on the frigate *La Felicite* with a revolutionary tribunal and the first guillotine to appear in the Caribbean. His interactions with Sir John Orde in Dominica are true to the historical record, as is his use of the guillotine on arrival in St. Lucia. The way he used revolutionary pamphlets to further the ends of the Revolution in St. Lucia were also real.

Captain La Crosse went on to use the same tactics of fear and propaganda in Guadeloupe and Martinique with success against the demoralized royalist supporters and, of course, he lived considerably longer than the villain of my story. In reality, royalist supporters fled Guadeloupe to Martinique as soon as the pamphlets arrived, leaving the way clear for La Crosse to focus on Martinique. This island took longer to sway, but capitulated to him early in 1793.

Baronet Captain Sir John Laforey was also a real person, but with one crucial difference. The real man was actually *Admiral* Sir John Laforey, in charge of the entire Leeward Islands Station at this time in his career. As the Admiral on station he would likely have spent far more of his time in Barbados. The Admiral was indeed involved in several disputes over prize money, which held his career and ascension to flag rank back. His penchant for enriching himself worked well with the story, so I decided to use him instead as senior Captain on station in Antigua and have someone else serving as Admiral in Barbados.

The shadowy French agents Montdenoix and Linger were real, as were their actions culminating in the desperate flight to safety by the real royalist Governour de Gimat. And who knows? Given they were real French spies, Evan Ross may well encounter these fellows somewhere in the future.

The island of St. Lucia was indeed given the appellation of 'The Faithful' by the revolutionary government, courtesy of being one of the first of the French Caribbean islands where the population largely embraced the ideals of the Revolution. Royalist supporters throughout the Caribbean and Europe fled the Revolution and the guillotine, which was very much in use, in an all too real diaspora of thousands dispersing to countries around the world.

The Revolution in France was a pivotal event in the history of this era, spawning a host of consequences no one involved could realistically have foreseen. These consequences were by no means confined within the borders of France. In the Caribbean the Revolution was a tsunami of change. While changes to the established order from the Revolution didn't happen as fast as they might in the hyper connected world we know today, the French islands like St. Lucia experienced dramatic change with what at the time must have seemed an incredible speed nonetheless.

The change was most extreme on the French possession of St. Domingue, known in our times as Haiti. I think what was happening there kept civilian and military authorities on every island in the rest of the Caribbean awake at night, wondering where it would all lead and whether the instability of St. Domingue would grow to encompass their islands too. The behaviour of Leger Sonthonax when he arrived to take charge of St. Domingue didn't help. Plantation owners throughout the Caribbean must have despaired for their future in the face of this new threat to their existence. Already beset by unstable prices for sugar and a slowly growing abolitionist movement around the world, the possibility of being murdered in their beds by slaves beginning to believe freedom was actually possible would have been higher than ever before.

Maximilien Robespierre was a well-known, outspoken, and controversial leader of the French Revolution. His famous suggestion it was imperative for the Revolution to keep its principles, even if it meant the colonies were to perish, served as inspiration for the title of this book. France paid a heavy price for this thinking, as St. Domingue in particular was a source of vast wealth because of the scale of its sugar production. The country lost enormous revenue when the flow was disrupted.

The book title is of course a metaphor. The sugar sacrifice refers not only to the lost wealth from sugar production. In this context I suggest the extremist Robespierre made a sacrifice of his humanity with his willingness to say or do *anything* to achieve the goals of the Revolution, regardless of the impact to others.

I doubt the new French administration realized how much change would be wrought by their Revolution in the Caribbean and whether this initially was really what was intended or foreseen. Because of the importance of St. Domingue in the history of the Caribbean you'll be reading more about it in future installments of this series.

But first, Commander Ross and Lieutenant Wilton will be off to a different Caribbean island on their next mission. The island of Grenada produced sugar like all the rest, but even today it is also known for the production of spices. Walking through a street spice market in the capital St. George's is an amazing treat for your sense of smell. The rich aromas of a bewildering array of spices envelope you with a tantalizing mix of potential flavours for your food. So please do look forward to the fourth book in this series, *The Sugar Rebellion*, coming soon.

68623459R00182

Manufactured by Amazon.com
Columbia, SC
05 April 2017